DEBUTANTES
❦
IN LOVE

Cora Harrison worked as a head teacher before writing her first novel. She has since published forty-seven books – ten for adults, thirty-three for children and four for young adults. Many of her books for children deal with the history and mythology of Ireland, while her love of history is also shown in her young-adult novels about the teenage years of Jane Austen, *I was Jane Austen's Best Friend* and *Jane Austen Stole My Boyfriend*. Cora lives on a farm near the Burren in the west of Ireland.

Debutantes: In Love is the sequel to *Debutantes*, set in the roaring 1920s.

Also by Cora Harrison

I Was Jane Austen's Best Friend

Jane Austen Stole My Boyfriend

Debutantes

DEBUTANTES

*

IN LOVE

CORA HARRISON

MACMILLAN

First published 2013 by Macmillan Children's Books
a division of Macmillan Publishers Limited
20 New Wharf Road, London N1 9RR
Basingstoke and Oxford
Associated companies throughout the world
www.panmacmillan.com

ISBN 978-1-4472-0595-1

1 3 5 7 9 8 6 4 2

A CIP catalogue record for this book is available from
the British Library.

Printed and bound by CPI Group (UK) Ltd, Croydon CR0 4YY

This book is dedicated to my dear friend Prish Hawkes with gratitude for over thirty years of loyal friendship and in memory of her charming mother, Eve Fontaine, formerly The Honourable Evelyn Dickinson, who was a debutante in 1924 and wore a very, very short dress for her presentation at Buckingham Palace.

Chapter One
Friday 1 February 1924

Poppy and Baz had been playing New Orleans rhythms for an hour, but now there was silence in the little cottage. They sat gazing into the fire, sitting side by side together on the large, old sofa – threadbare, but beautifully soft and deep. Baz propped his bass against the table, where Poppy had laid her clarinet.

Music was Poppy's security. Music had rescued her when the world had swirled into chaos on the death of her mother; it had brought order into that turmoil. Music had given her courage, but it was jazz that had set her free. The persistent beat had slowed the anxious fluttering of her heart, steadied her nerves and brought a thrill of happiness tingling through her veins. She smiled at Baz as he picked up his bass again and bent over it, an untidy lock of smooth black hair falling over his forehead and fringing his large chestnut-coloured eyes. He was the boy next door, the youngest son of an earl whose lands fringed theirs in west Kent. They had known each other all their lives, had played together, grown up together, even discovered a passion for jazz together. Poppy could not imagine life without him. The kitchen of the small cottage at the heart of the beech wood on this February day was warm and cosy with the heat from the ancient black range. Soon the other members of the jazz band would be here for their morning practice, but for the moment it seemed as though they were alone in the world.

She saw him look at her. An odd feeling, a sort of nervous tension that she had not previously experienced, ran through her as she looked into his dark eyes.

'If only we lived here and I didn't need to go home ever again,' she whispered. The cottage that housed her father's young chauffeur was so much warmer than her own home. Beech Grove Manor was a beautiful, grand old building, but living in a house where the ceilings of the huge rooms were twenty feet high and where a fire in one of the enormous fireplaces barely warmed those sitting directly in front of it was not so pleasant. And then there was her father's gloom and Great-Aunt Lizzie, who lectured the girls as though they were five years old.

Baz, sensing her mood, put down the bass and stroked her hand gently. He said nothing, but his eyes were full of understanding.

'Do you remember when we ran away together when we were eleven?' said Poppy, trying to smile at the memory. 'We were going to live in the woods – and I left a letter on my pillow saying that I had gone away for ever and ever – but Daisy tracked us with one of the hounds and persuaded me to come home.'

Typical Daisy, she thought. She had always been the more sensible one of the twins. At least they had thought themselves twins until last year when the true story of Daisy's birth had been uncovered, although

2

that had made no difference to them.

Suddenly Poppy stopped thinking about Daisy, stopped thinking about her troubles. Baz had put an arm around her shoulders – but not in the careless, half-affectionate, half-brotherly way of the past. Her heart racing, she turned her face towards him. His nearness seemed to be sending shocks through her. He reached out and put both arms around her, moved them up so that his wrists softly caressed the column of her neck, his face tilted towards hers. Poppy lifted her mouth and . . .

A log dropped with a clatter against the iron side of the stove and then flared up with a sudden flash of light. Poppy felt the warmth from the fire all over her body. Baz's lips were soft, gently pressing against her own. Her fingers ran over the shape of his shoulder blades, the warmth of the back of his neck, the satin-silkiness of his hair. After a long moment she broke off and lay her head against his shoulder, amazed at the way her heart was pounding. Baz laughed softly and untied her long plait of dark red hair, combing it out with his fingers and pressing his cheek against hers.

'We could run away together now; needn't live in the woods either – not now that I've got my own house in London. We could get married, Pops.' He caught her eye and smiled tentatively; there was a tremor in his voice and his eyes were golden in the firelight.

'Don't,' said Poppy, but it was too late. Reality had crept back into the little warm kitchen. They were no longer eleven. She was seventeen years old. It might be

1924, but her father and Great-Aunt Lizzie were still firmly rooted in the age of Queen Victoria – the days when an offer of marriage had to come before the first kiss and when a man had to show his future father-in-law how wealthy he was before he was allowed to talk of weddings. The chances of her father or her great-aunt allowing her to marry an eighteen-year-old boy, with no income and who had only just finished school, were nil.

'You might have a house,' she said trying to sound sensible, 'but where would we get the money to buy food? In the woods, when we were eleven years old, we were going to live on beechnuts and blackberries and wild mushrooms. Not too many of those on the streets of London.' Poppy tried to laugh, but she could hear a wobble in her voice so she bit her lip hard.

'We won't need to buy food: we'll have parties every night,' continued Baz, taking her trembling hands in his. 'We could ask people to bring something to eat and something to drink,' he went on. 'That's the latest thing these days. When you are going to those debutante parties with Daisy you'll make lots of friends. They'll all get tired of those stuffy affairs and they'll be delighted to come to our parties, which will be different and fun – and we'll be playing jazz – which is the latest thing at really wild parties, or so my sister Joan says. And when we're married they'll all keep coming and bringing food and drink with them. Bound to be enough left over to keep us going until the next party.' He looked at her closely and asked, 'You are going to have a season, right,

Pops? You haven't had bad news, have you?'

Poppy shook her head. 'Not bad news; just no news. We had expected to hear from Elaine by now. She did promise to come back from India and take a house in London for the season and present us.' Surely, she thought, Elaine would not let them down. She had been the only sister of Poppy's mother, Mary. But as well as that – and Poppy now knew the carefully hidden secret – she was Daisy's mother.

'Well, if you don't go to London, I'll stay down here too,' said Baz in determined tones. 'Mother wants me to go so that I can escort Joan, but I'd rather be . . . wherever you are.' He smiled at her reassuringly. 'But you might still hear. I saw the boy from the post office cycling up the avenue to your house when I was coming over.'

'Today might not be a good day,' said Poppy with a sigh. 'Father has to go to court this afternoon. Daisy is terribly worried about it because she's convinced that things will turn out badly. It's all too horrible. I don't want to think about it now! Let's play something instead.' She picked up her clarinet and waited until he had his bass.

'I say, Poppy, try this. It's called "Rhapsody in Blue".' Baz played a few notes.

Poppy picked up her clarinet, looked blindly at the music and put it down again. She had no heart to play. Beech Grove Manor, splendid though it looked from the outside, was just so miserable these days. Violet, their eldest sister, had got married last summer and rarely came near the gloomy place, and since their wealthy

Aunt Elaine had paid for Rose, the youngest of the four Derrington girls, to go to school in Switzerland, only Daisy and she remained.

Poppy felt guilty that Daisy was so often left to bear the double burden of her father and their great-aunt while she sneaked off to the cottage in the woods to play jazz. Still, Daisy had her own dreams of producing wonderful films and spent hours in the old dairy pantry with her camera, her film tank and developing dishes. Poppy admired the way that Daisy always made the best of things. Since she had no opportunity of working with real actors, she was shooting a comic film about hens where one young hen, called Jane, was being bullied by her cousins, a pair of aggressive Rhode Island Red pullets, and their brother, a swaggering young cockerel. It was to be a chicken version of the famous novel *Jane Eyre*, according to Daisy.

'Pops?' Baz had stopped playing and was looking at her worriedly.

'Tell me again about your grandfather's house,' she said softly. She knew all about it; Baz had talked of little else ever since the will had been read. The old man had bequeathed the small London mews house to his youngest and favourite grandson. Baz would have no money of his own, as the main estate and the house belonged to his eldest brother and the rest of the family property had been handed to his other brothers as they had come of age. But finally Baz had a house of his own, and that house was filled with his dreams of setting up a jazz club. It had been built originally for a coachman, his large family and a number of stable lads, so it was surprisingly roomy.

'Four bedrooms, a big, big basement for the jazz club and a coal cellar absolutely chock-full of coal so that the place will keep nice and warm for years; great place for parties – right in the middle of the West End of London,' recited Baz. 'Oh, and, I've been thinking, Poppy: those two big attics – they've still got iron bedsteads in them that were used for the stable lads. Well, I'll dig out some old mattresses from our place and get them up to London somehow or other, and then after parties people can sleep until daybreak if they like – one attic for the men and the other for the girls.'

'Oh, Baz, it sounds wonderful,' said Poppy wistfully. 'I just wish there was some way I could . . .' She stopped herself, knowing it would be futile to continue.

Baz put down his bass and pulled her into his arms. 'That you could set up the club with me?' he finished the sentence for her. His voice shook nervously, but his eyes were full of love. 'I say, Pops, will you marry me? I'm serious. Then it would be our house, our jazz club. Your father couldn't object to that, surely!'

'Baz!' cried Poppy, kissing him passionately for a moment before breaking off with a sob. 'I wish I could!'

'Why not?' said Baz, smoothing her long hair away from her flushed cheeks.

'Because you're eighteen and I'm still only seventeen,' said Poppy. 'The law of the land says that we can't marry without our parents' consent until we are twenty-one.

And you know that your mother wants you to marry money and I have none. And Great-Aunt Lizzie will have a fit if neither Daisy nor I makes a good match this season. And Father . . .' she trailed off, overcome with tears. Baz didn't, she thought, quite understand how bad things were at home. Great-Aunt Lizzie had fallen for his boyish good looks and charming manners and was always in her best humour when he visited. Even her father made an effort to be normal when the youngest son of his old friend was around. Baz's home was cheerful, noisy and fun, whereas hers was tense and unhappy. If it were not for Daisy, she would go mad.

'Well, who cares about being married then?' Baz chuckled softly, drying her tears with soft kisses. 'Let's just live together. After all, this is 1924. We're not back in the Victorian age. The old queen has been dead for more than twenty years – that's half a lifetime, remember.'

Poppy lifted her head to look at him in shock. Could they really just go off together to live in *sin*, as Great-Aunt Lizzie would put it? She tried to imagine being like her elder sister, Violet, and her husband, Justin. Although Great-Aunt Lizzie had been very disappointed that Violet, the beauty of the family, had not made what she would call, a *good* match, nevertheless she had to admit that Justin had a steady job working as a lawyer in London and was able to maintain a wife and family. Her sisters knew that Violet was very happy and had never regretted her choice.

Once again all her thoughts were forgotten as Baz

lifted her chin with his fingers and kissed her lovingly.

With a creak of ancient hinges, the door to the kitchen suddenly swung open.

'Oh, Morgan,' said Baz nervously, jumping up, 'we've been waiting for you. Glad you've come.'

Morgan did not look pleased.

'How did you two get in here?' he asked.

Poppy gazed at him, surprise widening her unusual amber-coloured eyes. 'We took the key from under the flowerpot. What's wrong, Morgan? You never normally mind us coming in.'

Morgan frowned. 'I don't mind when it's the whole lot of you, when George, Edwin and Simon are here, but I don't want you two slipping in here by yourselves and using it as a place to kiss and cuddle, which is what you were doing when I came in, so don't deny it.'

'We weren't doing anything – not really; you don't need to worry,' said Poppy, blushing furiously. She had little fear that Morgan would say anything – after all he was only a few years older than they were – but she added pleadingly, 'Don't mention this to Father, will you? He would be furious with me.'

'Well, your father will give *me* the sack if he hears about it; that's what worries me.' Morgan bent down to put another chunk of wood into the range. 'I don't want to be forced out of my job because of you two,' he said over his shoulder. 'Where else would I find a place for a chauffeur that allows me to play my drums and disturb nobody?'

'You could come and live with us at my house in London,' said Baz. 'I have plenty of spare bedrooms. Edwin and Simon are thinking of coming too.'

'He means to live with him and Tom,' put in Poppy hastily. Even though Bob Morgan wasn't much older than they were, he was sometimes a bit old-fashioned.

'And you and your brother will pay me a good salary, I suppose.' Morgan did not wait for Baz to answer, but began filling the kettle and glancing through the 'Rhapsody in Blue' music. He tried out a few taps on the drums and Baz accompanied him with his bass and after a few minutes Poppy came in with her clarinet. By the time that they had played it through once, Simon with his saxophone, George with his trombone and Edwin with his trumpet had arrived, and the Beech Grove Jazz Band was in full swing. Morgan did not give them a moment to rest – only stopping once to say breathlessly, 'I have to go at twelve, so let's make this last one the best.'

'Where are you going, Morgan?' asked Simon when the chords died away and they all stretched and drank the cold tea from their mugs.

'I have to take the Earl into Maidstone,' said Morgan briefly, his eyes on Poppy. 'Your sister says that she's coming too.'

The court case, thought Poppy, and for a moment felt ashamed of herself. She had woken with the thought of it in her head, but somehow it had gone, swamped by her rush of feelings for Baz. This court case was being brought against her father by the heir to the Beech Grove estate – Denis Derrington, or Dastardly Denis as her youngest sister, Rose, called him. He was suing the Earl for cutting down woodlands without his agreement. It could be very serious if the judge could not be brought to see that her father had no other choice in these bad times. Optimistically, the family hoped that the judge might order Dastardly Denis to give permission for a few farms to be sold. Other families had done this, but other families had sons to inherit their estates – and these sons had been willing to oblige their fathers. Michael Derrington only had four daughters so his heir was a distant cousin. Now everything depended on whether the judge was sympathetic to her father's situation.

'Do you want to come as well?' Morgan asked her, and Poppy shook her head decisively.

'No, he'll be better with Daisy; she calms him down. I seem to put him in a bad mood these days.' She avoided the chauffeur's eyes. Deep down, she knew that she was her father's favourite of his four daughters, but it was true that she agitated him. Although they shared a great love and talent for music, he felt guilty about not being able to afford lessons for her any more and was irritable about her wasting her talents on jazz. Also, since she was the image of her dead mother, she reminded him of how he had squandered the fortune of Mary Derrington on an ill-advised mine in India. With Daisy he was at ease, viewing her film-making with amusement and even allowing her to advise him on estate matters from time to time.

'We'll stay and practise,' said Simon, his voice

breaking into her thoughts. 'We'll manage without you, Morgan. The rest of us don't know this piece as well as you do.'

'I'll have to go soon too,' said Poppy. 'Great-Aunt Lizzie will be expecting me.'

I need to be careful, she thought as she packed away her clarinet. Her feelings for Baz and his for her *must* remain hidden, or Father and Great-Aunt Lizzie might stop her from going to London for the season – should the invitation ever arrive. Worse still, they might even forbid her from playing in the jazz band. To miss out on having a season would be terrible, but to lose Baz and the jazz band would be unendurable.

Poppy made her way back along the well-trodden path between the cottage and the house, pushed open the door into the hallway and was struck, as usual, by the icy chill of the place. Without bothering to change she strode into the dining room, where Great-Aunt Lizzie had already taken her place.

Great-Aunt Lizzie had brought up the orphan sisters Mary and Elaine Carruthers, had looked after the considerable fortune that the sisters had shared and had come to live at Beech Grove Manor House when Mary Carruthers had married Michael Derrington, eldest son and heir to the old Earl. She had remained there with the younger sister, Elaine, when Mary and Michael had gone out to India, and apart from a brief visit there herself to see Elaine safely married to a wealthy Anglo-Indian gentleman, she had stayed at Beech Grove Manor ever since. She was there when the news came that Michael's younger brother, Robert, had been killed in the Boer War, and had been there when the old Earl, Poppy's grandfather, had died and Michael had come back to his inheritance in England. And then when Mary Derrington in turn died, leaving four daughters ranging from twelve-year-old Violet, through the two ten-year-olds, Poppy and Daisy, down to five-year-old Rose, Great-Aunt Lizzie took over the care and education of the four motherless girls.

And yet . . . thought Poppy. None of them loved her very much – all wanted to escape her rule. She eyed the stately old lady with apprehension. She knew what was coming as soon as she saw the look of incredulous fury on the lined face.

'Poppy! How dare you come into lunch looking like that! Go straight to your bedroom!'

'Very well.' Poppy turned on her heel and went out through the door, almost knocking down the elderly butler.

'Sorry, Bateman,' she said remorsefully as she saw his worried old face. She waited until he had gone into the dining room. Once the door closed behind him, she moved fast. Not up to her bedroom to change into some shabby and darned frock, deemed suitable for lunch by Great-Aunt Lizzie; where she would be expected to comb and brush her unruly hair and bind it into two braids, and then to reappear meek and full of apologies and sit through a long lecture on her untidiness and bad manners.

No, Poppy slipped out through the front door, ran down the steps and across the weed-filled gravel to the stables. Quickly she saddled her pony and within a few minutes was galloping through the beech woods along the pathway that led to the boundary between Beech Grove Manor and the Pattenden estates.

She knew a place where she would be welcome to lunch.

Chapter Two
Friday 1 February 1924

Baz had only just arrived and was still in his riding breeches and tweed jacket when Poppy galloped down the avenue that led to the Pattenden house. He had just joined his mother and an elderly gentleman in formal black clothes on the lawn in front of the stately building. Poppy checked her pony, slid from its back and handed the reins to a groom who had appeared at her side.

'Darling Poppy, how lovely to see you. Have you come to lunch? Come and advise me, dear child.' Lady Dorothy was a vague, well-meaning woman who did not have very strong views on anything, but floated through life in a happy dream, allowing her numerous offspring to do whatsoever they wanted. She made an elegant figure, a tall, fashionably dressed lady who did not look like the mother of eight children. In fact, thought Poppy affectionately, she always seemed to act, speak and dress as though she were the same age as her two youngest children: Baz and his sister Joan, just a year his elder. Today Lady Dorothy was wearing a short skirt with an elegant cashmere twinset and a string of the finest pearls that hung down to waist level. Her hair was shingled close to her head and dyed an improbable shade of gold.

'You know this dear man, don't you, darling?' she

said, addressing the air between Poppy and the black-suited man, who bowed and muttered something about being his lordship's solicitor.

'Mother is thinking about building a wing on to the old house.' Baz grinned at Poppy.

The solicitor cleared his throat. 'No doubt his lordship will be interested to listen to any suggestions that your ladyship might like to make to him regarding any improvements,' he said diplomatically.

'His lordship,' said Lady Dorothy with a puzzled frown. 'Oh, you mean Ambrose. It's too, too amusing, darling girl –' she addressed herself to Poppy – 'but my Ambrose has got himself engaged to be married. It seems only the other day when the dear boy was in his pram. And now he has been snapped up. I don't know what possessed him – one of the Berkeleys, my dear! I'm very easy-going, as you know, but I can't live with a Berkeley and he is planning on moving down here to Kent, so I am going to have to build my own wing.'

The solicitor cleared his throat again. He had a harassed look, Poppy noted with amusement. Ambrose had inherited the estate from his father who had died the previous year, but it was apparent that Lady Dorothy reckoned she was still in charge and could direct any alterations to the estate or the house.

'I have come for lunch,' said Poppy with one of her most charming smiles. 'Will I be in the way? Shall I go away again?'

Lady Dorothy shrieked with dismay. 'No, no, I'm relying on you to help me; you're such a sensible little thing. I really need your advice about this building.'

Only Lady Dorothy, thought Poppy, unable to suppress a giggle, would refer to her as 'sensible' – or, given that she was the tallest of the family, as 'little'. However, she did her best and surveyed the handsome house with interest.

'You could build your wing on the front and then Ambrose and the Berkeley girl would have to use the servants' entrance at the back,' she suggested.

'Oh, you naughty little puss,' trilled Lady Dorothy, giving her an impulsive kiss. 'You know I wouldn't do that. I am determined to be the most wonderful mother-in-law in the world.'

'Just so, just so,' said the solicitor, looking uncomfortable. He turned with an air of relief to Baz and told him that his grandfather's will had been proved and the house in Belgravia was ready whenever he wanted to look over it and decide what he wanted to do with it – 'No doubt, his lordship your brother will advise you,' he concluded.

'So sweet of Papa to have left the little house to Baz, wasn't it?' said Lady Dorothy to Poppy. 'You know, I used to worry about this boy; his father wanted him to be a lawyer or something. All the other boys have had estates, but there was nothing left by the time that Baz turned up. You should have been another girl, darling,' she said to Baz.

'Good profession, the law,' said the solicitor slightly stiffly.

'Yes, that's what I used to say to him, didn't I, Basil darling? *Poor dear boy, you will have nothing – you know that you really should go to university and get some sort of profession; what a pity you are not clever*. That's what I used to say.'

'Yes, Mama. You used to say that every time his school reports arrived!' Joan, the youngest of the Pattenden girls, had come out of the house and joined the others on the lawn.

'Well, at least I was never expelled from school like you were,' said Baz.

'Not for dancing in the nude or anything,' explained Joan in a confidential whisper from behind her hand to the solicitor. 'It was just for smoking.'

'And setting the dormitory on fire,' put in Baz as the man tittered uncomfortably.

'That was completely unintentional,' said Joan airily. 'Just a mistake that anyone could have made! Anyway, will you stay for lunch, Mr Duckett? Or do you want to get the two o'clock train back to London? I'll get one of the stable lads to drive you to the station if you do.'

'Oh, I must get the two o'clock,' Mr Duckett insisted, and then, with the air of man nerving himself to dive into an icy sea, said very rapidly, 'And you do understand, your ladyship, that his lordship the Earl wants the house completely vacated of all of the family for four months after Easter so that it can be thoroughly decorated according to his instructions and a new boiler and central-heating system installed.'

'He's turning me out of my house, my own son,' said Lady Dorothy sadly.

'Oh, don't be ridiculous, Mama,' said Joan. 'You've already said that you plan to spend a few months from April in the London house – there's my presentation and my season coming up, you know. And Baz will *have* to come with us, won't you, Baz? You'll have Poppy there at the same time, because she'll be being presented with me. You can dance with her at parties – as long as you make sure first that I have a partner, of course. We'll all have such fun, won't we, Poppy? We'll set London on fire.'

Poppy looked helplessly back. If that letter did not come from Elaine in India, if her father did not give permission, then she would not have a London season at all. Up to now she had felt comforted by the thought that if she didn't go to London, then Baz would not go either. Now she knew that he would have no choice.

She said goodbye mechanically to the solicitor and followed Joan into the house and up the stairs to wash her hands.

I *must* get to London for the season, she thought. I can't bear to be without Baz for three whole months.

Chapter Three
Friday 1 February 1924

Daisy was nowhere to be seen when Poppy returned, but the car was in the stable yard so Poppy guessed that she was in the bedroom they shared. She sneaked up the back stairs in order not to have to meet Great-Aunt Lizzie, opened the door very quietly and found Daisy lying on her bed, sobbing quietly.

'What's wrong?' They had had such fun, herself, Baz and Joan, during the afternoon that, to her shame, she found that she had once again forgotten about the court case. She had been timing her arrival in order to give herself just enough time to get ready for dinner and to encounter Great-Aunt Lizzie in the safe presence of the servants waiting at the table.

'Tell me what happened,' she said nervously. 'Was it very awful?'

Daisy sat up and wiped her eyes. 'Terrible,' she said. 'From start to finish! When we got there the street was full of reporters. I expect that Denis Derrington must have tipped them off. They were awful, shouting questions and pushing notebooks in front of Father. And then all those cameras going off in Father's face – it was an agony for him. It was a good job that we had Morgan with us,' she said. 'He managed to park fairly nearby and you know what he's like; he stands up to people and he managed to clear a way through the crowd for Father and myself. He took no notice of the reporters and cameramen, just shouldered them out of the way.'

Poppy nodded. Morgan was a powerfully built young man and he would not hesitate to tackle the bravest reporter.

'*The Kent Messenger* already had banner headlines: *Local Peer Sued by Heir*,' Daisy went on. 'I hurried Father past, but you can guess what it was like.'

'And what happened in the court?' asked Poppy. She started to tidy her hair, running the comb ruthlessly through the tangles. Somehow it hurt her more than she had anticipated to hear of her father's humiliation.

'Well, Denis Derrington was there, of course – even the lawyer remarked on how happy he was looking. He kept roaring with laughter. I'd never seen him in person before today. He's got very unusual green eyes, and strange eyebrows, sort of winged, going up at the sides . . . Reminded me of someone, but I couldn't think who.'

'How was Father?' asked Poppy anxiously.

'Not good,' said Daisy flatly. 'You see the thing is,' she explained, 'that in theory Father needs to get Denis Derrington's permission before he sells even a single tree. It's just stupid, really. The Pattendens and the Melroses and the Frimleys are selling off farms and using the money to ride out this time of poor prices for the food grown on the farm, but Denis keeps refusing.' She

21

shrugged. 'And then, of course, Father took no notice and went ahead with the sale of some mature woodland – well, you know what he's like, he . . .'

'What happened in the end?' interrupted Poppy. She could guess, but she had to know for sure.

Daisy hesitated. 'Father was very odd in court,' she said eventually. 'He seemed to take no interest in the evidence or the swearing of documents. In the end, when the judge asked him whether he denied receiving the letter from Denis refusing permission to sell any land, Father just stared straight ahead of him and made no answer for a long time. And, you know, Poppy, up to that minute, I thought the judge might be sympathetic to him, going on about Father's large family and he being a widower and everything, but suddenly Father just shouted out, "That's my business." And he was glaring at the judge. And then he said, "I came here for justice, not to be interrogated." And of course the judge didn't like that and told him that he could sit down.'

'And then?' Poppy wished that she didn't have to hear of all of this.

Daisy dabbed at her eyes again with her handkerchief, took a deep breath and said, 'Well, he was fined and told that if he sold any woodland or other property without the written permission of Denis Derrington, then he could be sent to prison.'

Poppy gazed at her with horror.

Daisy started to cry again. 'I hate myself,' she wailed, 'but all the way home the one thing that I kept thinking was: we'll never get to London now for our season, and I'll never have a chance to make a film with Sir Guy. I did so want to become a film director and make some money and now I don't think it will ever happen. We'll be stuck here until we are as old as Great-Aunt Lizzie and nothing good will ever happen to us.'

Resolutely she went across to the washstand, dabbed cold water on to her eyelids and stood for a moment with the towel pressed to her face. Then she walked to the door. 'I'd better go down,' she said over her shoulder. 'Bateman has sounded the gong. Hurry up and change. We don't want any more trouble tonight.'

Chapter Four
Friday 1 February 1924

By the time Poppy came into the dining room the others were seated around the table in the cold, gloomy dining room. They had finished their soup and the battered silver spoons had been replaced into worn china bowls. Poppy slid into her place beside Daisy and stiffened as Great-Aunt Lizzie turned angry eyes towards her. But Bateman, the butler, immediately came forward and ladled soup into her bowl, and Daisy, after one rapid glance at her, continued reading from a letter in her hand.

"'*I must now tell you all the sad and tragic story of a girl who went wrong*," – it's Rose, Poppy,' said Daisy hastily, as if to stop Poppy from saying anything, and Poppy gave a reluctant smile. Ever since Rose had gone to boarding school in Switzerland in January, the family had been bombarded with letters, each of them filled with the terrible deeds of the girls at the school. It had started with a certain Angela, who had daringly greased the floor outside the staffroom with a pot of Vaseline – causing the teachers to go skidding in all directions down the corridor; then it had moved on to Barbara, who had stood up at the end of dinner, rung the headmistress's own hand bell and then publicly decried the food in terms so like Rose's language that Barbara was either briefed by Rose, or else invented by her. Next came Caroline, who daringly sold photographs of ten of the prettiest girls in the school to a white slave trader – even the Earl expressed doubt over that story, though Great-Aunt Lizzie could believe any wickedness of this modern world of 1924. There had also been tales of Dorothy who had stolen the silver cups from the library, pawned them and run away to Paris on the proceeds, and now there was Edwina . . . Michael Derrington was chuckling loudly over her exploits while Great-Aunt Lizzie sat rigid with shock.

Poppy swallowed her soup, and thought of Baz. Odd sentences from Rose's letter wandered into her mind:

'. . . *a young lady of weak will and mislaid morals . . . seduced by the thought of a party in a hot-air balloon . . . an experience as yet totally unknown in her dull and eventless life . . . to the horror of the headmistress and the terror of the teachers!*'

A snort of laughter from the Earl recalled Poppy to herself. Even Bateman was smiling at the vivid picture of the hot-air balloon landing on the hockey pitch at six o'clock in the morning, delivering an inebriated Edwina back to school in time for early morning prayers after she had deposited ten empty champagne bottles on the windowsill of the headmistress's study.

'That girl should be expelled,' declared Great-Aunt Lizzie.

She probably will be, thought Poppy, rapidly finishing her soup, if she's not simply a figment of Rose's fertile imagination. She half heard Daisy tell Great-Aunt Lizzie that Rose had received a prize for having submitted the most book reviews in the first half-term. Poppy peered over Daisy's shoulder and read:

'I gave that boring book five out of five stars as it is so immensely fat that it was useful as a second pillow underneath the thin old thing they give us. I made up the review and the librarian had obviously never read it either as she wrote: EXCELLENT WORK.'

Poppy chewed thoughtfully on the crust of her roll, admiring the way that Daisy skipped bits of Rose's letter and just read out the sections that would amuse or interest the Earl or Great-Aunt Lizzie. Her mind went back to her own concerns. Would the girls be able to have a season? Certainly her father could not afford it since the bank had told him that he could borrow no more money. He probably had not enough money to pay the fine and the court costs. She and Daisy had almost given up hope that their mother's sister Elaine, Daisy's real mother, would, as she had promised, come back from India in order to present the two girls at court, as she had done for their elder sister, Violet. Perhaps Violet would have me to stay, thought Poppy, but that was unlikely. Violet was too busy to be bothered with her younger sisters, not to mention the fact that she also did not have the money to launch the girls into society. Violet and Justin had barely enough for their own needs, although Violet had been hoping that Justin might get an increase in his salary soon.

'Poppy, I've already asked you twice where you have been all of this afternoon,' said Great-Aunt

Lizzie, breaking into her thoughts.

'In my bedroom,' lied Poppy, and crossed her fingers that the old woman had not gone in search of her. The jolly afternoon that she had spent with Baz's family seemed a long way away.

'I've another letter too,' said Daisy hurriedly. 'It's for Poppy and myself – from India.'

A glow of excitement came over Poppy and suddenly she felt full of optimism. Perhaps she was going to get away after all. How clever of Daisy to get Father in a good mood before she broached this one. She watched as Daisy slit the envelope and saw the words inside: 'Dearest Daisy and Poppy'. Unlike their father, Great-Aunt Lizzie had never been told that Daisy knew that her real mother was not Mary Derrington, the mother of Violet, Poppy and Rose, but Elaine, younger sister of Mary – and that Michael was not her father. After the death of Elaine's young lover, she had chosen to bear his child in secret and to transfer Daisy to her sister Mary. Even now Elaine was terrified of her aunt discovering that she had told the truth to her daughter. So whenever she wrote to Daisy there was always a pretence that the letter was for both girls. Poppy's heart began to thud with nervous excitement as she waited for the letter to be read out.

But Michael Derrington had raised a hand. 'Not now, please, Daisy,' he said, and waited until the butler had left the room before saying quietly, 'Elaine has also written to me – I got the letter on my return from court and I wrote

27

back immediately to say that you are both far too young for this nonsense. Next year, when you are eighteen, I may consider it, though I don't like being beholden to another man to launch my daughters into society. After all, Elaine's fortune is now the property of her husband. It was different when Elaine launched Violet. Then she was still a member of this family and not under the care of a husband.'

Poppy gazed at him open-mouthed. 'Father, how can Elaine's money belong to Jack? Her money comes from her legacy and from her first husband's fortune. Jack only has his salary as Chief of the Indian Police – and that's probably a good one, but Elaine is seriously rich. If you think that money belongs to Jack, you are going back a hundred years,' she said impatiently.

'And your great-aunt agrees with me.' Michael Derrington's face had turned dark red with anger. He hated to be contradicted.

'Seventeen is far too young,' said Great-Aunt Lizzie obligingly. 'It's a very bad idea for girls to have a season before they are old enough to behave with decorum. I sometimes wonder whether Violet wasn't a bit young for it all. She certainly didn't take her obligations to the family seriously.'

'It's nothing to do with that,' shouted the Earl. 'I'll look after this family and I'll decide what's best for them. Anyway, I don't like what is going on in London at the moment. I've been reading in the newspapers about all those "Bright Young People" and what they are getting up to. It seems to me that you girls are better off staying down here in the country.'

Poppy stared at her father. The congested face, the staring eyes; how could she get through to him? How could she make him realize the agony that he was causing? Any minute now he would complain of a headache and go off to the library.

'Violet had her season; you allowed her,' she said, trying desperately to keep calm. She felt a lump in her throat. I have to get away, she thought. Baz can't go to London without me!

'And look what came of that,' said Great-Aunt Lizzie caustically. 'She threw away all her chances, the loveliest girl of the season, and married a young man who had been hanging around the house for months. When I think of all the expense, all the money, all the hard work . . .'

'It wasn't your money and it wasn't your hard work,' snapped Poppy before she could prevent herself. She felt Daisy grab her wrist under the table, but she couldn't stop.

'What have you ever done for us but scream and shout and torture us?' she burst out, glaring at the old woman. 'I hate you worse than I hate any living being. I hate you, I hate you, I hate you!' She suddenly felt overwhelmed by her feelings. It had been bad enough when they thought Elaine had forgotten about them, but now that she had at last written, it seemed unendurable that her offer should be turned down. If only Great-Aunt Lizzie would keep out of it, her father could be talked around.

To her horror she felt sobs welling up inside her. She made a dash for the door as Great-Aunt Lizzie shouted, 'Go to your room, instantly, Poppy, and stay there until I give leave for you to come out.'

Shaking with sobs, Poppy slammed the door behind her and raced for the back stairs, almost knocking over Maud the scullery maid as she went. A clap of thunder shook the house as she climbed up the narrow staircase and rain crashed against the windows. The butler called to Maud to put buckets under the drips in the attic and Poppy stood back, pretending to look out of a small window on the landing to allow the girl to pass. The rain was coming down in sheets and the sky was filled with lightning. A blocked drain in the yard below overflowed and a large pond began to form in front of the scullery door. One of these days, she thought savagely, this house will just rot away. There were patches of mould on the walls of the back stairs that kept coming back no matter how often Maud was sent to scrub them away. Poppy took a long breath to try to control her sobs and wiped her face with her handkerchief. She climbed the rest of the stairs, going quickly to avoid coming face to face with the scullery maid on her way back down from the attic.

'What am I going to do?' she said aloud as she closed the bedroom door behind her and threw herself on the bed. If it weren't for Baz she would wish herself dead. She thought briefly about a hunger strike but wasn't sure that she could keep it up for long enough to be effective. Great-Aunt Lizzie's anger at Violet's marriage to a penniless young lawyer, at her failure to make a good match and tow her family out of their crippling poverty, had been voiced before now, but Poppy had not realized that it would affect the chances of Daisy and herself having a season and escaping this terrible house. She moaned softly to herself and curled up on the bed, her arms hugging her shoulders as though she had been mortally wounded. Once April came, Baz would be ferried off to London by his mother, Lady Dorothy, and would be kept busy there going to party after party with his sister Joan. Perhaps he might even meet another girl there and forget about her. She remembered the portraits of the pretty girls in the magazines that Joan collected, that they, all three, had been looking through after lunch. Baz had been admiring some of them. She had not minded then – but what if she were stuck down in Kent while he was there in London, going to parties every night? Surely it would be too much to ask that he not dance with these pretty girls, flirt with them . . . At that thought she began to shiver and then realized that she was cold and pulled the eiderdown over her. She wished she could sleep but sobs kept shaking her. Her pillow was soaked with tears. The agony seemed to last for a very, very long time.

Finally the door opened and Daisy hurried across to her.

'I got away as soon as I could,' she said with her arm around Poppy's shoulders, holding her tightly and dropping kisses on Poppy's head. She, of all people in the house, understood the violent emotions that ripped

Poppy in half and seemed almost to threaten her sanity. 'It's all right, my pet,' she murmured again and again, until Poppy drew in a deep breath and sat up. Daisy relaxed her grip a little and dropped another kiss on her dark red hair. 'Don't worry,' she said. 'I would have come earlier, but I had to calm things down a bit. I told Great-Aunt Lizzie in a whisper that it was your time of the month – and that embarrassed Father so much he got all red in the face. Then he told me to tell you not to upset yourself and that he would try to arrange some little treat for you.'

'A new dolly, I suppose,' said Poppy, wiping her eyes.

'He adores you,' said Daisy. 'Don't forget that.' Something in her voice made Poppy remember that Daisy's father, Clifford, died at the age of seventeen, leaving his beloved Elaine pregnant, in the middle of season as a debutante, to the mercies of her aunt. For a moment Poppy felt almost ashamed of herself; she did know that her father adored her, but what good was adoration if he was going to try to keep her as a little girl, hidden away in a crumbling old house?

'It's just that Baz has no choice but to go to London for four months,' Poppy murmured. 'His brother is remodelling the house. If we don't get to have a season, I won't see him . . . or the rest of the jazz band, for months,' she added hurriedly.

'I'll do my best,' said Daisy.

'I know,' said Poppy, and she squeezed Daisy's hand. 'Baz and I . . .' she began shyly and then, 'You'll never 'guess,' she said, looking into Daisy's cornflower-blue eyes.

'I think I might,' said Daisy with an amused smile.

'He kissed me,' went on Poppy in a whisper. 'You can't imagine. I still can't believe it.'

Then she drew in a deep breath and hardened her heart; she had to do it – her life or her sanity depended on getting away from this house and away from Great-Aunt Lizzie.

'There is one thing that you could do, Daisy,' she said, hating herself and yet telling herself that she was doing this for Daisy's sake as well as her own. Daisy needed to get away from this house and go to London if she were ever to fulfil her ambition to be a film director. 'You do want to go too, don't you?' she asked.

'Of course.' Daisy's voice was emphatic. 'I can't wait. It's not just the season, though I know I'd enjoy that. It's everything else – it's being independent, leading my own life, starting my directing career.' Daisy stopped and Poppy could tell from the half-smile that trembled on her lips that she was seeing visions of that future.

'And you're not willing to let this vision go; that's right, isn't it?' Poppy heard a hard, rather calculating note in her voice, but she didn't care. Daisy was right; they both had to fight for their future happiness. They could not leave it to others to arrange their lives for them.

'Well then,' she continued in a steady voice, 'Elaine is the only one who should decide whether you should have a London season. She *is* your mother. You should send her a telegram and . . .' Poppy hesitated, then drove herself on, 'and then, once we've done that, you can go to Father and tell him he has no right to forbid you to do what your mother wants.' Poppy stopped. Daisy had a stricken look.

'I'm sorry,' she said quickly.

'No,' said Daisy slowly. 'You're right. It's funny, isn't it? When you're young you think that grown-ups must always be right, but then, when you grow up, you realize that they can be wrong sometimes. Father is wrong about this, and I think that I must tell him.'

Despite her confident words, her face was very white and her blue eyes were wide and frightened-looking.

With a cry, Poppy threw her arms around Daisy. She suddenly realized that, to Daisy, Michael Derrington's good opinion was important – that she needed his favour to feel part of the family.

'I'm a pig,' Poppy cried remorsefully. 'Don't do it, Daisy, unless you are really doing it for yourself.'

'I'm doing it for both of us. When things are not fair, one has to remedy them.' Daisy's voice was steady. She bit her lip and tried to smile. 'But I'm not going to sneak down to the post office and send a telegram without talking to him first.'

'Let me do it,' begged Poppy.

Without waiting for an answer she burst out of the room and ran down the stairs, safe in the knowledge that Great-Aunt Lizzie always had a snooze after dinner. Daisy followed slowly.

'Father,' said Poppy dramatically as she burst into the library, 'I must speak to you.'

She threw herself at his feet on to the rug before the miserable fire of wet timber that smoked in the fireplace. His high colour had faded and now he just looked pale and miserable.

'It's not just about me,' she said, as calmly as she could. He could not bear too much emotion and was quite liable to get up and walk away if she wept all over him. She heard the door open and Daisy come in, but she did not look around. 'You see,' she said more calmly, 'Elaine has been longing and longing to come back over to see Daisy.' She hesitated for a moment and then said bravely, 'I know that Daisy is her daughter and that Justin's uncle, Clifford Pennington, was her father; Daisy told me when she first found out. Elaine has been waiting for the excuse of a season to come back over again and see her only daughter, and Daisy . . .' She stopped.

On the desk she could see a letter lying open. She recognized the handwriting. It was from Denis Derrington, the heir to the Beech Grove Manor estate. The script was large and the words jumped out at Poppy.

I hope that you intend to pay the fine that was fixed by the court. If I do not get the money within one month then I will drag you through every court in the land and I will make you penniless. Your daughters will be without a home and you will have to beg in the streets for all that I care.

And do not imagine that you can sell any part of the estate without my knowledge. You are trying to destroy the heritage that should be mine and I will not stand for it.

See you in court again!

And below that was the signature: *Denis Derrington*.

No wonder that her father was depressed. He stared silently into the fire.

'Father, I know that you are worried about money,' Poppy said gently, 'but Daisy should see her mother again.'

He lifted his eyes at that. 'I suppose you would both be better off without me,' he said unexpectedly. He looked at Daisy, hesitated and then seemed to force the words out. 'I'm sorry, Daisy. I had no right to refuse – it's up to your mother. I'm sorry that I acted on impulse and replied to that letter without consulting you. But it's gone now, I'm afraid.'

'Let me ride down to the post office and fetch your letter back,' said Daisy softly. 'It won't go until nine o'clock tomorrow morning. Don't worry about it. I'll tell Mrs Jefferies that you meant to enclose something,' she added in a matter-of-fact way.

Somehow this practical suggestion seemed to work wonders. He turned his eyes away from the letter and looked at Daisy properly for the first time. He even smiled a little. She perched on the arm of his chair and put an arm around his shoulders. Poppy sat on the threadbare rug beside his feet and put her arms around his knees, hugging him and resting her head on his knee.

'You'll be proud of us one of these days,' Poppy whispered. He had said nothing about her having a season, but his eyes were soft and affectionate now and she knew that he would not disappoint her. Elaine has invited me as well as Daisy, she thought and then her mind went to Baz. First of all, the jazz club had to be a huge success, and then her father would see that she would be better off married. Violet and Justin were not rich, but no one ever bewailed their lot, these days. They were happy, well-fed and lived in a snug little house – not in a fashionable part of London but that did not seem to matter. They had lots of friends and went out to parties all the time. Great-Aunt Lizzie might deem Violet's marriage a failure, but no one else in the family, looking at her happy face, could think like that.

'Won't you say yes?' Poppy murmured, lifting her head to look at her father. 'I'll die if you won't.'

There was a struggle on his face. Daisy watched him anxiously from under her eyelashes. Suddenly he got up, disentangling himself gently from their arms, and walked over to his desk. He picked up the letter from Denis Derrington and flung it into the fire. There was a momentary flash of heat as the letter burned and then the damp wood went back to sizzling slowly. Her father had picked the telephone receiver from its perch and stood holding it. In the quiet room the girls could hear the postmistress's slightly breathless voice, saying, 'Yes, my lord,' in respectful tones.

'Get me Fuggle, will you, Mrs Jefferies?' It was typical of him that he had never bothered to memorize the telephone number of his estate manager but treated the exchange as though it were part of Beech Grove Manor.

'Fuggle, that you? I've made up my mind. Get in touch with those timber merchants. I'm selling the Binton Wood timber; yes, that's right.'

Poppy could hear the estate manager's agitated voice and looked apprehensively at Daisy. Was everything to go wrong now, just as she thought that they had talked him around? What had made him think of Binton Wood, the finest of all the beech woods on their estate? Surely he had been told that he was not allowed to sell any more of the woods. She wished that Mr Fuggle would stop talking. Any opposition to his decisions these days sent the Earl into such towering fits of rage. Now he looked as though shortly he would foam at the mouth.

'Sir Denis!' he yelled, his mouth close to the receiver. 'What has Sir Denis to do with this? It's my property still, I would remind you. I'll sell Binton Wood if I want to sell it. You take your orders from me, man, or you can start looking for another job.'

And then he slammed the phone down, turned to the two girls and amazingly he smiled broadly and said: 'I'm damned if I'll allow another man to pay for my daughters' coming-out dresses.'

Chapter Five
Tuesday 1 April 1924

It had been snowing overnight. The bright light streamed through the threadbare curtains of the shabby bedroom Daisy shared with Poppy. She woke up, put a hand out and quickly pulled it back under the blankets. The air was freezing.

Beech Grove Manor was such a beautiful old house, but what a pity, thought Daisy drowsily, that the Earl did not have the money to heat or repair it. Even though it was April, the rooms were still freezing cold. This bedroom had been designed as a nursery for the two girls over seventeen years ago and neither the furniture nor the carpet nor the curtains had been renewed since. Years of almost no fires through the winter months had brought out patches of damp in the faded yellow wallpaper.

Still, thought Daisy, today we are going to London. She hoped that the snow would not prevent that, but then reassured herself. April snow seldom lasted long. She and Poppy had spent weeks dreaming of the day when they would finally leave Beech Grove Manor for London. Once they got there it wouldn't matter how cold it was.

She and Poppy would be staying with Elaine, just back from the heat of India, and there was no doubt that she would have hired a luxurious and warm house and that there would be fires in every room as well as central heating. Elaine was a rich young woman. She had inherited a fortune, married a wealthy Anglo-Indian from whom she had inherited another fortune, and her second husband, the Honourable Sir John Nelborough, had recently been knighted by the dashing young Prince of Wales.

Daisy smiled. London would be wonderful. They would wear lovely clothes and have fun shopping, going to balls and perhaps even meeting handsome young men. She pictured herself in a smart short dress and short coat, with one of these head-hugging little hats, dashing through London on her way to the film studios. The thought gave her courage. Rapidly she jumped out of bed, washed in icy water from a bowl in their dressing room, pulled on a pair of ancient and well-patched riding breeches and added two large jumpers on top. She gazed at herself in the mirror for a moment. She looked rather well, she thought – very like her mother, Elaine. Perhaps, she mused, with a smile at her reflection, she would, like her mother, marry a very rich man and be able to rescue the family fortunes. She knew how it all worked out. First of all, in just over a month's time there would be the great day. THE GREAT DAY, Elaine had written, giving it the dignity of large capital letters – the day when she and Poppy had their coming-out ball. And then another great day when they would be presented at court! And sometime at one of the balls or dances that were held during the following couple of months, an incredibly handsome man, rather like Mr Darcy in Jane Austen's *Pride and Prejudice*, would be attracted to her, would ask for an introduction and then would fall madly in love with her and ask her hand in marriage.

This vague figure of her imagination would be so very rich that it would be nothing for him to rescue the Beech Grove Manor estate; he would build a house somewhere on the outskirts of the beech woods, or perhaps near to the lake, and they would spend a few weeks there every year – as well, of course, as having a house in London with a special darkroom and studio for her film work and perhaps a small apartment in the fashionable part of Paris.

She sat for a moment with a smile on her face and the comb in her hand and laughed at herself and her visions. Then she went out, leaving Poppy still sleeping, her magnificent sheaf of red hair spread on the threadbare pillowcase.

The snow covered everything. Daisy stopped at the large window halfway down the stairs, rubbed the frost patterns from the glass and peered out. The weed-spotted gravel avenue, the neglected lawns and unpruned shrubs were all covered in a light blanket of snow that made them look almost magical, and the frozen lake sparkled with white crystals.

There was no one in the dining room when Daisy came in, but she was glad to see that the scullery maid had lit a small fire in the fireplace. The table was laid for breakfast and the post boy must have made his way up from the village, because there were letters already on the table – a pile of bills beside the Earl's plate, a letter from Violet and, placed centrally between her place and Poppy's, a letter with a Swiss stamp.

'Letter from Lady Rose, my lady,' said Bateman, who had followed her in. The elderly butler was trying to conceal a smile. Daisy picked it up and chuckled. The envelope said:

THE DEBUTANTES
BEECH GROVE MANOR
WOOLSDEN
KENT

And in the left-hand corner, in tiny letters, was written:

FROM A LONELY PRISONER IN A FOREIGN LAND.

Daisy tucked the letter into the wide pocket of her riding breeches without reading it. If she opened it at table Great-Aunt Lizzie would want to know all about it and would be bound to find fault with something that Rose had said in the letter – she might even write to the headmistress. Rose was going rather over the top with her dramatic stories these days. Daisy had written to tell her to tone them down or there would be trouble, but Rose could not resist inventing new exciting happenings and dropping hints that it was not a suitable place for a well-behaved girl like herself.

'She's not really unhappy at that boarding school, Bateman,' she said reassuringly, knowing he would have read the pathetic message in the corner of the envelope. 'You know what she's like; she always makes a drama out of everything. Switzerland will be very good for her coughs and colds.' Rose's health had always been a worry to her father, and that was the only reason why he had consented to Elaine's plan to pay to send her to the same boarding school she had attended when she was Rose's age.

At that moment she noticed on her chair an ancient book with a mould-spotted leather cover.

'What on earth . . . ?' she began to say and then saw the title in faded gold lettering: *Etiquette for Young Ladies*.

'Lady Elizabeth desired Nora to find this in the library, and to place it on your chair; she thought you would wish to take it with you to London, my lady,' observed Bateman in his most non-committal fashion.

Bother, thought Daisy. I'm certainly not taking this smelly, dusty old book with me. However, it would be best to show an interest and then to tuck it away in some place where Great-Aunt Lizzie would be unlikely to find it during the next few months. Daisy settled herself on a chair as near to the fire as possible and began to turn over the pages.

'*Never remove your gloves when making a formal call*,' she read aloud, and yawned.

We shouldn't be burning this wet wood, she thought as the fire hissed. Morgan, the chauffeur, who did all the odd jobs around the estate, had told Father that the timber, from one of the ancient stands of woodland, should be stacked for at least another year before burning, but they had no choice. The Earl could not afford much coal, so trees had to be cut down and the timber burned within weeks of being sawn and split.

Daisy flicked through the dusty pages of the book, skipping the sections about letter writing and country-house visiting and moving on to Court Presentations.

'*Names have to be submitted to the Lord Chamberlain*,' she read. '*Only those bearing the white flower of a blameless life will pass his scrutiny. No girl who has been born out of wedlock may be presented to their majesties and admitted to the court as a debutante*.'

Daisy felt the book drop from her hands and she gazed into the fire.

What was she going to do if her secret was revealed?

If that happened, any chance of meeting a wealthy young man and making a wonderful match would be destroyed.

Chapter Six
Tuesday 1 April 1924

It was only when they were halfway to London in the old-fashioned Humber car that Daisy remembered the letter from Rose.

'Bother,' she said aloud, and Maud, who was coming to London with them to act as their maid, turned her head to look over the back seat and Morgan's eyes left the road momentarily to meet hers in the mirror.

'What's wrong?' asked Poppy.

'I left a letter to us from Rose in my old riding breeches and I hadn't even opened it,' said Daisy. She and Poppy had not packed any of the shabby clothes that they wore at home. Elaine had bought them elegant new outfits on her last visit to London and these they had kept wrapped in tissue paper and sealed into a trunk, so that they would be pristine for their next visit. Daisy, who was plump, had been conscious that a few of the clothes were a little tight on her. Still, Elaine had promised shopping trips in order to have everything right for their debut into London society.

'Won't be anything of importance,' stated Poppy. She was fizzing with excitement, swinging her foot and humming fragments of jazz. 'We're going to be different, Daisy,' she said. 'We're going to be the leaders of fashion – we're going to have parties that will make all the other girls envious.'

Daisy giggled. 'I can't imagine Elaine throwing wild parties for us, and as for Jack – well, can you imagine Sir John, His Excellency, the High Commissioner of Indian Police, allowing his wife to do anything of the sort?'

'We'll find a way.' Poppy tossed her splendid mane of red hair over her shoulder and smiled to herself. She lowered her voice to a whisper, glancing at the broad back of the chauffeur, and gave a quick giggle. 'Baz and I have been making plans,' she said, and looked out of the window.

'You might as well put wild parties out of your head,' Daisy said. All sorts of promises had been made and it was only when Elaine's husband, the newly decorated Sir John, had added his plea and had undertaken to make sure that the girls were well looked after that Michael Derrington felt totally reconciled to the plans. He had made as many conditions as possible before agreeing though. They were always to be chaperoned. Morgan was to drive them everywhere. Skirts were not to be too short. And above all, they were not to get themselves labelled in the newspapers as Bright Young People. Elaine would be keeping a strict eye on them.

Poppy shrugged and grinned slyly. Daisy frowned slightly. What was Poppy up to? Baz's sister Joan was being presented at the same time as them. Their mother had taken a house for the season and Baz was coming too, to keep his sister company and to be away from the

Pattenden estate during the refurbishment works. Joan was nearly twenty, a little old for a debutante – she had gone down with pneumonia halfway through her season the year before – but she and her married sister had a reputation of being in with rather a wild set in London.

Daisy looked closely at Poppy. 'You're up to something,' she said. Once again she could see Morgan's dark eyes in the driver's mirror and knew he thought so too. 'I don't see Baz's mother throwing any wild parties either, whatever his sister is like,' she added.

'You've forgotten that Baz has his own house,' said Poppy mischievously.

Daisy's eyes widened. But she said nothing as Morgan was negotiating a tricky path between a bus and a speeding sports car full of young people. In any case, if Poppy and Baz were planning something like that, perhaps the least said the better.

'Be there in few minutes now,' announced Morgan. 'We'll be half an hour early. I hope Lady Elaine will be in. They were due yesterday, weren't they?'

But when they arrived at the stylish house in Grosvenor Square only the butler came to the door, a newly engaged starchy young man with an air of self-importance, who introduced himself as Tellford and looked amazed to see them.

'I regret that neither Lady Elaine nor Sir John is here yet,' he said in answer to Morgan's query. 'Their ship has been delayed. They won't dock until tomorrow or the next day. We had a wire the day before yesterday, as you did, I presume,' he added frostily, ignoring Morgan and holding out a telegram to Poppy.

She took it and uttered an exaggerated exclamation of surprise. Perhaps, thought Daisy, Poppy was practising for her London season when, judging by the group that their sister Violet had been part of, all the girls shrieked in astonishment or made noises like peahens. Daisy held out her hand for the telegram and read aloud:

ARRIVAL DELAYED FOR THREE DAYS STOP
HAVE TELEGRAPHED THE EARL STOP
NELBOROUGH

'What!' exclaimed Daisy. 'We received no telegram at Beech Manor. How odd!'

'Perhaps, I should take you ba—' began Morgan, but Poppy quickly interrupted him.

'That will be all, thank you, Morgan. I hope that you find your quarters comfortable. Perhaps you will ask a footman to direct our chauffeur to where he should put the car and his belongings, Tellford; I presume our rooms are ready?'

Maud gave them a quick glance and then disappeared towards the back stairs, like a well-trained lady's maid.

'Yes, indeed, my lady.' Tellford was a little overawed by Poppy's frosty manner. 'Everything has been prepared for your ladyships. It's just that—'

'But . . .' interrupted Morgan, at the same moment; the two men looked at each other.

'Thank you, Morgan,' said Poppy, raising her eyebrows in a lofty manner, and Daisy said hastily,

'We'll be fine, Morgan, thank you,' and the chauffeur said no more.

'This way, your ladyships,' said Tellford, and he escorted them upstairs to their rooms, which both overlooked the square and had fires burning in them.

'I'll send your ladyships' maid to unpack for you,' he murmured, and then left them both in the room that Daisy had selected. She warmed her hands at the fire and waited until he had closed the door almost noiselessly behind him before saying to Poppy, 'Where is it?'

'Where's what?' Poppy turned her large eyes that tried to look innocent, but were brimming with mischief, towards her.

'Don't try to fool me,' said Daisy, trying to repress a grin. 'I'm not stupid. I know what happened. You got that telegram. I saw you meet the post boy a couple of days ago. I forgot about it afterwards. And all that talk about parties. You knew we would be on our own for a day or two.'

'Lucky, wasn't it?' Poppy wore a wide smile. She took from her handbag a post-office form and held it out.

ENGINE TROUBLE STOP SHIP DELAYED FOR AT LEAST THREE DAYS STOP SUGGEST GIRLS WAIT UNTIL NEXT WEEK STOP ELAINE, read Daisy.

'Sounds more like Jack than Elaine, doesn't it?' said Poppy thoughtfully. 'Can't imagine her being so forceful. Anyway, why should we miss a week of our lovely, lovely time in London just because that silly ship has engine trouble? Well, let's get rid of this, now, before anyone can see it,' she said, throwing the telegram into the fire. 'I just saved it for you because I thought you'd be so grateful to me that I would be able to bend you to my will in all things. Otherwise, you know, you'd still be back in Beech Grove with Great-Aunt Lizzie instructing you how to act like a young lady. And who knows, Father might have decided to cancel the whole business. You know what he's like, especially at the moment!'

'Morgan wanted to take us home again,' said Daisy warningly.

'I'll talk him around; anyway, he has the boot of the Humber full of his own drums and Simon's saxophone and things like that. He'll have to take them over to Baz's place. It's all arranged. I can't see him being serious about taking us back to Kent, can you?'

Typical Poppy, thought Daisy, always thinking about her music and the jazz band that the chauffeur ran in his little cottage in the woods behind Beech Grove Manor House.

'Still,' said Daisy, half to herself, 'it's not as though we're on our own. I suppose there is a housekeeper and then there's that butler and the footman, and probably a cook and a lady's maid, as well as Maud. And we'll both have to swear that no telegram arrived.' She was beginning to weaken. London would be such fun on their own. However, some things had to be established.

'Listen, Poppy,' she said as Maud came silently into the room and looked around, 'you can forget about going out at night alone to a wild party. If that ever came out, then our reputations would be ruined, we'd be bundled straight back to Kent and Father would refuse permission for us to have a London season, not just this year, but for ever and ever. You remember all the fuss there was – all those letters and telegrams to India during the last couple of months. And there are things that I want to do in London; I'm not going to put that at risk just for one wild party. I suppose you and Baz have planned it for this evening, haven't you?' Daisy saw a flash of amusement in Maud's very green eyes and guessed that she was sounding a bit elderly, but if she was going to make a good match with a rich young man, she would have to be careful. *A reputation, once lost, can never be regained*, was one of Great-Aunt Lizzie's favourite sayings. She would not worry too much about romance, she thought firmly. Her destiny was to marry money and rescue her family. 'Tell me what's going to happen, Poppy?' she said firmly.

'It's all settled,' said Poppy sulkily. 'Oh, come on, Daisy. It will be all right. Morgan will be there. And you know what a mother hen he is, always clucking over us and making sure that we behave like young ladies.'

Daisy bit back a smile. Nothing was less like a mother hen than Morgan with his broad shoulders and determined jaw, but it was true that he was protective of them.

'Morgan is all right to drive us to a party,' she pointed out now, 'but not even Elaine would consider that he was the correct person for a debutante's escort. What do you expect him to do: sit on a little gilt-legged chair with the other dowagers and watch us dance?'

Poppy giggled. 'It's not going to be that sort of party. Oh, come on, Daisy, don't be so stuffy. We're going to have fun, fun, fun! I'm sick of leading a dreary life with Father in his moods, the house freezing cold, Great-Aunt Lizzie lecturing if we raise our voices above a whisper. I want to be wild for just one night. Just one night, Daisy! That's not much to ask, is it? It's all arranged. And I'll never forgive you if you spoil things. Don't go if you like; I don't care, but I'm going and you can't stop me.'

Daisy opened her mouth, but then shut it again. She knew Poppy was stubborn and once she had made up her mind there was little use in trying to shift her. Daisy still remembered the battles when she had given up classical music on her violin and had demanded a clarinet and jazz lessons. Great-Aunt Lizzie had a steely will, but she had met her match in her great-niece. Daisy crossed over to the window seat and stared down to the street below while she tried to think of a way out.

'I know,' she said eventually. 'We'll take Vi and Justin. She's a married woman, therefore must be able to chaperone her sisters. Let's telephone her now and tell her about the treat in store for her.'

Poppy might not care about what people think, she thought to herself, but I can't let *my* reputation be injured if *I* am going to make a splendid match.

Chapter Seven
Tuesday 1 April 1924

As soon as Morgan pulled up outside Baz's little house in Belgravia, Poppy jumped out of the old Humber, leaving Morgan to unload the drums. The misty London midday sun was doing its best to shine through a haze of fog as, followed by Maud, she ran up the steps and banged on the knocker of the front door. Simon opened the door to her; Edwin was lugging a suitcase up the bare boards of the staircase, but came back down to greet Poppy. Then George swung himself down from over the banisters, landing with a loud thud in the back hallway, and rushed towards the front door. Poppy's face lit up at the sight of them and she hugged the three boys vigorously.

'Baz is downstairs, Pops,' said Edwin, giving Maud an inquisitive glance and then shaking her gravely by the hand when Poppy casually said, 'This is Maud,' before flying down the basement steps.

'Baz!' she cried delightedly, as she pounced on him at the bottom of the stairwell, before hurriedly disentangling herself when she heard voices nearby.

Morgan had gone down the outside steps to the basement to unpack his drums, and when they looked into the kitchen he was already lighting a large old stove. Baz's sister Joan was there too, gazing worriedly at the dirty ceiling and the blank walls. She looked despairingly at them when they came in.

'My dears,' she said uncertainly, 'are you sure that this is quite right for a party? I know it's a perfectly sweet house, but this basement! Of course, the cobwebs do give it atmosphere, I suppose . . . and those filthy windows shut out the view of that dirty wall and the pavement above, but, my darlings – I don't like to say this – and it may be the latest fashion to have peeling whitewash on the walls and a floor thick in dirt, and spiders everywhere, but I do think that there is rather a strange smell, and it's . . . well, I have to say it – this place is positively filthy.'

'What are we going to do?' said Baz, looking worried. 'Joan and I sent out the invitations; we have to have it tonight. You said that we should give it a go as soon as you came to London, didn't you, Morgan?'

'I anticipated a little more notice,' grumbled Morgan, 'but it's the music that will count.'

'The party is supposed to start at nine,' wailed Joan. She looked around the desolate basement with despair. 'What are we going to do?' she said gloomily. 'I was thinking about Christmas decorations, but they are all down in Kent. I suppose it mightn't look too bad when it's full of people.'

'I've got an idea,' said Poppy eagerly. 'We'll just cover up the walls. I wish we had money for silk. Violet said they went to a party where the hostess had lined the walls with strips of silk.' She thought about it for a moment while the others looked at her doubtfully.

'Silk is definitely out, I'd have thought – too expensive,' put in Morgan, striking a match.

'What about newspaper?' Joan looked at *The Daily Express* beside Morgan and said rapidly, 'That would be too, too unique. We could cut out all the gossip columns and stick them on to the walls. Everyone could go around reading about themselves. *The Daily Express* is full of pictures of all of us Bright Young People.' She seemed cheered by the idea, but the others raised eyebrows and looked at each other doubtfully.

'What about artificial silk?' Poppy felt excited. There was no doubt that the walls covered in flaking plaster looked very dreary. 'Do you remember, Baz, Great-Aunt Lizzie was talking about how silk was becoming déclassé because these days all the shop girls dressed in artificial silk since it was so cheap. I wonder where you could buy artificial silk and how much it would cost.'

'What about going to Petticoat Lane and buying some there?' said Maud, giving her opinion in way that would have shocked the housekeeper back at Beech Grove Manor.

'Petticoat Lane – the very place,' said Poppy enthusiastically.

Joan stared at her. 'Petticoat Lane,' she said uncertainly. 'Darlings, where's that? Never heard of it, and I know everywhere in London.'

Poppy ignored Joan. She had never heard of it either, but she wanted to keep things moving.

'How much money have we all got?' asked Baz. He

took an old plate from a shelf, put a ten-shilling note on it and then passed it around. By the end he had collected two pounds.

'Too, too shaming to have to ask for money,' said Joan vaguely. 'Why didn't the silly old man leave you a fortune as well as a house, Baz baby?'

'Because he gambled it all away – he had to sell the big house, poor old fellow. I was lucky to get even this,' said Baz. He looked perfectly happy as he stuffed the money into Poppy's bag.

'You girls go and buy the silk and we'll scrub the place and wash the windows,' he said.

'In a minute.' Edwin took up his trumpet and blew an exploratory note into it, but Poppy snatched it from him and placed it on a shelf.

'I think that Maud should stay and make sure that they do it properly,' she said. 'Now, boys, no playing jazz until we get this place looking shipshape.'

'I say, would you like me to lend you my riding whip?' Joan asked Maud. 'Are you sure you will manage?'

'I'll manage,' said Maud firmly. 'Give me a shilling or two and I'll go and get some soap and anything else that we need.' She opened a cupboard and found an immense array of mops, brooms and dusters.

Joan gave a squeal of delight. 'A witch's broom!' she said. 'That has to go across the window.'

'Let's go,' said Poppy. She thought that they should move quickly before Morgan had any doubts about taking the two girls without a maid in attendance. If the place was to be cleaned up, then Maud's supervision was essential.

'Too, too sweet of you,' said Joan, smiling warmly at Maud. 'I say, I hope you don't mind my remarking, but I do love your eyebrows. Most unusual. How do you get them to have that sort of tilted-up shape? Do you go to a beauty parlour?'

'No, my lady.' Maud gave a giggle. 'I wouldn't know a beauty parlour if I saw one, but I do know plenty about cleaning.'

'She'll lick this place into shape or my name is not Bob Morgan,' said the chauffeur with a grin.

'Do you like the name Bob?' said Joan with interest. 'I suppose it's got a solid, reliable, sensible sort of sound to it, but it is quite boring, isn't it? Oh dear, am I embarrassing you? Do say if I am.'

'Not at all,' said Morgan politely. 'I don't like the name Bob either. Reminds me of the orphanage. My middle name is St Clair, if that would suit you better.'

'Bettermost,' approved Joan. 'I shall call you St Clair. It's got a nice ring to it. I say, Poppy darling, does your papa have one of those tubey thingamajigs in your car. I do fancy calling "St Clair" down it.'

'Take no notice of her,' advised Baz. 'Lots of insanity in my family. We try to keep it quiet, but it does tend to seep out. What colour silk will you get, Poppy? What about a sort of flame-coloured red like your hair? What would you think about that, Joan?'

'Oh dear,' said Joan again. 'I do so hate decisions.

Can't we leave it all to St Clair?'

'You choose the colour,' said Morgan decisively. 'I'm buying a hammer and some tacks. That will be my part in the shopping.'

'I have an idea,' said Poppy, suddenly inspired. 'Why don't we call for Violet and Daisy? Violet has great taste and she always knows which colours go together.'

Violet was pleased to go, and Poppy was glad that she had thought of it. She had forgotten how good Violet was at anything practical. Joan passed the time between Violet's house and Petticoat Lane by pretending that the bumper-to-bumper jam of cars on the Strand was a racing track and that number twenty-nine, driven by an intrepid racing driver called St Clair, was edging into the lead.

'I would so love to have a car,' she said with a sigh. 'Dearest St Clair, you must teach me to drive. I feel, deep within me, that I was born to be a racing driver. I'll even give up smoking in order to achieve my ambition. The steward at the racing track where I went last Sunday was such a bore about my throwing cigarette ends over into some barrels full of water – or rather they weren't full of water, but petrol, but how was I to know that, my dears? Oh, that looks like the market, doesn't it? Now, St Clair, imagine that I'm waving the little blue flag and that means you must pull over.' And then, in a loud whisper to Daisy, she said, 'Doesn't St Clair have the most wonderful eyes? So beautifully brown, just like moorland pools.'

*

By the time that they got back from the market, the place no longer smelt of mould and mice but very strongly of carbolic soap. It was clean, but still rather dismal.

Violet's presence was an inspiration, thought Poppy. It was Violet who organized everyone to open all the doors and windows, Violet who had the good idea of soaking a sponge in eau de cologne, which was then set into a bowl behind the warm stove. By that stage everything began to smell much more party-like and then they all set to work on transforming the basement. Coral-red swathes of artificial silk were tacked on to the beams and draped down the walls by Morgan and the boys; Joan stood on a chair with an old deaf-aid trumpet which she had found in a cupboard and called out orders to 'St Clair'; Daisy and Simon draped short lengths of black silk over the small windows; Poppy blew softly into her clarinet and imagined the scene that night.

'Candles better be kept away from this stuff,' called out Morgan, as Baz came back from the store cupboard with a few dozen, mice-nibbled plain white ones. 'I'd say that is very flammable,' he commented, running the silky material between his finger and thumb.

'Dear St Clair; the man knows everything,' intoned Joan into her deaf-aid, and everyone looked startled as the booming sound echoed around the room.

'Fix them into bowls of water with some of that eau de cologne thrown into it,' said Violet authoritatively. 'Wait a minute – did I see some old bottles of red food colouring in one of the cupboards, Maud? Yes, that's the one. Good job that there are all those white bowls stacked up in the crockery cupboard. I'll cover that terrible old table with the last piece of black cloth and we'll put the bowls and the candles on it. When people come in, tell them to put the food and drink on the table. It'll look great. They are bringing food and drink, aren't they, Baz?' Violet's tone was crisp and efficient, but for once she did not annoy Poppy. There was no doubt that her eldest sister had been a great source of ideas.

'Told them it was a house-warming and they'd be turned away if they did not come with both hands full,' confirmed Baz.

'And they'll believe him. He's a funny fellow,' said Joan, looking at her youngest brother with affectionate amusement. 'He's the only person in the world who never tells lies. He's famous for it. Now, dears, I need to get back and start my beauty routine. Dear St Clair, when I come back you will be stunned at the sight of me. You will kneel at my feet and worship me with your wonderful dark eyes. Come on, Baz, dear Daisy is getting an irritated look and I always know when people are getting tired of me.'

Chapter Eight
Tuesday 1 April 1924

Back at Jack and Elaine's house in Grosvenor Square, Poppy smiled at her reflection in the full-length looking-glass in her bedroom. Her gown was a straight shift with narrow shoulder straps. It was made of sunset-coloured silk chiffon; the bodice and dropped waist of coral pink shading into a pale purple, and both colours were misted over with a lace overdress. Its length just skimmed her knee and Poppy felt like a princess as she moved across to Daisy's bedroom.

'Oh, I'd forgotten how nice you looked in that black net over the pink satin,' she said spontaneously as soon as she saw Daisy.

'It's not as fashionable as yours, but it's the only one that fits me properly,' confessed Daisy. 'I've been eating too many potatoes.'

'Nothing much else to eat at Beech Grove,' mused Poppy, but then added hastily, 'but it's gorgeous, really suits you – the flowers made from sequins make it look so sophisticated.'

'Perhaps we'll both meet rich suitors who will be possessed of a good fortune and will fall madly in love with us, and then we'll have twin weddings in June.' Daisy added a pair of earrings with tiny diamonds which

Elaine had bought for her and then tilted her head to see the effect.

'Daisy . . .' said Poppy, taking a deep breath, 'Baz and I want to get married. We've got it all planned out.' She knew that there was a note of defiance in her voice, but Daisy, of all people, had to understand, had to be with her in this. 'We are going to have a jazz club in Baz's house – it could be a great success, Daisy, don't you see? That's what I want for the future – just me and Baz working together. After all, it's all turned out well for Violet and Justin, hasn't it?'

Even as she spoke, Poppy realized that there was, of course, one difference.

Justin was a qualified lawyer and he did have a job.

'Oh, Poppy,' said Daisy with a joyful laugh, 'I should have guessed! I've just been so wrapped up with my own plans for the season and my film career that I didn't even think . . .' She stopped, suddenly. Her face, porcelain pretty in the mirror, looked appealingly at Poppy. 'But, Poppy, you do see that now I *must* marry money, since neither you nor Violet will. Someone has to save the house and the estate. We must go through the presentation and be popular debutantes so I can make a good match – for Father's sake.'

The little house in Belgravia seemed transformed when Poppy and Daisy, chaperoned by Violet and Justin, arrived in good time for the party. The boys had been busy after the girls had left. The scuffed bare wooden steps leading down to the basement had been painted black – still slightly sticky to the sole of the shoe, but dry enough to walk on. Tin trays, placed in the corners of the steps, had been filled with dyed green water where nightlights floated. The whitewashed walls of the stairway had been decorated with strange paintings drawn directly on to the walls; one was of a huge human eye, another of the backbone of a fish.

'Bad imitations of cubist paintings,' murmured Violet, but a crowd from a couple of taxis were behind them and they shrieked with hilarity at the sight of the paintings. For a moment Poppy wished that Daisy had not insisted on having Violet as a chaperone – she was spoiling the mood of excitement.

'Joan! Darling!' shrieked one of the girls, and then her voice rose up to almost a scream.

'Oh, I say, how too, too stunning!'

'Too, too amazing-most!'

'Joan, you pig, you've been hiding this place from us.'

Poppy pushed ahead of Violet and went in. It had looked good when they had left, but in the darkness of the evening it looked spectacular.

The windows of the cellar were draped with black artificial silk and the many candles seemed to draw pools of palest silver on their glossy surface. Packets of glitter had been sprinkled over the cement floor of the cellar. The result was a bit haphazard, but quite enchanting. The gorgeous sheets of flame-coloured material draped over the walls from the ceiling gleamed like the most expensive silk.

Poppy gave a little shake to her sunset-coloured dress. Last year she, Daisy and Violet had sewn coral-coloured glass beads to the hem and they shimmered and flashed in the candlelight. Morgan, she noticed with approval, had shed his chauffeur's coat and cap and now appeared in a dinner jacket with a gleaming white shirt and a smart bow tie. He had told her that he had sold a drum backing for a film and had used the money to buy proper evening wear – just like a real band leader. The three boys were turned out in the same way and Poppy went forward to take her place among them. The trestle table at the side of the cellar, covered with its length of silky black, was filling up nicely with bottles and cake boxes and small tasty savouries. There would be plenty for supper.

'Jam jars!' exclaimed Violet, staring at the rows of well-washed glass containers that were lined up beside the bottles.

'The latest fashion from New Orleans,' said Joan with aplomb. Maud's discovery of a stack of jars in a dusty cupboard had solved the embarrassing problem of what to do about glasses.

'Let's go,' whispered Morgan, tapping his drumsticks together to count the band in.

That was enough. The crowd started to jig around the floor, heads waggling, feet pointing, hands shaking. More guests arrived. Greetings were shouted over the music, the newcomers joined in, the fire in the stove died down a little, but it didn't matter – the room was gloriously warm.

'We should have charged an entrance fee,' said Poppy when the band paused for a rest.

'Not yet,' said Morgan. 'Have a few more parties, Baz, and then get the thing on a proper footing. Pay the band out of the entry fee, do some more decorating and then start saving.'

'This will be most famous club in the whole of London,' said Poppy. She felt herself tingling all over with excitement. The music seemed to be rippling through her blood and she felt incredibly thirsty, but also as though she could play for hours more without tiring. She crossed over to the table and ladled out a scoop of a punch that a girl called Annette had been making in one of the old cookery bowls probably belonging to the long-dead wife of the coachman. It tasted fantastic and she had some more, and then some more again.

When she went back to the band she felt her legs wobble with exhaustion, but the most wonderful variations on the tunes came floating through her brain. When the band started up again she let those tunes come, very quietly at first, and then blew more strongly when she saw smiling faces looking at her over shoulders. It felt as though she had entered into a new world, a fairyland where all her dreams had come true.

Chapter Nine
Tuesday 1 April 1924

'If your father gets wind of this I'll lose my job; I never thought that it would get as wild as this. It's these London girls – they get up to anything these days.' Morgan accepted the drink that Daisy brought to him and surveyed the scene with a worried look. Couples were huddled in dark corners, and Baz's sister Joan was teaching a group to do a raucous Charleston, the latest fashionable dance.

'Right foot back one step,' she was shouting. 'Now kick backwards with the left foot; move right arm forward. Feet and arms back to the start position; right foot kicks forward while the right arm moves backwards. Go, on, Squidgy, do a little hop in between steps!'

Morgan's dark eyebrows met in a frown. 'And now I hear that the telegram about the ship's delayed arrival did come to Beech Grove after all.'

'That wasn't my idea,' said Daisy guiltily. 'I honestly didn't know that my aunt would not be here in London. And Poppy wanted . . .' Her voice faded away as she wondered how to explain.

'None of my business,' said Morgan, eyeing Poppy. 'I'm only the chauffeur. But you know what your father is like – thinks of the two of you as little girls.'

'We *are* chaperoned,' said Daisy defensively. She was surprised how much she minded his criticism. 'By a married woman too.'

He raised his eyebrows and then glanced across the room at Violet. 'You would think that she would have more sense,' he said. 'She should take you both home now that things are getting a bit out of hand. Do you want me to drive you?'

'No,' said Daisy. 'Poppy would never forgive me. Don't worry. We're old enough to look after ourselves.'

'You might be; she's not,' he said shortly.

'Actually,' said Daisy defensively, 'Poppy is older than I am.'

'By ten minutes,' said Morgan with a grin.

By six weeks, thought Daisy, wondering how it would feel to carry this secret with her for her whole life. Elaine, her mother, would die if it got out, and Michael Derrington would be devastated after all the years of pretending that she was his daughter.

'Anyway, what about all the attention you've been paying Joan? You can't suggest that you've been perfectly behaved,' she said with spirit. 'She's not much older than us!' Without waiting for an answer she turned her back on him and joined the group around Joan, taking Edwin's hand; he was doing his best to follow Joan's instructions and to put in the little hop between the steps.

'Time to start the music again,' shouted Morgan. 'Come on, band members.' He went across to his drums, performed a quick flourish and settled down to a fast beat, his drumsticks moving at an incredible speed. Obediently the jazz band, including Baz and Poppy, came and joined him. In a moment the tune of 'Running Wild' filled the crowded room and the couples lying on cushions, or kissing in dark corners, leaped to their feet.

There was something hypnotic about jazz, thought Daisy as she danced the Charleston. Morgan led the band through tune after tune without any break. The little house almost rocked with the strange music and Daisy found that she could no longer think about anything at all but seemed in a strange sort of trance, her head and arms swaying, her feet performing the kicks and the steps back and forth with the little hops almost of their own accord.

A moment later, Morgan ceased his frenetic drumming, held up a hand and the other instruments immediately stopped.

'Twelve o'clock – that's all, ladies and gentlemen,' he said decisively. He walked across to the gas lamp, struck a match, turned the switch and a tiny flame appeared. After a few seconds it flared and lit up the cellar. 'Always leave them wanting more,' he said in low voice in Baz's ear.

'Taxis, gentlemen, please,' he continued out loud. 'Ladies, if you would be so kind – a quick tidy-up – we must get ready for the next party,' he said with a charming smile at Joan. She immediately got to her feet with an exclamation of 'Dear, dear St Clair, anything for you!'

Daisy suppressed a small grin when she saw even Poppy was obediently putting her clarinet into its case and then joining the group picking up cushions, albeit in a somewhat wobbly fashion. Perhaps she had taken a little too much wine. There were many empty bottles on the table and lots of half-finished food, all of which, under Morgan's orders, went into a dustbin in the arena outside the basement window.

'That was fun,' said Violet with an elderly sigh as Morgan drove them home. 'Made me feel young again. Not like an old married lady.' She leaned across to Justin, who was sitting in the front beside the chauffeur. 'Let's have a party next week, Justin. Morgan, will you bring your drums? And the jazz band, of course?'

'Depends on what Lady Elaine says, my lady,' said Morgan stiffly, slowing down and looking to his left. 'This house here, is that right, sir?' he said to Justin.

'You're very starchy, Morgan. What's the matter?' asked Poppy once Violet and Justin had gone up the steps to their little house.

Morgan pulled away from the pavement and inserted the Humber into the stream of cars coming home from a large cinema nearby. When he spoke his voice was very firm.

'You're lucky things didn't get even more out of hand than they already did tonight. Things are different for girls than they are for boys. You've got your reputations to think of. You don't want to miss your season as debutantes, either of you, and Daisy has her career to think of. She's going to be a big name in film-making one day. She needs to be in London, don't you, Daisy?

My lady, I mean,' he added in a perfunctory tone which amused Daisy. Morgan normally called Poppy by her first name when they were practising jazz in the cottage – or even 'Pops' as Baz called her – but in the car and around the house he was quite formal with both of them. She was touched by his thought for her though.

'It was just the once,' she assured him. 'And no one need know. My . . . my aunt will be back in a day or two and then everything will be normal. We'll be going to parties like two demure little debutantes and we'll be very well chaperoned. That's right, isn't it, Poppy?'

I hope, she thought as Poppy did not answer. She was staring out of the window at the busy London scene. Young girls in short coats and tightly fitting hats were everywhere, hanging on to the arm of an escort, by themselves, mounting the high step of a bus, disappearing down the steps to the underground, girls twirling on the pavement, even one singing at the top of her voice as she swung with one hand around a lamp post at the roadside. A taxi driver hooted violently as she almost swayed into him. Daisy understood what Poppy was feeling, but saw Morgan's lips tighten.

'Let's get you both home,' he said abruptly.

When they reached the pavement in front of the rented house at Grosvenor Square Daisy saw to her relief that the light outside the door was still switched on and the hall, through the pane of stained glass in the front door, appeared to be lit up also.

Morgan said tersely, 'Wait here,' and then jumped

out of the car, ran up the steps and pressed the doorbell. The footman opened the door almost instantly and Morgan exchanged a pleasant nod with him and ran back down the steps and had the car door open and his hand extended to Daisy before the footman could make up his mind whether they were important enough for him to come out in the cold.

'Straight to bed now, and say your prayers that no one finds out,' he murmured in a low voice as he handed Poppy out.

'Yes, Grandpa, certainly, Grandpa,' murmured Poppy with an innocent smile. 'What a pleasant evening that was with Violet and Justin,' she said in loud tones, though Daisy did not know why she bothered. It was unlikely that the footman cared.

The loud voice, however, took the attention of a lady across the road who was just getting out of a taxi. Daisy saw her look over and then, to her horror, come straight over to them.

'My dears,' she said in tones of amazement, 'so you came to London after all! I understood you had been informed that Sir John and his wife were detained. Engine trouble on the ship, I understand. So, so horrid for them.' She peered inquisitively at them.

'We didn't get their telegram,' said Daisy, trying to sound as natural as possible. 'It doesn't matter though. We've spent the evening with our married sister. Our chauffeur drove us over and collected us.' She gave one quick look at Morgan, but he was standing stiffly to attention, looking the embodiment of discretion.

'Oh, but why didn't you stay the night with your sister? It can't be suitable for two young girls to be alone in the house,' shrilled the lady.

Daisy stifled a giggle. Not exactly alone, she thought. There must be at least six servants in that house.

'House full up with guests,' said Poppy laconically and then she began to laugh. 'We'd have to perch on the roof like a pair of little birds.' Daisy cringed. Poppy's breath smelt of alcohol.

'I must introduce myself,' said the officious lady. 'Lady Cynthia de Montfort. I am a cousin of Jack, I should say of Sir John Nelborough. My son Charles had been with him out in India and they are coming home together. It was so disappointing when I got the telegram. I am so looking forward to my son's visit; still, one hopes we have only a few more days to go. And it is so lovely to meet dear Elaine's two little nieces.' She shook hands with Poppy, who was at least a head taller than she was, and then with Daisy, saying, 'Now which is which?'

'Guess,' muttered Poppy, and Morgan cleared his throat warningly so Daisy went into a hurried explanation about the flower names for all of her sisters. By the time that she had finished Lady Cynthia was beaming again.

'So, what do you say?' she enquired. 'What about coming to stay with me until Sir John and his wife come home? I'm just across the road. Wouldn't that be cosy?'

Poppy hiccupped. This seemed to finish her off and she began to laugh without restraint.

'How very kind of you, Lady Cynthia . . .' Daisy started to say, but she could feel a storm of giggles rising within her also. She bit her lip hard and tried to keep the lid on them. Lady Cynthia eyed them both coldly. There was a flare of suspicion in her large blue eyes.

'Excuse me, your ladyships,' said Morgan stiffly. He touched his cap respectfully to Lady Cynthia. 'It appears that the footman has a telegram in his hand. Perhaps there is good news from the ship.'

'Oh, the ship!' cried Poppy. There was a slight note of hysteria in her voice. 'Perhaps Sir John has fixed her. He's such a useful man, your cousin,' she said to Lady Cynthia.

'Oh, perhaps they'll be home tomorrow. That would be wonderful news,' gushed Daisy. 'Do come quickly, Poppy. Lady Cynthia will excuse us.' She grabbed Poppy's arm in a firm grip and dragged her up the steps towards the waiting footman. Morgan followed, carrying Poppy's discarded handbag and keeping his broad back between them and the lady on the pavement. Before they knew it, he had almost pushed them inside and closed the front door firmly behind them.

It was true. The footman did have a telegram in his hand. It was marked as sent from Beech Grove at six thirty in the evening. Daisy took it and read aloud:

SCARLET FEVER IN SCHOOL STOP
ROSE ARRIVES LONDON NEXT TUESDAY STOP
DERRINGTON

'Scarlet fever! I bet there was something in that letter

from Rose that I left behind. Rose would get wind of something like that before anyone else. Now what are we going to do?' Thoughts ran around in Daisy's head. Michael Derrington would be waiting for an answer to his telegram.

The first thing, however, was to get Poppy to bed. The yawning footman was obviously impatient to retire. Luckily the lady's maid, engaged to attend on Elaine, had not thought it part of her duties to stay up for two girls who were so late home. No one else was about except Maud, hovering on the stairs.

'Thank you, James,' she said aloud. 'We'll leave you to lock up. Come, Poppy.'

'Make her drink plenty of water,' muttered Morgan in Daisy's ear as he handed her Poppy's handbag.

'That woman is priceless.' Poppy dissolved into another fit of giggles, but Daisy did not find it funny. She had taken some wine herself that evening – not as much as Poppy; just enough to give her a wonderful feeling of euphoria – but Morgan's words had turned her cold sober. It was true. Fun was all very well, but the prospect of three whole months in London and the opportunities to pursue her ambition to be a film-maker – director, scriptwriter and camera operator – were just too good to be put in jeopardy by a silly evening like the one that had passed. She wished now that she had telephoned Michael Derrington as soon as she had found out about the delay to the ship – but of course he would immediately have gone storming down to the post office and Poppy's theft of the telegram would have been discovered.

And that would have been the end of their long-awaited season in London.

Once Daisy had decided what was best to do she slept well, waking with a start when the housemaid carried in her breakfast. She ate quickly, had her bath, which Maud had already filled – such bliss to have a hot bath; *too, too divine*, as Baz's sister Joan would say, and then went into Poppy's room.

Poppy was eating her breakfast and looked quite recovered.

'Wasn't that fun last night?' she said with a chuckle.

'It was dangerous,' said Daisy severely. 'You do realize that we are within inches of being found out. Remember Father's telegram . . .' and she waved the piece of paper in front of Poppy's nose.

'That's all right,' said Poppy, chewing a mouthful of toast. 'It will be fun to have Rose here for a while.'

'Father is probably pacing up and down wondering why he has not yet had a reply. We must answer this immediately.' Daisy took a pencil from the table beside Poppy's bed and turned over the telegram. She wrote for a while – twelve words for a shilling, she said to herself. They had been given five pounds each – but that, according to Great-Aunt Lizzie, would have to last for the entire two months and there would be taxis to be paid for and tickets to concerts and cinemas to be bought, not to mention new stockings, tips to the servants and all of the hundred and one things that would come up while they were here. 'What about this?' she asked after a minute and read aloud:

WILL MEET TRAIN STOP WHAT TIME
AND STATION DOES IT ARRIVE STOP

'Two, four, six, eight, ten, twelve – twelve words,' she said with satisfaction. 'Father is so used to economizing that he won't be surprised that there is no name signed. He wouldn't want to spend more than a shilling himself.'

'Why didn't the silly chump say the time in his telegram?' Poppy tried to remove some of the worst tangles from her waist-length hair with her fingers.

'Think ourselves lucky that he didn't telephone.' The telephone at Beech Grove Manor was forever going wrong. She hoped this was one of the frequent occurrences of trouble on the line. 'He probably didn't like to ask if Elaine would meet her and keep her overnight,' she added. 'You know what he is like about asking for favours. If he told the time and station then it would be like he was expecting her to be met. Now I'm off.'

'Just going down to the post office, Tellford,' she said, meeting the butler in the hall.

'Yes, my lady,' he said respectfully, opening the hall door for her. 'Just down the road and then turn left.'

To her relief he showed no sign of thinking it odd that she went to the post office by herself. It's 1924, not before the war when women wore long skirts and girls daren't step outside their gardens without a chaperone. And it's London, not down in the country in Kent, she told herself as she walked quickly down the pavement, looking at girls everywhere, alone, many of them running for a bus or driving cars. Living down in Beech Grove with two elderly Victorians, one forgot how the world had changed. The thought gave her courage and she dictated her telegram in a steady voice, then bought a *Daily Mail* for a halfpenny from newspaper boy outside the post office.

She needed to be back in the house at Grosvenor Square before a telegram was delivered, or, horrors, a phone call came from Kent. The newspaper would give her an excuse to sit in the hallway and await developments.

I wonder, could I persuade Poppy to see a film with me this afternoon? she thought as she unfolded the paper and perched on a seat beside the telephone in the hall. There was *The Kid* by Charlie Chaplin – she would love to see that, but would Poppy? There was another film that she wanted to see: *The Iron Horse*; her godfather, Sir Guy Beresford, had told her about that. As a film-maker himself, he kept a close eye on what rival companies were producing. Her eye went down the line of cinemas. Goodness! London was full of them, she thought, and then jumped as the doorbell rang.

Resisting an impulse to answer it herself, she waited for Tellford.

'Two telegrams! Your lucky day!' Daisy liked the brisk sound of the boy's cheeky voice as he handed the telegrams to the butler. The post-office boy back home would never have dared to address Bateman in anything other than tones of deep humility. London was so modern, she thought as she rose from her seat and held out her hand for the telegrams.

One of them, she noticed, as Tellford reluctantly handed them to her, was addressed to Elaine; the other just had 12 GROSVENOR SQUARE on the envelope.

'Thank you, Tellford,' she said, resuming her seat and trying to look as if the hall were her favourite place to read the newspaper. She opened the Grosvenor Square telegram first. That would be from the ship.

ARRIVING THREE PM TODAY EAST INDIA
DOCKS STOP NELBOROUGH

'Oh, good,' said Daisy, 'they're arriving today, Tellford. They must have fixed the engine trouble more quickly than expected. My sister and I will meet them with our chauffeur, and . . .' she hesitated and then thought of what Great-Aunt Lizzie would say, and finished bravely, 'and I'm sure that I can rely on you to have everything ready for them.' She had to bite the inside of her lip to stop herself laughing into his affronted face.

'Yes, my lady,' he said in a wooden fashion, but she knew that he was bursting to tell her that he knew perfectly well how to welcome the returning travellers.

'That will be all, thank you, Tellford,' she said, still in Great-Aunt Lizzie mode. He would be unlikely to know what age she and Poppy were; and the older the staff imagined them to be, she thought, the less likely tales would be carried to Sir John. She gave him a haughty nod and waited until he had gone back downstairs before she moved. She certainly did not want to open the telegram addressed to Elaine in his presence or in front of the maid who had appeared to polish the brass knocker on the front door, so she took it and the newspaper up to Poppy's room.

'Well, thank goodness, you are dressed. How do you feel?'

'Did I seem a bit drunk last night?' Poppy yawned and then thirstily drained the glass of water on her bedside table.

'You are just so stupid,' said Daisy severely. 'How could you have taken that much wine? Lady Cynthia—'

'Never mind about Lady Cynthia,' interrupted Poppy. 'Did Bob Morgan notice anything?'

'What does that matter?' said Daisy impatiently.

'Of course it matters,' snapped Poppy. 'He threatened to throw Edwin out of the band if he got drunk again. "*You don't drink when you're on duty*" – that's what he said to him – "*and you're on duty when you are playing in my band.*"' Tears came to Poppy's eyes and she put her hand to her forehead. 'I've got such a headache. And I didn't drink much.'

'Yes, you did,' said Daisy unsympathetically, but then she relented. 'I'll have a word with Morgan and tell him that you thought the punch was only lemonade or something.'

'Thanks!' Poppy cheered up. 'He likes you and thinks that you are sensible. He's much more likely to believe you than me.' She turned to the mirror and began to comb her hair.

'I've got a great idea,' she began, but Daisy interrupted her.

'Prepare for a shock – no more wild parties.' She held out the telegram from Sir John and Poppy scanned it, pouting heavily.

'Oh, bother,' she said. 'Still, there's always lunchtime – and of course evening visits to Violet. Who's the other telegram from?'

'Father, I hope,' said Daisy. She held the gummed strip on the envelope to the warmth from Poppy's teapot and carefully separated the flap from the back of it. Then she peeled it away and pulled out the post-office form.

'Oh, good; it's about Rose's arrival,' she said, and held it out to Poppy who read it aloud:

TUESDAY VICTORIA 2PM TELEPHONE OUT OF
ORDER WIRE SHE CAN STAY OVERNIGHT

'*Wire she can stay overnight* – what does the man mean?' puzzled Poppy.

'He's trying to save a shilling,' said Daisy. 'He means to say *send a telegram if she can stay overnight here in London*. You know what Father is like about spending money on telegrams. I'm going to spend another shilling though, and you can pray that everything is going to work out.' Daisy grinned at her sister and added bossily, 'Now if you want to go out, take Morgan with you and stay with him. Tell him about meeting them at the East India Docks at three p.m. – tell him that first of all so that he can plan.'

She raced down the steps, trying out the words in her

mind. There must be exactly twelve so that her father would not wonder about the lack of a signature.

WILL MEET ROSE ON TUESDAY AND
KEEP HER FOR A WEEK STOP

Once the telegram was sent she could relax. She and Poppy would meet Elaine and Sir John at the East India Docks, explain about the lost telegram, implore them to say nothing to the Earl about it in case the unfortunate postmistress got into trouble and then they both would enjoy their time in London and be discreet about their activities.

Chapter Ten
Wednesday 2 April 1924

The East India Docks were crowded with people welcoming travellers after their long journey from India. Morgan parked the car at some distance and then made a way for them through the crowd until they were so near that the ship loomed high above their heads. After a moment they spotted Elaine, pretty in furs, standing against the railings of the ship, and Jack, the newly dubbed Sir John, by her side.

But on the other side of Elaine was a young man. And once she had seen him, Daisy looked no longer at the woman who was her real mother.

'Wow!' she murmured.

He was the most devastatingly beautiful man that Daisy had ever seen in her life. *Love at first glance*, she thought, seeing the words written on a film title board. But this was no film and her heart was thudding inside her warm coat.

Beside Elaine at the ship's railings was the man of her dreams. Not tall, half a head shorter than Sir John, very slim. The three were standing just above the dock, so near that she could even see his eyes – gorgeous eyes, huge and dark. Daisy's fingers itched for her camera. What a face! A perfect mouth, half open, made for kissing, thought

Daisy, a straight nose, masculine, but of such a faultless shape that it looked as though it had been taken from a Greek statue. And hair as blue-black as a magpie's wing.

'Elaine looks different,' said Poppy's voice from beside her.

Daisy looked at her in shock. Perhaps she was teasing; surely Poppy had noticed him too, but no, Poppy looked her usual, slightly indifferent self. She didn't show any interest in the extraordinarily good-looking young man beside Elaine and Jack.

The three were walking down the gangway now, Elaine hanging on Jack's arm and the Greek god on her other side, laughing now and displaying a splendid set of white teeth. Daisy felt her cheeks glow. Poppy moved forward and Daisy had to follow. Elaine had seen them now. She waved with her free arm and then pointed them out to the young man. Sir John waved also and nodded to Morgan, who was approaching them, ready to take Elaine's dressing case from her husband.

'Darling!' Elaine flung her arms around Daisy's neck and held her very close for a long minute. 'How I have missed you!' Then hurriedly she turned to Poppy and bestowed the same embrace on her.

'You're looking well, Daisy. Grown a bit, I think.' Sir John broke off his conversation with Morgan about the trunks and the suitcases that were being carried down by a couple of porters.

Idiot, thought Daisy, talking to me as though I were about ten years old, but it didn't matter anyway. He, the gorgeous man, the Greek god, wasn't looking at her; wasn't listening to Sir John. Elaine was saying, 'Girls, this is Mr Charles de Montfort; Charles, these are my nieces, Lady Poppy and Lady Daisy.' The Greek god was smiling and his hand was outstretched and his beautiful eyes – now that Daisy was near to him she could see that they were a wonderful shade of dark blue – were firmly fixed on Poppy. And it was Poppy's hand which he held reverentially, giving her a half-bow and a wonderful smile.

For the first time in her life, Daisy almost hated her twin.

'Have you been out in India for long, or was it just a holiday?' Poppy was asking politely.

'A few years.' His voice, too, was wonderful. Quite deep and very musical. And his tanned skin suited him, thought Daisy.

'And this is Lady Poppy's sister Lady Daisy,' Sir John broke into the rapture on the young man's face with a slightly abrupt note in his voice.

'Lady Daisy.' He took her hand, but his eyes strayed back to Poppy, who said impatiently to Sir John, 'Oh, never mind all of this "Lady" stuff, Jack – it's so old-fashioned. Call us Poppy and Daisy. It's lovely to meet you, Charles.'

Her tone, to Daisy's relief, was unemotional and indifferent, but the gorgeous young man continued to stare at her.

'You and Daisy will have a lot in common, Charles,'

Jack was saying. 'Charles has been in quite a few films in India, Daisy.'

'You like films, Daisy?' His smile was perfunctory – that of an elder cousin.

'I'm a film director,' said Daisy coolly, and could have blessed Poppy when she chimed in with, 'Daisy has a film called *Murder in the Dark* running in a cinema just now.'

Daisy tried to smile modestly and hoped he would not ask where. Somewhere up in Scotland, Sir Guy had told her. 'I've done well out of your film,' he had added, 'doubled the price that I paid you for it. But these days the film-going public needs something new all the time. Films only last a few months on the whole.'

'What films did you star in?' she asked.

'Quite a few,' he said, with a weary air that Daisy thought very attractive, though not as attractive as the boyish smile that followed it. 'That means nothing that you would have heard of, I'm afraid.'

She smiled back. 'Perhaps you'd star in one of my films and we'd both make a fortune,' she dared to say.

'Daisy's godfather is Sir Guy Beresford and he owns a film studio,' put in Elaine. 'He thinks that she is very talented. I knew that you two would have a lot in common.' She put her arm around Daisy and suddenly Daisy felt a little thrill run through her. Almost like having a mother, she thought. And then had to smile at herself. Elaine *was* her mother. Perhaps, like all mothers, Elaine was doing a spot of matchmaking. Perhaps Charles was rich – he must be if his mother took a house in London for the season though she did not appear to have a daughter. A Greek god – and rich too! Who minds marrying money, if money comes looking like this? she thought as she smiled up at Charles. He smiled back at her and started to ask questions about her films and did not glance again at Poppy.

'Here comes Morgan,' interrupted Sir John. 'Come on, girls. Can't offer you a lift, Charles, I'm afraid. We'll be crowded out.'

'Oh, Mother will be here in a few minutes. She is always late. And if she doesn't turn up, I'll get a cab. I'll call tomorrow, if I may.' Despite the talk about films, his eyes still went back to Poppy with that expression of admiration. However, Daisy was hopeful. Poppy was only interested in men who played jazz – film-star good looks were of no importance to her. In any case, her whole mind was focused on Baz. No other boy had ever meant anything to Poppy, and Daisy had the feeling that none ever would. Once Charles saw Poppy with Baz he would realize that he had no chance with her.

'Yes, let's go before the car gets blocked in,' said Daisy hurriedly. She seized one of the packages that Elaine was fumbling with, tucked it under her arm and urged them all forward. It had occurred to her that it would be better to be out of the way before Lady Cynthia arrived on the scene.

'Aren't you surprised to see us?' she asked as she settled into the back seat of the Humber, between Elaine and Poppy. She gave her mother's hand a little squeeze.

She had never admitted to Elaine that Poppy knew their secret so any gestures of affection had to be those of an affectionate niece to an indulgent and loving aunt. Elaine was so desperately ashamed of having had an illegitimate baby that she would hate to know that anyone other than her aunt and her brother-in-law knew of her secret, thought Daisy.

'Yes, we are. Though very pleased, of course,' Sir John was saying from the front seat. 'Especially Morgan. I was all ready to share a cab with Charles de Montfort. Apparently his mother has taken a house in Grosvenor Square also.'

'Well, according to your butler you sent a telegram to Beech Grove, but we didn't get it,' said Daisy, trying to sound as though it were a trivial matter. 'Don't say anything to Father, will you, Elaine?' she added. 'He's not well at the moment; his nerves are not in a good state and he'd have a fit if he thought that we had stayed up in London without you two – but as a matter of fact we managed fine. We went to see Violet and Justin.'

'No, of course we won't say anything to Michael; I know how he worries. I'm glad that you were so sensible. And of course you had Morgan here to drive you over to Violet's place and take you home again; I know that he would look after you well.' Elaine gave Daisy's hand a little pat and cast a look at Morgan, who nodded his head and raised his hand to his cap in thanks at her praise.

'Telegrams have been flying.' Daisy decided to get all the confessions over during the drive while the noise of engines revving and horns blowing distracted attention from her words. 'There's an outbreak of scarlet fever in Rose's school and the girls have been sent home a week early. They are arriving from Dover into London on Tuesday. I sent a telegram to Father saying that she can stay here. Phone's out of order at Beech Grove – as usual! Was that all right?' Elaine, she guessed, would not mind that she had opened a telegram addressed to the Nelboroughs.

'Perfectly.' Elaine looked genuinely pleased. 'But that will be wonderful. Dear little Rose! Tell me, how is she getting on in Switzerland? I must say that I loved that school.'

'Very well, I think, but she'll be able to tell you herself.' Daisy made a private note to bribe Rose to give very good accounts of the school to Elaine. After all, Elaine was the one paying the bills, so that all this stuff about '*a lonely prisoner in a foreign land*' would be a bit disappointing for her. And certainly Sir John would immediately want to investigate stories about white slave traders buying photographs of boarding-school girls.

'You don't mind, dearest, if Morgan takes a detour around by Westminster? I have something that I need to drop off at the office of a member of parliament.' Sir John addressed Elaine over the back seat of the car.

'Not at all, Jack. We're quite cosy here.' Elaine was the perfect wife for a successful man, thought Daisy. She obviously adored him. All of the time that he was in the House of Commons – and to give him his due he was not long – she poured out a hymn of praise about him. Poppy grew bored and yawned, but Daisy was glad for her mother. From time to time she had felt a little guilty about refusing the invitation to go to India to live with them, but now she could see that her presence was not at all necessary and that she might even have been in the way.

'Does Jack want to stay on in India? Or would he think of coming back to England?' she asked the question, knowing the answer.

'India suits his talents,' replied Elaine firmly. 'He is so highly thought of there. Why, the Maharajah . . .' and she embarked on another story about her wonderful husband.

Did Elaine ever have regrets about giving up her baby to another woman, even if that woman was her sister? Did she ever wish that she had had the courage to stand up to the world and keep her child? Daisy thought not, and she tried not to mind. She saw Poppy looking at her and remembered with a little warm feeling in her heart the words uttered by her – '*I've decided that we will always be twins*'.

'Here's Jack,' said Elaine, and the look on her face told Daisy what a success this second marriage had been. Impulsively she kissed her mother's cheek. 'He can't stay away from you for too long,' she teased, and saw Morgan tighten his lips to keep the grin from his face.

'Affairs of state, Jack?' she queried when he got back into the car. It was important, she felt, to keep the tone light and not to wear the look of an abandoned child. Elaine was too prone to guilt about that. After all, what else could she have done? And it was Daisy's own decision not to live with them in India.

'Oh, much more important than that!' said Jack in shocked tones. 'Well, I did have a parcel to deliver, but the main purpose was to recruit a few young men for your coming-out ball. I have three under-secretaries, a promising young member of parliament and the three sons of an old friend who has retired from India. All handsome young men, I assure you, girls.'

'Seven, and with Charles de Montfort that makes eight,' said Elaine. 'I've got all sorts of ideas about your ball – Jack and I have been talking them over during the voyage. I want it to be splendid for you both. Suitable young men are always the problem though – so eight for starters is wonderful.'

'And there's Baz, Simon, Edwin and George,' said Poppy, for whom the members of the jazz band would be the most important people present. 'That will make twelve – how many are we going to invite for this ball?'

'We'd like it to be a big affair,' said Elaine with a look at her husband. 'It's just a matter of getting enough young men – girls are always easy.'

'I'll get you so many young men that we'll probably end up scurrying around London recruiting girls,' prophesied Jack, but there was a laugh in his voice, and Daisy guessed that he was quite looking forward to putting his formidable organizing talents to this ball and was probably determined to make it, for the sake of his new wife, the event of the season.

'By the way, we've already met Charles de Montfort's mother, Lady Cynthia,' said Daisy. She tried to sound casual, but she felt her heart bump uncomfortably at the mention of the Greek god's name.

'Bit of a—' began Poppy, but Daisy interrupted her quickly, with, 'A very pleasant woman, very friendly and hospitable to us. She even invited us to stay, but we told her that your housekeeper was looking after us very well.' She risked a quick look at Morgan, but the chauffeur's profile was rigid, his eyes, beneath the peaked cap, fixed on the road as he swung into Grosvenor Square.

'Charles must have had quite a queue for a taxi,' exclaimed Jack, looking out of his window. 'Look, he's only just arrived.'

'And there she is,' said Poppy, looking with disfavour at the charming picture of a mother embracing her son on the pavement at the bottom of the steps. 'Right across the road from us,' she added, and Daisy knew what her twin was thinking. All their comings and goings would have been noted. What if Lady Cynthia gave the game away?

They saw both the heads turn when the car drew up in front of number twelve. Lady Cynthia took her arms from around her son and they both came across the road towards them.

'I'll make sure that Morgan knows what to do about the luggage,' said Poppy. As soon as the car stopped she was the first to jump out and she was around the back of the Humber before the two de Montforts were halfway to the stately old car.

Here goes, thought Daisy. She followed Elaine out of the car, smiling sweetly and hoping sincerely that the woman would not say anything bad about her and Poppy to Sir John or, worse still, to her son. How very good-looking he was, she thought again. He seemed to light up the dull square on the dull spring day.

Lady Cynthia obviously had more pressing things to discuss than the scandalous behaviour of Sir John's nieces-in-law. She seemed very anxious to impress the great man himself and embarked on a long story as to why she had thought that the ship was going to arrive at the East India Docks at four o'clock, rather than at three.

'A good thing that darling Charles is not as woolly-headed as his mama,' she said, looking coyly up at Sir John. She was obviously expecting him to say how efficient Charles was, but he just gave her an inscrutable smile while Charles looked uncomfortable.

'It doesn't matter, Mother,' he kept saying, but Lady Cynthia had to go through all the times in her life when the wrong hour had lodged itself in her head.

'I saw a wonderful film about someone that this happened to. It meant that she escaped being murdered,' said Daisy eventually, smiling encouragingly at Lady Cynthia, who was quite taken by that idea. While her son was helping Daisy to recount details of the film, Sir John managed to exchange a few words with his new butler and then steer his wife away from the de Montforts with the firm assurance that they would all being seeing lots of each other in the very near future.

'You and I have to have lots of talks about films,' said the handsome Charles, giving Daisy's hand a very warm shake.

'Yes, do come over tomorrow morning,' said Daisy bravely.

'I won't disturb Sir John on his first morning in London,' he said politely. 'But you and your sister must pop around and see us. That will be all right, Mother, won't it?'

And with that Daisy had to be content. There was, she thought, a look of calculation in Lady Cynthia's eyes as she looked from Daisy across to Sir John. He was an important man, and women like Lady Cynthia respected men of power – especially when their sons worked for them. Of course, it would be well known by Charles and therefore his mother that Sir John had married a woman with a large fortune. All in all, Daisy thought, Lady Cynthia might overlook a little indiscretion, especially if the girls were now impeccably behaved.

Tomorrow, she thought. She would make sure that Poppy understood the full significance of the visit and that she would have to stay for the regulation time, or, better still, perhaps Poppy might concoct some prior arrangement with Baz and the jazz-band boys and would stay to entertain Elaine while her husband was busy with his affairs.

Chapter Eleven
Thursday 3 April 1924

Daisy had slept little the previous night. When Elaine had retired to bed, Poppy had come into her room and they had spent ages talking.

'What did you think of Charles?' Daisy had asked, after waiting for what felt like hours to see whether Poppy would bring up the subject, but all Poppy had wanted to talk about was the jazz club and the success of their opening night. As far as she was concerned, the day had been a wasted one as neither she nor Morgan had been able to join the boys in the little house in Belgravia for jazz practice.

'I hope Jack isn't going to keep Morgan too busy,' she said darkly. 'I could see that he liked having a car and a chauffeur.'

'But what did you think of Charles?' Daisy repeated.

Poppy looked at her. 'Well ... he's a bit of a ... You like him, don't you?' she said opening her eyes very widely with the air of someone who has just made a surprising discovery.

'Why not?' said Daisy. She could hear her voice sounding defensive. She picked up Poppy's comb and fiddled with her hair in order to avoid meeting Poppy's eyes.

'I suppose he's good-looking,' said Poppy after a moment. 'And of course he's interested in films,' she added when Daisy didn't reply. Now she seemed more enthusiastic. 'Yes, I can see what you mean. I do think that he is good-looking. Pity about his mother, but then people can't help their relations, can they? Look at us with Great-Aunt Lizzie! And Baz even knows her well and he still loves me and wants to marry me! You wouldn't think that possible, would you?'

'I think Charles's mother is all right,' said Daisy defensively. 'And Great-Aunt Lizzie is not too bad if you handle her the right way. The trouble is that you keep crashing head first into her.'

Poppy had said nothing for a minute, and when she did speak she sounded a little odd, as if she were searching for the right words. 'You think that he might be interested in you . . .' was what she said. It wasn't a question, but it wasn't a statement either. It hung in the air as Daisy brushed and re-brushed her hair.

'I don't know yet,' she said eventually, before silently walking back to her own room. Things had been easier, she lay in her bed thinking, at Beech Grove, where she and Poppy shared a bedroom. Sooner or later the subject would have been resurrected and from then on they would have continued to talk about Charles. Daisy was so used to being the leader of the twins – the sensible one, she was always called, even by Great-Aunt Lizzie – that it had come as a shock to her to realize that Poppy knew so much about love and that she knew so very little. She had fallen in love with Charles the moment she set her eyes on him, but what about him? Had he shown anything other than a polite interest? Daisy now didn't think so, and had resolved not to mention his name to Elaine, but to be full of plans for their coming-out ball and their court presentation. Lady Cynthia, she had decided, was the type to be impressed by a magnificent debut. Soon, she hoped, Charles would be as openly in love with her as Baz was with Poppy. You only had to see the look in Baz's eyes to know that there was only one girl in the world for him.

To her shame she spent half the rest of the night trying to devise ways to persuade Poppy not to join her on her visit to the neighbours across the road. After all, she told herself, Poppy had Baz. Let them go off together, out on the London streets and enjoy each other's company, and let Charles not fall in love with Poppy and overlook the more ordinary Daisy.

But as it happened, Baz came with them.

He turned up at half past ten in the morning, wearing a large flower in his buttonhole, a sleeked-back, man-about-town hairdo, copied from his elder brother, and carrying a large and very limp bunch of daffodils, which he insisted on presenting in person to Elaine.

'Welcome to England, what,' he said nervously. He had obviously been schooled well by Poppy, who was regarding him adoringly. 'Thought you'd like these, Lady Elaine; hard to get flowers in the city,' he ploughed on, the words jerking out with a rapidity that implied that he had been memorizing them on the way. He took a quick look at the exquisitely arranged vases full of exotic blooms that decorated the morning room and seemed to feel that some explanation was necessary.

'From Kent,' he explained. 'Real country flowers.' He whipped the daffodils from under Elaine's nose and rushed forward to shake hands with Sir John. Daisy suppressed a giggle. The flowers received another few mortal wounds as they swept a small cigarette box from a low table.

'Rushed down to Kent in order to pick them first thing this morning while the dew was still on them, did you?' enquired Sir John.

Baz looked a little confused. 'No, no,' he was saying now. 'It's about fifty miles,' he explained patiently. 'No motor. My brother won't let me borrow his.'

'Ever since you drove it backwards around Tunbridge Wells,' put in Poppy.

'So how did you get those . . . those daffodils from Kent?' Sir John was someone who did not like to let go of a point until it had been answered to his satisfaction.

'Covent Garden market; but they were picked this morning in Kent,' said Baz with simple pride. 'That's what the woman told me anyway.' He gave a slightly worried glance at the wilting bunch.

'They're lovely,' said Elaine, but her voice did lack conviction. She now had the bedraggled bunch in her hand and did not appear to know what to do with them. A trail of slime oozed out from the sheet of newspaper that was wrapped around the stems.

'I'm sure they were,' said Sir John. 'Daisy, do you think . . . ?'

Daisy took the flowers from Elaine's limp grasp. Baz was looking a bit abashed – he had understood the significance of Sir John's use of '*were*' – so she made a bit of a show of burying her nose in them and exclaiming what a real smell of the country they had and how she would find a good vase that would show off their beauty.

'Let's go, Poppy; we're due next door,' she said when she returned. She had not bothered the efficient housekeeper but had found a tall, slender vase that supported the limp stems and only allowed the bright yellow trumpet heads to be seen. 'Baz will like to meet Charles de Montfort. He's just back from India, Baz, and he's about our age or a few years older.' It would be cruel, she thought, to leave poor innocent Baz to be a butt for Sir John's witticisms.

'Does he play piano?' asked Baz, for whom the world was divided into two groups – those who played jazz and those who didn't. 'Morgan says that we need someone on a piano. I say, is Morgan . . . ?' He looked around the smart, trim morning room as if he expected to see the chauffeur sitting on one the comfortable easy chairs.

'Let's go,' said Poppy hastily. She took Baz by the arm and steered him out while his good manners were making him try to take leave of both Elaine and her husband simultaneously. 'Daisy wants us to see Lady Cynthia first,' she said to him soothingly. 'She's a horribly boring woman but Daisy likes her son, although I'm not quite sure why – he's so, so, sooo ugly . . .' She gave Daisy a mischievous grin. Daisy stiffened but then laughed. Typical Poppy.

'Now, Poppy, you have to be very, very polite to her,' she cried. She surveyed Baz. He was the epitome of the well-dressed young man about town – and he was the son of an earl – youngest son, of course, but nevertheless Lady Cynthia would probably like him. He looked a suitable companion for Poppy, and when Charles saw them together, perhaps he would turn his attention to Daisy once and for all.

'Come on,' she said in a low voice, with glance at the closed door of the parlour. 'You can see Morgan afterwards, but don't bring up the subject of jazz in front of Lady Cynthia.'

'And don't say anything about the party the other night,' warned Poppy.

'And nothing about telegrams,' said Daisy, adding, as he looked confused, 'That's three things not to mention.'

'I say,' said Baz, 'do you think that I should bring this Lady Cynthia some flowers? Mother always says that a gentleman paying a morning call on a lady brings flowers.'

'Give her that thing in your buttonhole; it looks stupid,' said Poppy impatiently.

'King Oliver wears one of these,' said Baz, squinting down at his buttonhole as they walked up the street. 'I say, Pops, Morgan says that King Oliver is coming to London next month. We must go to hear him. He's got a marvellous new trumpet player called Louis Armstrong.'

He took out his flower, bestowed a worried glance on it and then plunged across the road to the locked enclosed garden for the use of the residents of the square. In a second his long legs had scaled the railings and scattered a few nursemaids and small children. In a few minutes he was back with a handful of violently coloured spring polyanthuses.

'That's good,' said Poppy, surveying them critically. 'They freshen up that orchid of yours. It looks like it's dying on its feet.'

'Well, it came from a bouquet that someone brought to Joan. It was the only one of them that wasn't completely dead,' confessed Baz. 'I snaffled it off the housemaid when she was doing the rooms this morning.'

'I'm glad you haven't spent any money on it,' said Poppy severely. 'You know that we need all of our money to furnish your house.'

'I suppose you got the daffodils from another one of those gardens.' Daisy was giggling helplessly, but she managed to find a bit of string in her bag and to tie up the little bunch of flowers into a neat small bouquet.

Lady Cynthia was alone when the maid introduced them. She welcomed the girls coldly, but unbent when Daisy introduced Baz as a neighbour from Kent and made sure to give his father's title.

'Dear boy, how very, very kind of you!' She gave the

small bouquet a perfunctory look and laid it on a side table. That would finish off the wilting orchid, and probably the outdoor flowers as well, but it had broken the ice and they chatted amiably until Charles arrived, looking even more attractive than ever, thought Daisy.

'I haven't been in bed! Honest!' He came in with his hands raised as though a pistol were pointed at him. He greeted them with pleasure and shook hands with all three, explaining that he had been visiting his tailor. 'Look!' he said dramatically. 'Look at this suit! Three years old, if it's a day. How can I go around in a three-year-old suit? What film director would ever look at a man in a three-year-old suit? I've spent the last few years in uniform so I've nothing fit to wear.'

'Nothing fit to wear!' exclaimed his mother. 'Charles, what a fib! Your wardrobe is bulging!'

'You don't play any instrument, do you?' asked Baz, already bored with talk of clothes, and Charles immediately turned to him. He had had a friend in India who played the trumpet and he told a good tale about how amazed the native Indians were when he decided to go out and play by the river at moonlight. He had the sort of face that showed every expression so clearly, thought Daisy, as she listened to the story. Despite his laughing denial, she thought that he would have been a success as a film star. *We have no sound, no words with which to tell the story; only pictures*, her godfather used to say. A leading lady or a leading man needs to tell the story by the expressions on their face.

'But do you play the trumpet, yourself?' interrupted Baz.

'Trumpet! Good gracious, no,' interrupted Lady Cynthia. 'Why should he do a thing like that?'

'Why indeed,' said Daisy sweetly. 'Baz is interested in music. All kinds of music,' she said, wishing she could kick Poppy or something. It was obvious that this was not the kind of household that would be interested in jazz. However, she saw that Charles gave Baz a long look and then turned to smile at her. Obviously he had realized that Baz and Poppy had a close relationship. It would be impossible to miss the loving looks that Poppy gave him as they sat together on the sofa, shoulder touching shoulder.

Daisy returned Charles's smile and said politely, 'Tell me, Charles, how long will you be staying in England?' Elaine had told her last night that Jack felt Charles was not suited to the Indian Police, but had warned her not to let Charles suspect that she knew. Daisy intended to show him that he had not been betrayed.

'Oh, I'm back for good,' he said pleasantly with an uneasy glance at his mother. 'I'm not a brainy bloke, like Sir John. The Imperial Indian Police is not the right place for me – have to keep on passing those wretched examinations.' He gave a careless laugh. 'A man can only repeat so many times,' he said. There was an uncomfortable note in his voice as he looked at his mother again, so Daisy changed the subject to talk about their plans for the season.

Lady Cynthia was very enthusiastic about the question of the ball. She beamed happily at Daisy while she was telling the story of Sir John's visit to the House of Commons and hoped archly that her little Charles might get an invitation also.

'And your frocks?' she queried.

'Oh, Elaine, our aunt, has the most wonderful taste. The last time that we were in London she had the whole of Harrods running around until she found the perfect dress for me.' Daisy smiled at Lady Cynthia and had the satisfaction of seeing her eyes widen. Only seriously rich people made an impression at Harrods, the most expensive and most exclusive shop in London.

'Beg your pardon, my lady.' The maid who had let them in was at the door now. 'The butler from number twelve says that Sir Guy Beresford is waiting in a taxi for Lady Daisy.'

'Better go, too – c'mon, Pops; rude to stay so long when you're so busy. Glad to have met you, Lady Cynthia; hope you have a good stay in London; Mother sends her regards.' Baz was on his feet, his fingers clutching Poppy's wrist as he pulled her towards the door in a determined fashion.

'How very kind,' murmured Lady Cynthia, looking somewhat surprised at this message from Baz's mother, but sending a return message, hoping to call on her ladyship as soon as was possible. Poppy gave Baz an exasperated look but went willingly to the door.

Daisy mustered up her courage and turned to Charles.

'I suppose that you are very busy with tailors and things,' she said tentatively, 'but I wondered whether you'd like to visit the film studio. My godfather, Sir Guy Beresford, will be delighted to meet you. I'm on my way there now. Would you like to come with me?' And if Sir Guy did not particularly want a potential young film star added to his party, well, she was sure that she could talk him around.

'Would I not!' exclaimed Charles. 'What a pity that my new suit is not ready. I'm so shabby.' He cast a disparaging look at his neatly tapering trousers and his highly polished shoes. 'But such as I am, I'd be delighted to come. You're sure that Sir Guy won't mind.'

'Not too natty a dresser himself – Sir Guy, I mean,' confided Baz. 'Will you ever forget him on that horse of your father's, Pops? Do you remember, Daise?' He went off into a fit of laughter and Lady Cynthia looked at him indulgently. She had, thought Daisy, registered that Poppy and Baz were quite a couple, and so was especially cordial towards Daisy, patting her hand after she shook it and expressing a hope that they would see lots of each other during the coming months.

'We'd better go. Sir Guy won't want to keep the taxi waiting.' Daisy ushered them all out into the street. She introduced Charles to her godfather before installing him next to Sir Guy in the back seat. Baz climbed into the front seat and turned around to assure Sir Guy that they would not be all descending on his film studios.

'Just going as far as . . .' he began.

'The British Museum,' put in Poppy quickly, and Baz beamed over his shoulder in admiration at her quick-wittedness.

'Bit of a squash back there,' he commiserated. 'Want to come in the front with me, Pops? You could sit on my lap.'

'We're all right,' said Daisy. She was very conscious that she was wedged in very close to the beautiful Charles de Montfort, who was being so respectful to Sir Guy that he had left him about half of the back seat in which to stretch himself. 'Tell Sir Guy about your films in India,' she said to him.

Charles was modest, mentioning a well-known film, but hastily adding that he was only one of the many young rajahs in it, but by the time that Baz and Poppy slid out of the taxi outside the British Museum he and Sir Guy seemed to be talking in a very friendly fashion. Daisy giggled a little as she saw Poppy forcibly drag Baz inside the black iron railings that surrounded the museum. He looked to be protesting vigorously.

Boys! she thought, and then hastily asked, 'What did you say, Sir Guy?'

'I was thinking that I could get Tom to do a screen test on Charles when we get there. Nothing elaborate: just a bit of acting. Would that be all right, Charles? Match you up with a blonde, perhaps. That would contrast nicely. '

Daisy could see that Charles looked thrilled and wished that she could warn him that Sir Guy had forty projects a day and only carried out about ten in the year. The chances of him using Charles as a star were small, but then, thought Daisy, on my films I can do my own choosing and, who knows, I might make us both famous.

Chapter Twelve
Thursday 3 April 1924

Although Sir Guy was enraptured by the idea of Daisy's chicken version of *Jane Eyre* and immediately got on the phone to various cinema owners, the film test for Charles did not look as though it was going to be a success. Daisy's heart ached. Poor boy, she thought, and longed to comfort him as Charles began to get a stricken look in his eyes. It had been all right in the beginning when they took a few shots of him, full face and then of his left and right profile. But Charles had become increasingly wooden as Tom tried to film him in various poses with studio crew – obviously they were considering him as a romantic hero; on his knees presenting a bunch of paper roses to an embarrassed Fred, kissing Harry's chemical-stained hand, and, worst of all, ordering him to throw his arms around James's neck.

That was the moment when Sir Guy took charge.

'C'mon, Daisy,' he grunted. 'Let her do it, Tom. It's no good filming him with James. James is too tall. At least with someone the size of Daisy you can get a good profile shot.'

His voice was impatient and Daisy's heart sank. Sir Guy, she thought, was not seeing any potential in Charles. He had wonderful looks, but that seemed to be the total sum of his assets. She stepped forward eagerly. She was surprised at herself, but she felt so sorry for Charles that she was not even conscious of any feelings of embarrassment.

At least, unlike the lanky James, she was smaller than Charles, and Tom would be able to film his profile over the top of her head. She moved close to him. The top of her head came close to his chin.

'Put your arms around her, man,' said Sir Guy wearily.

Charles obeyed. For a moment his arms felt stiff, but then they gathered her in, close to his chest. He looked down and smiled, that wonderful smile of his, and without meaning to, she moved in even more closely. Now she could feel his warmth, could smell the soap that he had used, could feel the pressure of his hand on her shoulder blades.

Once she was securely held by him she felt her legs trembling and her whole being melting and dissolving into his. She looked up at him and found her lips had parted. Without any instructions from Sir Guy, Charles bent his head. His lips found hers. For a moment she felt a shock of embarrassment and then, as they pressed gently and firmly, she forgot where she was, forgot the film-studio boys standing around, forgot her godfather, her father's friend, standing looking at her.

I'm just making the kiss last for the sake of the camera, she tried to tell herself, but deep down she knew the truth. This was her first real kiss and she wanted it to go on forever. When they broke apart to breathe, she reached up and touched her lips to his again. This time she put her arms around his neck, standing on tiptoe so that he did not have to bend down. She reached out with one hand and stroked his hair. It was as she had dreamed – as glossy as thick satin.

'And cut,' said Sir Guy.

It took another second before Charles released her. He had a startled look on his face, but his beautiful dark eyes glowed. Daisy stepped back from him. She was conscious that her cheeks were on fire as she reached for her camera and lifted it. After a moment she realized her hands were shaking too much to get a clear shot, so placed her camera on a tripod and began to film him at the same time as Tom did. Charles's slightly wooden air was back again and she wanted to distract him quickly.

'If only we were out in India where the sun was blazing down and the light was really good,' she said, wildly grasping to make conversation, but at the same time visualizing how the glossy black wing of his hair would perhaps show deep tints of chestnut under the fierce Indian sunlight.

'Tell me about the place; what are the colours that come into your mind when you think of India?' Now her pulse had slowed and her mind was concentrated on the lens of her camera. He had replied, but she didn't listen. His eyes were on her. They travelled around her face and Daisy imagined that they were focusing on her lips. What a hit he would be in the cinema if he looked at the camera like that! She glanced hastily at Sir Guy, and when he turned to speak to James she touched her fingers to her lips and blew Charles a quick kiss and he blew one back to her, the beautiful mouth widening into a smile, the perfect teeth flashing white under the studio lights.

'At the lens, at the lens; it's the camera that you should be focusing on, not Daisy,' growled Sir Guy, and Charles obeyed, but the result was not good.

'Go on, Tom, you carry on filming,' said Daisy impatiently. She abandoned her camera, took Charles by the hand and drew him over to stand in front of the backdrop of a sparkling waterfall that Fred had just finished painting. Tom had lifted his camera again, although she noted that he sent an uncertain glance in the direction of Sir Guy.

'I dream of India,' she lied, frantically searching her mind for extracts from Rudyard Kipling that Rose had read aloud to her. 'Tell me what it's like in the early morning – when you get up – when you step outside your bungalow.'

He wasn't good with words – Rose would not have been happy with the few halting descriptions that he gave – but Daisy, watching with a cameraman's eye, could see how effective were the deprecating smile, the glowing eyes, his gestures when he told her how impossible it was to describe a sunrise over the River Ganges at the moment when water and sky turn pale pink and flocks of birds dip down to drink from its surface. His hand was warm in hers. His dark head was bent down towards her and she longed to return into his arms.

'And cut,' said Sir Guy. 'Good, good.' He nodded. 'Fred, take Charles out for a walk around our domain while Tom gets these shots ready. Daisy, I want to show you something in my office.'

Daisy watched Charles go out – he did move well, she thought, wondering whether she would tell Poppy about what had occurred today. Did Poppy, she thought, feel like this about Baz?

'I agree with you,' she said, making a great effort to breathe naturally and to slow down her thumping pulse as soon as she had closed the door between Sir Guy's office and the studio. 'He isn't a natural actor. He would have to be handled carefully. Needs a talented director like you,' she added.

Sir Guy grunted. 'Don't try to soft-soap me, young lady. What were you up to – kissing that young chap like that?'

'You told Charles to put his arms around me,' countered Daisy, although she had to admit that Sir Guy probably had not anticipated it would result in a passionate kiss.

Sir Guy waved a hand. 'You didn't need to put your heart and soul into it,' he said severely. 'If your father had seen you in there, in front of all the lads too, well, he would have had a fit of apoplexy.'

'And he would have had a fit if he saw that film you were shooting the last time I was here. All that walking around in underwear! That glamorous lady! I don't know what you were thinking of, Sir Guy,' said Daisy severely.

He chuckled. 'You should have seen some bits of that film *Witchcraft through the Ages* – came out last year. Now that . . . ! But this is all beside the point. I'm talking about my goddaughter, the daughter of my great friend Michael Derrington, who is not one of your Bright Young People, but is a man who was born in the reign of Queen Victoria and stays firmly planted there. If he knew that I allowed you to kiss a young man in my presence – for the sake of a screen test, no less – he would be after me with a horsewhip.'

'Don't be ridiculous.' Daisy gave a light laugh. 'It worked, didn't it? You can see now what he is capable of. I was just getting the best out of a star.'

'As long as he can do it with any actress.' Sir Guy sounded wary. 'Nothing between you two, is there?' He gave her a shrewd look.

'Nothing whatsoever; only met him yesterday.' Daisy smiled sweetly at her godfather and wondered whether she too could be an actor. Listening critically, there was no betraying tremor in her tone. 'Don't say this to anyone, but I gather he failed his examinations for the Indian Police once too often,' she went on, lowering her voice. 'Jack is feeling guilty about him and would like him to pick up some work here in London; Elaine told me that last night. Jack is having a word with a few people that he knows to see if he can get him a position as a private secretary or something so that he can go off back to India with a clear conscience in a couple of months' time. But the trouble is that Charles just wants to make a career acting in films.' Daisy made her voice brisk and matter-of-fact. It didn't matter, she thought, telling this to Sir Guy, when Charles himself had said that he had failed his examinations.

'Well, if you're sure.' Sir Guy was always an easy man to convince. His mind was already focusing on a possible new star. 'He's certainly a very good-looking young fellow. We definitely need a blonde to go with him,' he mused. 'You two looked very good together. Now let's go and have a look at this screen test and see how the pictures turned out.'

This time Daisy took care to sit beside Sir Guy and keep her eyes away from Charles. All of the time while the pictures were being shown one half of her mind was registering how well the ones taken with her had turned out, in comparison to the earlier efforts, while the other half was busy thinking of the taxi ride back to Grosvenor Square. Sir Guy, she knew, was extremely busy; he would be expecting her to stay at the studios until five or six o'clock as she had done the last time that she was in London. And she did need to perfect the work on the hens film.

However, she plotted, if she left soon she could share a cab – and the cosy back seat – with Charles. Another day would do for working on her film.

Once the screen tests had been shown, Sir Guy's crew, as she had expected, obviously wanted to discuss them and were wishing that they could tell Charles to make his exit; she looked at her watch and gave a slight scream.

'Look at the time!' she exclaimed. 'And Elaine wants to go shopping to get ideas for our dresses for the ball. Charles, could I share a taxi with you?'

'James will get one for you; go on, James, find one and tell him Grosvenor Square and he can keep the change.' Sir Guy threw a coin at James and Daisy gave him a kiss.

'What a charming godfather you are,' she cooed. Elaine had given her spending money, but it was lovely to have taxis ordered for her, and paid for.

'Tell me about yourself,' Daisy had said as soon as she and Charles got into the taxi. 'Tell me all about those films that you starred in when you were in India. I'd love to find out what stars think about while they are being filmed. I've only worked with members of my family and friends – and the hens, of course. You are the professional.'

'Tell me about *you*,' he said putting an arm around her. 'I'm not interesting, but you are. What a wonderful thing it is for girl like you, with all that you have, to be so in earnest about making a career. Most girls just spend all their time thinking of parties and clothes.'

'I'm really in earnest about being a film director. I can do everything now,' she said seriously. 'I can film, I can develop the films, I can make up a story – though my little sister, Rose, is much better than I am at that, but one day I hope that I can just be the one who takes a story and sees how it might work out in pictures, the one who plans the film and decides on the stars and – and with a sort of vision in my mind about how it will turn out.'

'And is your father willing to set you up in your film studio? Or is he like all fathers and just wants you to be happily married to a nice man who will take care of you and of your children?' His arm pressed a little more closely and she nestled into him and in the dimness of the taxi cab smiled a little at the thought of her father affording the cost of setting her up to make films. Still, it was nice to talk about her ambitions for a change. At home no one listened to them.

'I want to be different,' she went on. 'I don't want to be like my mother and girls like that – I want to be responsible for my own future.'

And then she wondered whether she should have said that and looked at him uncertainly.

'I feel the same,' he said. 'I want to be independent. I'm very modern. I wouldn't mind my wife working.'

He reached down and squeezed her hand. And then he tilted his head towards hers and the kiss was so much better than it had been at the film studio. Eventually she broke away, feeling breathless and a little shy.

'Do you think that I will make a good film director?' she asked, trying to cover up her rush of emotions.

'Of course you will. And you'll fall in love, get married and have lots of lovely little blond babies,' he said softly.

Or dark-haired little boys, with wonderful brown eyes, she thought to herself and quickly his lips found hers again. He was very, very good at kissing, she thought, almost feeling slightly dizzy. Eventually she had to break away and gulp for air and then felt embarrassed. Surely there was a better way of managing. In films people seemed to kiss for a very long time and when they came apart it was a slow, graceful procedure as they gazed lovingly into each other's eyes. Perhaps she should practise more.

'Thank you for a wonderful day,' he said politely when he got out of the taxi. To her disappointment he did not invite her into his mother's house, nor did he accompany her up the steps, but just waved in a friendly fashion and went off briskly.

Morgan was washing the car in the mews and she wandered down there.

She wanted to talk to him about Charles, but didn't know where to start. Morgan was looking at her, waiting for her to say something. She smiled a bit as she remembered Joan being lyrical about his lovely eyes. They were rather intriguing, she thought. They seemed to change in different lights. Now in the gleam of the sunlight they were the colour of a chestnut newly peeled from its shell.

'Do you like London, Morgan?' she asked.

He shrugged. 'I enjoy it for a break, but I'm a countryman at heart.'

'Were you brought up in the country?' she asked. It seemed funny that she knew so little about him.

He shook his head. 'No,' he said. 'I'm a Londoner, in truth, but my mother was from Kent. She died when I was young, but I have memories of her telling me about Kent and about bluebells in the woods. That's why I applied for the job when your father advertised it. I liked the name of the place, Beech Grove Manor, and after the war I wanted to get away from London – hated the place. Still, the big money is up here in town. Young Baz could make a thing of this jazz-club,' he went on, 'but he's a bit under the influence of that sister of his, and she is in with a very wild crowd. I thought of having a talk with him this morning, but then I thought I would leave it until later.'

'So what did you do this morning?' asked Daisy.

He hesitated for a long time and then said, 'Well, when Lady Elaine said that she would not need the car this morning I walked down to the Strand and went into Somerset House.'

Daisy felt the colour drain from her face and she stared at him. She remembered the time when she and Poppy had gone there the year before and had found that only one baby, a little girl named Poppy, had been born to the Lady Mary Derrington on 11 October 1906. Had he guessed her secret?

'I thought about Maud finding out about herself there,' he went on, hardly seeming to notice her expression, 'and I thought I should like to find out about my parents – I never knew my father, but I just about remember my mother – actually it was that silly business yesterday with Lady Joan calling me St Clair that made me think about her.'

'She, your mother – she told you that your middle name was St Clair?' Daisy's voice was soft. Poor fellow; he must have grown up feeling very lonely in the orphanage. She was much luckier. She had grown up with the conviction that she had three sisters, a mother and a father. She said nothing however. It was not her secret to tell; Elaine would have to be happy for her to reveal the truth before she could share her history with her friends.

The chauffeur frowned. 'That's the strange thing about it,' he said. 'My mother told me that my middle name was St Clair, and another thing she told me was that I was born in June – "Born in June, silver spoon"; she used to sing a little song about that.'

'And did you find your birth certificate?'

'Well, yes, but on there it was noted, "Thought to be born in December 1900" and Robert St Clair wasn't my name – it said Edward Robert Morgan, son of Annie Morgan. And that's odd too, because the name "Annie" meant nothing to me. Still, I was only a little fellow when she died.'

'She didn't register you?'

He smiled. 'Apparently not. It's the old, old story, I suppose. I perhaps never had a father, or at least he didn't stick around to see me born.'

'Who registered your birth then?' asked Daisy.

'It seems that it was the orphanage. And the funny thing is that they didn't register me until I was almost three years old. I must have come into their care then. Perhaps my mum got herself another man and dumped me.' He sounded depressed.

'But you remember her – you remember her telling

you about Kent, and singing songs to you about "born in June", and telling you about your stylish middle name – it sounds as though she was fond of you,' urged Daisy. 'If I were you, I would go to that orphanage that registered your birth and try to find out some more details about yourself. Where was it?'

'In Bethnal Green . . .' began Morgan and then stopped as the butler came to the back door. 'You'd better go,' he said curtly.

Well, at least Elaine didn't put me in an orphanage, considered Daisy as she made her way back into the house. Her mind went to an earlier thought that she had had. What if Elaine, aged only seventeen at the time of the tragic death of the boy that she had loved, had gone to London and had her baby there under an assumed name. Would she have kept her, or would she perhaps have put her in an orphanage? Instead of being Lady Daisy, the daughter of an earl, she might now be Daisy the scullery maid.

'Elaine,' she said when she went in, 'would it be all right if I phoned Father? I'd like to talk to him. He was very depressed when we left.'

Without Michael Derrington's generous offer to rear her as his own daughter, what might have happened to the child of a weak-willed, rather self-centred seventeen-year-old?

Chapter Thirteen
Thursday 3 April 1924

'Don't look so disappointed, darling. Michael is always bad on the phone,' said Elaine when Daisy put down the handset after a brief conversation. She gave a little laugh. 'He thinks a phone is like a telegram – the more brief you are, the better.'

'He does sound low.' Daisy gave a sigh. It was hard to know what she could do. The phone call had seemed just to annoy him and he had seemed eager to finish.

'Let's go shopping, just the two of us. Shall we? It will be fun.' Elaine looked at her so anxiously that Daisy felt guilty.

'Yes, let's,' said Daisy, trying to summon up some enthusiasm. It was true that the Earl was never very good on the phone – he tended to worry about the cost, not just to himself but to anyone that called him, and so he was tense and gave one-word answers. He had sounded depressed though, even for him, and she felt worried.

And then there was Charles.

She turned impulsively to her mother. 'I really want to talk to you,' she said.

'Yes, of course, darling,' said Elaine. 'Just run upstairs and freshen yourself up and we'll have tea at Harrods and then look at the clothes. It will be lovely to have a chat together.'

Daisy did what she was told, and by the time she came back downstairs again, Morgan, very smart in his uniform, was at the door, ready to usher them into the car.

'We'll have some tea first before we exhaust ourselves,' said Elaine as they got out of the car at the stately entrance. 'Come back in couple of hours, Morgan.'

She hardly looked at the chauffeur as she spoke, and Daisy, after a quick smile at him, followed her up the steps. It was odd, she thought, how dismissive Elaine and Jack were of Morgan. For a moment she half wished that he would join them over tea, wished that she could ask his advice, certainly about her father, and perhaps he might have some useful thoughts on Charles also. He might laugh at her though, for being interested in Charles. Instinctively she felt that Charles would not fit in well with the jazz-band boys.

'So how was your morning, darling?' asked Elaine as Daisy bit into a cinnamon-sprinkled piece of shortcake and sipped the fragrant tea.

'Fun,' said Daisy, after a moment's pause. Elaine was but yet wasn't her mother. Daisy wondered whether to talk to her about kissing Charles. Looking back on it, perhaps it did seem a bit fast. Elaine might be shocked at her behaviour. 'Charles came to the studio too,' she said after a minute. 'He'd like to earn his living as a film star, I think.'

'Funny idea,' said Elaine. 'I wonder why he would want to bother. I got the impression from Jack that he was one of those rich, idle young men. Of course, Jack and his mother are only second cousins – or even further distant; I'm not sure. Jack doesn't have much time for Charles – they're not very alike. Jack is so dynamic and so hard-working – but I always found Charles perfectly amiable. Do you like him, darling?'

'Do you?' countered Daisy.

'Oh, of course; he is charming. And you have such strength of character. They talk about marrying someone like yourself, but I always think that the secret of a happy marriage is to marry your opposite. Look at us! We are so happy, Jack and myself!'

'And do you think that Charles and I would be happy?' Daisy asked, trying to laugh. She suddenly found herself feeling very self-conscious. Elaine seemed to have jumped to conclusions very quickly, she thought, and wondered guiltily where she had given herself away.

'What do you think, darling?' asked Elaine, holding Daisy's hand affectionately. She looked closely at her daughter. 'You're blushing,' she said with an amused smile. 'Don't say that—'

'I did kiss him,' whispered Daisy, 'but . . .'

'Well!' exclaimed Elaine. 'You modern girls. I must say that was very quick. Don't tell Jack that. He'll be shocked!'

Daisy giggled and after a moment Elaine giggled too. It was almost as if they were two girls out together, talking about young men. There was, thought Daisy, not much more than seventeen years between them.

'Tell me about my father, Elaine,' she said softly. 'Did you adore him from the moment that you met, or did you just gradually grow together? You would have grown up with him, wouldn't you? You were at Beech Grove with your Aunt Lizzie and he was over at Staplecourt. Justin Pennington used to stay at Staplecourt, too, didn't he? He was Clifford's nephew. I remember him telling us about it.' She prattled on, waiting until Elaine's colour came back. Perhaps, thought Daisy, I should not have mentioned my father like that, but we have never spoken of him and we should. She could imagine, though, the shock that it must have been to a pregnant seventeen-year-old to hear the terrible news that the boy who was father to her unborn child had been killed on the hunting field. She poured another cup of tea from the delicate china pot and handed the cup to her mother.

'You mustn't make the mistake that I made,' said Elaine after a minute.

Which mistake? wondered Daisy. Was it the mistake of allowing herself to be loved by someone, to become pregnant by him, or was it the mistake of giving her baby away and allowing her aunt to force her into a loveless marriage in order to stop the gossips' tongues?

'It's just been a kiss,' she said after a minute.

'A kiss can lead to other things – sometimes very quickly,' said Elaine with a sigh. 'I suppose that is why girls have to be chaperoned so closely.' She bit her lip and stared with unseeing eyes across the restaurant.

'It's natural at your age to think that people like Great-Aunt Lizzie fuss too much,' she said after a minute, 'but don't forget that these rules and regulations are there for a purpose. When you meet a new young man, don't be too forthcoming, Daisy, will you?'

'I suppose you saw a lot of Charles in India,' said Daisy, suddenly desperate to change the subject. 'Did he have a girlfriend there?' She could tell from her mother's expression that Elaine did not want to talk about Clifford Pennington, and in any case, she was interested in the answer to that.

Elaine brightened. 'Not that I remember,' she said. 'He's about twenty-four, I think. A perfect age for marriage,' she added jokingly. 'He'll probably want to settle down soon now that he is back in England. And don't say anything to him, but Jack feels that he might be able to do something for him. I'm sure that if, well . . . if there is any question of an engagement, then Jack will move heaven and earth to get him a position in the Foreign Office. Jack,' she said earnestly, 'thinks it's very bad for a man to have nothing to do, no matter how wealthy he is.' Then she looked at her daughter with a smile. 'And are you really interested in Charles then, darling?'

'Well,' said Daisy, trying to sound as though it were all a joke, 'since he looks like a Greek god, kisses like . . .' she ran a quick check of male film stars and ended with, 'kisses like Douglas Fairbanks, is incredibly rich and will be found a position in the Foreign Office by

Jack – how on earth could I resist him?'

That, she thought, had struck the right note. Elaine laughed and said, 'How wonderful it is to have this time to chat with you. Now let's go and look at some frocks. We need to think carefully about what you will need for your season.'

'I did see, as we came up the stairs, a lovely tea gown in black and silver . . .' Daisy knew her mother would be happier shopping for clothes than discussing serious matters – especially if they involved past history, and so it proved. They had a wonderful afternoon, with Elaine flushed and animated, and there were dozens of boxes for Morgan to load into the car by the time that they finally finished.

Poppy arrived home about half an hour after they did. She had Baz in tow, of course, and Daisy heard them arguing in the hall as she came down the stairs.

'You do it,' Baz was saying.

'Don't be stupid; you have to do it,' hissed Poppy. 'It's your mother.'

'No, it isn't,' retorted Baz, and there were muffled giggles from both of them.

'Shh,' said Daisy, coming on to the landing and putting her finger to her lips. She pointed at the yellow parlour, where the sound of Jack reading a newspaper article to Elaine boomed through the doorway.

'This is what *The Times* says: "*It is time that those antics ceased. Those Bright Young People and their ridiculous parties are giving London a bad name with their . . .*"'

'Go on, go in,' muttered Poppy, and gave Baz a firm push from behind as he hesitated on the threshold. Daisy followed, trying not to giggle at Baz's expression of horror. On their entry Jack laid aside the newspaper with a slight expression of annoyance crossing his handsome face, but Elaine seemed glad to see them and Daisy suspected that she was tired of being lectured.

'Card from my mother,' Baz muttered, after prolonging his greetings for as long as he could. He held out a gold-bordered card with his mother's name and address on it and then quickly reversed it so the handwritten message on the back could be seen.

Elaine scrutinized it carefully and Jack looked over her shoulder.

'Well, that's very kind of your mother to invite the girls.'

'It's just a supper party on Monday – very small affair,' stuttered Baz. 'Nothing formal – no chaperones,' he ended, giving Poppy the despairing look of someone who had forgotten his lines.

Elaine looked at him with surprise and Jack with suspicion.

'You must call on Lady Dorothy, my dear, of course,' Jack said to Elaine. 'It would be better to thank her in person.'

And find out what's *really* happening, thought Daisy, hoping that Joan would manage to prime her rather indulgent mother before Elaine called.

'What's this party, then?' she asked Poppy as soon

as they were alone upstairs.

'Small, informal supper at Lady Dorothy's town house,' said Poppy demurely, adding, 'Why don't you bring your camera? You know you want to make a film about the Bright Young People.' Joan will tell you all about them – she's one of them; she knows all about the treasure hunts and the parties in a swimming bath and things like that. Me and Baz won't do anything like that though, of course.'

Daisy gave her a suspicious look but decided it might be better not to know too much. Things could not get *too* wild if it really was a party held by Lady Dorothy.

'Would it be all right if I asked Charles de Montfort?' she asked casually. 'He doesn't really know many people in London and I think he would enjoy it.'

And then, as Poppy looked at her suspiciously in turn, she threw her arms around her and whispered in her ear, 'He kissed me and it was heaven!'

'Who?' Poppy sounded startled.

'Charles, of course,' she said trying not to blush.

'Charles?'

Daisy looked at her with annoyance. 'Well, who else?' she asked. She could hear her voice sounding defensive and that irritated her. Who was Poppy to sound so dubious? After all, she, Daisy, had never said a word against Poppy's plans to marry Baz, though personally, she could not ever visualize spending the rest of her life with someone who seemed so immature and unintelligent.

'Don't you like him?' she asked defensively.

'You're not just falling in love with him because he's rich, are you?' Poppy gave her a penetrating look.

'Of course not,' said Daisy firmly. 'It's not about the money at all. I truly am falling in love with him.' She couldn't understand why Poppy seemed unable to see how gorgeous Charles was, but she supposed her sister was blinded by her love for Baz.

'It's just that it all seems a bit sudden, but as long as you like him . . .'

Of course, Poppy and Baz had known each other for all of their lives and had only recently fallen so deeply in love that they were thinking about marriage. Perhaps her feelings for Charles were a bit sudden. Two days as compared with seventeen years.

Daisy shrugged. Love at first sight was more romantic anyway, she thought, and certainly more cinematic.

Chapter Fourteen
Monday 7 April 1924

Poppy snuggled in close to Baz and then sighed as she heard Joan's voice from upstairs. The town house belonging to Baz's family was very tall and narrow with numerous flights of stairs, and the large and noisy family were always tramping up and down them and calling to each other continually. All of Baz's family, except he and Joan, were married and had their own homes, but as soon as their mother came to London they all seemed to congregate at Belgravia Square.

'Sometimes I almost wish that we were back at Beech Grove,' she said, moving away from him reluctantly. Soon all Joan's friends would be arriving for this 'informal supper party' and then they would have no opportunity to be alone.

'Not taking a dislike to London, are you?' Baz sounded worried.

'No, not to London. If only we could just move into your little house – with no fuss, no plotting and planning. Planning makes my head ache. I just want to play music and to be left in peace.' She stared moodily ahead and drummed her feet on the ground. 'I'm so tired of telling lies and making up excuses,' she said apologetically as his arms went around her again. Daisy, she thought resentfully, seemed very happy. She spent most of her days at the film studios and no one questioned that because of Sir Guy being her godfather and a great friend of the Earl; certainly no one asked whether she was going there because of her ambitions to make a film or because she would be with Charles de Montfort. Poppy heard a lot about Charles de Montfort in nightly talks – all about the new film that Daisy was making about India, in which Charles was an Indian rajah, and Violet a young girl just arrived from England. Daisy, thought Poppy, was perhaps a little jealous of her elder sister's being so close to the wonderfully desirable Charles.

And then she forgot about Daisy as she felt the soft pressure of Baz's lips on hers.

'Oh, I say! Too, too shy-making . . . shall I go out and come in again? I can even cough in a tactful way and then tap on the door,' said a voice from behind them.

'Oh, go away, Joan.' Poppy pulled herself away from Baz. She quite liked Joan when she was in the mood for comedy, but just now she wanted to be alone with Baz. Everyone treated them like a pair of kids. She scowled at Joan, and then her eyes widened. For a small, informal party, Joan was very dressed up.

She wore a straight shift of midnight blue, lightened by three panels of iridescent sapphire shimmering against the background of the darker colour. Circles and half-circles of dark and light blue ornamented the bodice, and the hem dipped on both sides and rose well above the knee in the middle. On her head she wore a close-fitting elfin cap with circles of blue beads stitched into the silver lace. It curved around her forehead, finishing in two points on her jawbones, enhancing the colour of her eyes and giving her face an innocent and childlike expression.

Poppy glared at her. She and Daisy were just wearing ordinary tea gowns – after emphasizing how small and informal the gathering was going to be, neither had liked to dress up too much.

'I say, cheer up,' said Joan. 'There was a poem that governess of ours was always quoting: "*To be young is very heaven*", something like that.'

'Well, it's a lie,' said Poppy fiercely. 'To be young is very hell. Why should we be bossed and bullied and hemmed in with rules and regulations? We're adults. I stopped growing four years ago. Why can't we be treated like grown-ups?'

'Can't say it bothers me.' Joan yawned.

'Well, you're lucky then,' snapped Poppy. 'You just want to get married to a rich man and your mother wants that for you too so you have no problems.'

'And have some fun, while I'm waiting for him to turn up,' said Joan, peering at herself in the mirror and rubbing gently at a spot of excess colour on her right cheekbone. 'Too, too sickening, making up one's face in daylight,' she murmured. 'Why can't sun be more like electricity?' She blinked her mascara-coated eyelashes several times, then shut each eye in turn and peered at the navy-blue lid with satisfaction.

'I've got an idea,' she said brightly. 'Trust me. I will take your affairs in hand and bring them to a satisfactory conclusion. Do you know that Annette is thinking of setting up as a marriage broker? They have them out in India. She says that she has got three clients already. I shall be her rival.'

'Oh, go away, Joan,' Baz groaned.

'Joan!' Her mother's voice called from downstairs. 'Here come some of your young people. Do come down, dear; I never know which is which. These girls change their appearance so quickly.'

'Just chaperoning the young couple, Mama,' called back Joan, adding in a whisper, 'Don't worry; she's going out. I persuaded her that having supper with us young things would bring on one of her migraines. She telephoned Sarah and her husband to come and take charge. Funny, isn't it, that only last year Sarah was just a debutante to be chaperoned and this year, just because she's married, she's trusted to take care of her sister and brother and all of their friends.

And then she was gone, ostentatiously leaving the door wide open.

'Wonder how much she charges for marriage broking – Annette, I mean.' Poppy tried to smile, but she knew from the gentle concern in Baz's eyes that the attempt was a failure. She gulped a little and went over to the mirror and painted her lips. She looked pale, she thought, and there were dark shadows under her eyes. Still the closely cut black shift dress did look quite nice.

Carefully she outlined her lips with a firm stick of bright red lip rouge.

'Think about tonight,' he suggested. 'We'll just have to endure the supper party. Then we'll go over to my place and get the music going. Joan has it all fixed. It will just be a few friends.'

Poppy nodded and smiled. Baz kissed her on the forehead and she felt overwhelmed with love. Yes, it would be fun.

'It would be so good to be married,' he said wistfully.

'We'll manage somehow or other,' she said fiercely as Joan came running back up the stairs.

'Now, darlings,' she said with a businesslike air, 'let's try to make you interesting.'

Poppy frowned. 'Why interesting?' she asked.

'Trust Aunt Joan, dear. Tell me about your coming-out dance – you and Daisy.'

'Going to be huge,' said Poppy emphatically. 'Elaine's husband is insisting on making a big, big affair of it. First it was going to be in the house, but now it's going to be at the Ritz Hotel. We are going to have very special dresses!'

'The Ritz, hmm, a bit stuffy, but always worth a story – there'll be plenty of newspaper reporters and photographers popping flashlights,' said Joan thoughtfully. 'You'll have to make it different though, to every other coming-out dance. These affairs are such a yawn; I've been to a million of them and I swear that they are getting duller and duller; I was never more bored in my life than at Charlotte Muskery's do in the Savoy.

We'll have to think of something exciting. My plan is to make you two the most talked-about couple in town. Get people used to having your names paired together. Then when you get engaged, no one will be surprised,' she ended, and Poppy looked at her with sudden interest.

'But more of that anon; now let's go down to supper,' said Joan briskly. 'Daisy and her young man have just arrived. My dear, what does she see in him? He looks and acts like a tailor's dummy.'

Chapter Fifteen
Monday 7 April 1924

'I don't think that I have ever been so happy in my life,' said Daisy defiantly.

Violet looked at her with narrowed eyes. 'Has he got any money?' she asked. 'You do know that it's your duty to marry money? Someone must, and Poppy is flying headlong into this business with Baz, who is the youngest of five brothers! Rose is too young, so it's up to you to save Beech Grove. How old is he?'

'He's twenty-four. And he doesn't have any brothers – or sisters. His mother must be rich – she's taken a house in Grosvenor Square for the season and she doesn't even have a daughter to present. Anyway, Elaine got the impression from Jack that Charles is rich. He certainly looks well off – you can see that from the way he dresses.' Daisy felt defensive and rather sorry that she had said anything to Violet. 'His father is dead,' she added. Violet was an expert on things like inheritance and she was frowning now. She sprayed her neck and shoulders with Lady Dorothy's expensive perfume – Joan had thrown open her mother's bedroom to all the girls and urged them to help themselves to scent and powder.

'De Montfort,' said Violet thoughtfully. 'I will make enquiries. There's money in the family, of course. The mother is some sort of cousin of Jack's, isn't she, and he inherited a big sum last summer when one of that family died – Justin saw it when probate was asked for,' she added, in her usual irritating fashion of knowing so much more than her younger sisters. 'That's not to say that Charles is well off though. Still, the fact that he threw up the Indian Police business might show that he has come into money. Whatever you do, don't rush into anything. You are far too young and you're only at the beginning of your season. There will be plenty of fish in the sea and you're not too bad-looking these days,' she finished in a condescending way that made Daisy long to slap her.

'I'm perfectly happy with Charles,' she said shortly.

'Well, as I say, don't rush into anything; it could be fatal at this stage,' said Violet, who had, thought Daisy, an annoying habit of repeating her mediocre thought processes over and over again. 'I'll get Justin to make some enquiries,' she added.

'Don't,' said Daisy, but Violet wasn't listening to her and was now eager to explain why she couldn't meet Rose tomorrow afternoon at Victoria Station as she would be too exhausted after a morning's filming.

'It takes so much out of one,' she murmured, trying the effect of Lady Dorothy's powder and then wiping it off with a shudder. 'You have no idea what we actresses go through,' she added as she left the room.

Left to herself, Daisy grinned. Violet was no actress. Only this morning Daisy felt as though she had been through a wringer while she tried to get performances from her sister and from Charles. She had to admit that Charles too was no actor, but that fact had to be concealed from Sir Guy, who was looking at him with an increasingly sceptical eye. Violet had once had a screen test with a Hollywood producer, but nothing had come of it. No doubt her inability to act had outweighed her lovely face; Sir Guy had said so privately to Daisy. All their hopes were now based on this new film, *The Rajah and the Lady*. Daisy brooded on Sir Guy's words:

'The story is all right – I've seen worse – and the filming is great, and young Fred has done some genuinely good backgrounds on those screen boards that would make you almost think that you were in India, but neither of them can act, my dear.'

Deep in thought, she made her way down to supper.

'Does anyone mind if I film?' she asked, raising her voice a little and looking around the table. There must be about twenty people there, she thought – the men in their black and white and the girls in daringly short low-cut dresses would make a great scene.

'I say,' said the girl called Annette, 'a real film. How too, too marvellous.' She adjusted her bejewelled headband and waved her long cigarette holder, making a trail of smoke which Daisy immediately filmed.

'Too, too swoon-making,' said Joan, not to be undone.

'What a shame that Eve is not here,' said another girl, called Lottie, who was wearing a particularly short black dress, made almost entirely from net and trimmed haphazardly with bunches of fur. 'Dear, dear Eve – she does have such wonderful cheekbones. She's so proud of them. And she does so love to be photographed.'

'What has happened to that young man of yours, Lottie?' enquired Annette, with what Daisy thought was the professional interest of a dedicated matchmaker. 'I don't see him around these days.'

'He has left me, darlings!' said Lottie dramatically. 'Isn't it too, too shame-making!'

There was a chorus from around the table while Daisy filmed the animated faces, the waving hands and the clouds of cigarette smoke.

'Dear, dear Lottie, how devastating!'

'How ungentlemanly!'

'How cur-like!'

'How shaming, Lottie, darling!'

'How sick-making!'

'How too, too awful!'

I wish that Rose was here, thought Daisy with a slight pang as she lowered her camera. She would so love Joan and her friends. She would have material for a new novel just from the way they spoke. The pages would be peppered with '*too, too*'s. Still, she would be here tomorrow – and she would just have to meet them then.

'Just ignore me,' she told everyone as they kept glancing her way, but she knew that there would be a certain amount of posing. Still, the wonderful thing about being able to develop your own films was that you could use what you wanted and cut out the rest. The long hours in the dairy pantry at Beech Grove House had been of great value. She was quick at picking out worthwhile shots from small negatives and expert at the developing, cutting and pasting procedures that formed the backbone of film-making. Sir Guy was astonished at the speed with which she was putting together her new film about India.

'I hope you mean to dance with me and not to spend all night filming,' whispered Charles.

Daisy felt a little conscience-stricken. How could she think of giving up the pleasure of being in his arms or hand in hand with him for the whole evening, just in order to shoot a film? However, there seemed to be more girls than men at the table so Charles would not be left standing by the wall if she did snatch a few camera opportunities. Luckily Annette was on his other side and she was an incessant chatterer, so Daisy was able to plan her film in peace and only came out of her reverie when the meal finished and the girls all trooped to mirrors and the bathroom and the young men straightened their ties, tugging at coat tails or at moustaches.

'Joan, darling, how many taxis do you think?' called Sarah, Baz's eldest sister, as she went towards the telephone.

Joan gave a hasty glance around. 'Just four, darling. We'll all pile in.'

That will be a sight, thought Daisy. Twenty-four people in four taxis!

'Don't get out until I get in position,' she warned them as their taxi turned the corner towards Baz's little house.

It had been too cramped to film them inside the taxi, but she would get them pouring out of it, she decided.

'Here, do I get paid for this?' shouted the taxi driver as she filmed.

Daisy ignored him; she was busy with her thoughts and plans. She would join this footage with the shots of the occupants of the next taxi and the next, so that it would look as if an unending stream of partying young people poured out from the one car. Luckily all these London cabs looked alike.

'Dear man, you will be famous all over the world after this,' called out Joan, her sleekly dressed head sticking out from the next taxi's window. 'People from New Orleans will come to London especially to ride in your cab. Make sure that you film his number, Daisy.'

Chattering and laughing they ran up the steps, and Morgan opened the door. He let them in and then came down and joined Daisy, waiting for the others to arrive. Annette, Daisy noticed, had tucked her arm into Charles's and borne him up with the rest of the crowd. For a moment Daisy stared after them and then she shrugged. I suppose we have to trust each other, she thought, but she did wish that he had looked back at her. Still, once she had finished her filming there would be time for them to dance together. She thought of that perfect profile, and knew that it was inevitable that other girls would try to take him from her.

'You filming it tonight?' asked Morgan.

'Yes. Is that all right, Morgan, do you think?'

He thought about it for a moment. 'No harm in it, I'd say. That lot –' he jerked his thumb towards the house – 'they're all mad for publicity. Think themselves badly done by if they haven't been in the newspapers for a week.'

'Here comes the next taxi.' Daisy's eyes went to the corner of the little back street. Joan was hanging out of the window of the first floor of the little house and waving madly, shouting messages that could not possibly be heard by those in the car. 'Don't you wait, Morgan,' Daisy said.

'Yes, I'd better get back inside,' he said. 'Maud and I have got everything ready – candles and all. I've made a sort of punch – mainly orange juice with a couple of cheap bottles of white wine thrown in. No strong drinks tonight so it shouldn't get too wild. After tonight we'll have to charge an admission, but we'll see how this one goes.'

And then he was gone and Daisy concentrated on filming the arrival of the next two taxis, trying to get different types of shots from each of them – a glimpse of nude stocking, a sheen from the lamplight on a dark dinner jacket, a girl's heavily lipsticked mouth and then a tousled head of brilliantine-clogged hair, sticking up in spikes like a porcupine's, belonging to a very tall young man stooping to emerge from the cab.

Chapter Sixteen
Monday 7 April 1924

'I say, Daisy isn't doing much dancing with that fellow Charles de Montfort, is she?' Baz handed Poppy a jar of orange punch and sat down again, his forehead shining with sweat. Morgan was working them all very hard that evening, leaving only a few minutes between dances. 'You tired, Pops?' he added.

'No, it's wonderful!' Poppy felt a glow right through her. She gave an indifferent glance at Charles de Montfort chatting to Annette and then another towards Daisy. Her twin looked perfectly happy as she aimed the square black camera at the guttering candles. Daisy, she knew, would make something special out of those channels of twisted wax, in the same way as she, Poppy, could make something special with her clarinet. She smiled across at the serious face behind the camera and then glanced over towards Morgan. He had consented to this party because they were being chaperoned by two sets of married couples, but only on the understanding that Poppy and Daisy promised not to drink. He was, thought Poppy, with an amused smile, relaxing his rather old-fashioned attitude and seemed excited about the success of their parties. Perhaps Joan's flirtatious attitude was having a good effect on him.

'What's next, Morgan?' she asked.

'Let's take a break,' he suggested, mopping his forehead.

'Hope there's not too much of a queue for the bathroom,' she said, getting to her feet.

'I'm afraid that it leads all the way down the stairs to the hall,' said Simon, who had just returned.

'There's another WC under the stairs,' said Baz. 'Grandfather had it put in for the servants.'

'Maud will show you the way; she's been cleaning it,' said Morgan, beckoning to Maud, who, in one of Daisy's old dresses, was practising the steps of the tango.

'I do wish that we could pay you for all your hard work, Maud,' said Poppy as they went out together. 'It's not that we're mean; it's just that we're so poor.'

'I like it,' said Maud, her green eyes shining with an intense enjoyment. 'I wouldn't mind working here if you do set up your jazz club. It's more fun than Beech Grove – especially since Rose, Lady Rose, I mean, went away.'

'You must come to the station with us tomorrow to meet her. She'll be really pleased to see you. I miss her too,' she added. A wave of euphoria spread over her and she felt at peace with the world, even remembering to thank Maud when she pointed out the location of the tiny WC. The girl had a good speaking voice and a striking appearance, with her dark green eyes and those winged eyebrows. Perhaps Baz could try her out as a singer.

Morgan had such great plans for this jazz club. He had heard a story about the owner of some night club who was earning twenty thousand pounds a year, even after paying his musicians and all the other expenses. Twenty thousand pounds, she thought. Baz and she could live like kings on that! And, she observed with a mischievous grin, the prospect of earning that kind of money had rather changed Morgan's attitude towards having his employer's daughter playing in the band. Her clarinet, she knew, considerably enhanced the sound that they made.

She went into the small room and shut the door quietly. It would be good to keep this place a secret or else there would soon be a queue here too.

She checked her face in the mirror and then stiffened. There was a voice coming through the thin wall.

It must be the room where the telephone was, thought Poppy. Baz's grandfather had not wanted to put it in the hall, where all of the stable lads could use it, so it was placed in a little locked room to which only the coachman and his wife would have had the key.

'Fleet Street 1000' said the voice and then, 'Chomondley here.'

Poppy frowned. Baz must have told that silly ass Chomondley, one of Joan's crowd, that he could use the phone – summoning a taxi, she assumed, but quickly realized that she was wrong.

'Ready?' asked the voice and then began to speak fluently:

'Headline: *Mr Gossip Lets Us into a Secret* <new paragraph>*There is a tired feeling among the party goers* <comma> *the* <italics> *Bright Young Things* <end italics> <comma> *and the movers and shakers on the London scene* <full stop> *There often seems nowhere to go and nothing new to experience* <full stop> *What I am going to reveal to you tonight is secret even to* <quote> *those in the know* <unquote> <full stop> *Hidden in the basement of a tiny mews house in Sutcheley Street* <comma> *Belgravia is the most delicious nightclub that your correspondent has ever seen* <full stop> <new paragraph> *Decked out in black and red silk and lit only by candles* <comma> *it forms the perfect background for London's most fashionable young people who gathered there tonight* <full stop> <new paragraph> *Lady Poppy Derrington* <comma> *looking gorgeous in black with her Pre-Raphaelite hair* – what? pre P-R-E hyphen – you know – a dash R-A-P-H – oh, OK, yes, that's Poppy as in the flower – *was there with her constant companion the Honourable Basil Pattenden* <comma> *youngest brother of the Earl of Pattenden* <semi-colon> – yes, that's the dotty-comma thing – *A little bird tells me that an interesting announcement may be expected soon* <full stop> <new paragraph> *Also present was her equally talented sister, the film-maker Lady Daisy Derrington* – yes, that's Daisy as in the flower – no, no *z* in it . . . <full stop> <new

paragraph> *Lady Poppy is a debutante* <comma> *and* <comma> *wait for it* <comma> *plays in a jazz band with the Honourable Basil Pattenden* <full stop> *The band* is *led by the well-known impresario – one s – just over from New Orleans* <comma> *that talented drummer Bob Morgan –* I don't care if it doesn't sound like a New Orleans name, that's my information – who cares anyway? <comma> *the Honourable Simon . . .*'

The voice went on in a dreary monotone while Poppy sat and stifled a giggle as all the outfits were commented on and then, quite abruptly, in a natural tone of voice – 'That's it; nighty-night.' The telephone clicked back on to its bar receiver, the door opened, brisk footsteps sounded in the hall and the front door slammed shut.

Wait till Daisy hears this, thought Poppy as she flushed and went back into the basement. Morgan (from New Orleans!) was flourishing his drumsticks, and Poppy hastily took her place. Once again she lost herself in the beat and the rhythm of the drums, the dark sultriness of the saxophone, the plaintive chords from the bass, the fizzy brassiness of the trombone and the rich, smooth notes of her clarinet.

It was the next morning before she thought of telling Daisy about the gossip columnist.

Chapter Seventeen
Tuesday 8 April 1924

'A gossip columnist! Oh my God, Poppy, why on earth didn't you stop him – snatch his notebook from him, get Morgan or something?' Daisy, half dressed, stared at her sister in horror.

'He didn't have a notebook; he just dictated it through on the telephone – the fellow at the other end wanted to spell your name with a *z*.' Poppy started to laugh. 'In any case, how could I stop him? I was in the lav, remember? He was out of the front door before I even flushed it.'

'Oh my God,' said Daisy again. She pulled on her other stocking and buttoned the straps of her low-heeled shoes. 'I must get down and look at the papers before anyone else. What paper was it?'

'Dunno,' said Poppy. 'He asked the exchange for some number in Fleet Street. Wouldn't be *The Times*, I'd say, and that's the only paper that Father ever reads – and he cancelled that in one of his economy fits.'

'What about Jack? And Elaine? Don't you remember what Father said about no mentions in gossip columns?' Daisy gave herself a quick glance in the mirror. Poppy had not bothered replying to her frantic questions but had gone back to her own bedroom, yawning.

Daisy hurried down the stairs. It was too early for breakfast, but the papers would have arrived.

The butler was still blotting the damp print on the newspapers with his hot iron and a piece of paper when she came downstairs. She stood beside him for a moment and then forced herself to ask nonchalantly, 'Any gossip columns in those, Tellford?'

He gave an almost human smile. 'No, my lady. You'll have to wait for *Vogue*, or *The London Illustrated News* for accounts of your parties. Sir John only takes *The Times* and *The Financial Times*.'

Daisy beamed at him, almost weak with relief. As long as there were no headlines to catch Jack's eye, then they should be safe for the moment. The reporter that Poppy overheard was probably from what Jack described as the gutter press.

Last night, thought Daisy, had been a success for her as a film-maker – she had got some great shots and had even begun to sense how the storyline could evolve – but as for her relationship with Charles, well, that had not gone so well. She had only had one dance with him; he had been monopolized for the rest of the night by Annette, who had seemed to be doing a bit of matchmaking on her own behalf. Still, she thought defiantly, it wasn't Charles's fault that Annette was a man-eater.

'I'll have my breakfast now,' she said to the parlour-maid who had appeared. She would call for Charles – get him out of bed if necessary, she decided. The afternoon would have to be devoted to meeting Rose at Victoria, so there was a lot of work to be got through this morning on the Indian film.

And if there was any spare time she wanted to be able to work on her new film. *Bright Young People*, she would call it, she decided. It would be a treat for her because she knew that there were some wonderful shots among the strips of film now carefully wrapped in the special box that her godfather had given her for keeping film dry and unscratched.

As the parlourmaid busied around bringing hot toast and pouring tea, Daisy heard Elaine's light step in the hall outside and made up her mind to be honest with her mother about what had happened last night. She sat up very straight and smiled a welcome as Elaine came into the room.

'How was last night, darling? We heard you come in, but I didn't want to disturb you and Poppy talking over the party. Was it good?'

'Very,' said Daisy. And then, with a quick gulp, she said bravely. 'It was one of those affairs where we moved on to another place – it was all fine though. Morgan drove us and Baz's married sister and her husband were there, as well as Violet and Justin, of course.'

'Oh, I see. Well, so long as you were both sensible.' Elaine seemed to be quite satisfied with the explanation and Daisy felt glad that she had told some of the truth anyway.

'There's something else that I wanted to talk to you about,' she went on, and then stopped as heavy footsteps sounded on the stairs. Still, she thought, Elaine will want to talk it over with Jack so I might as well mention it now. She swallowed some tea and, as Jack opened the door, she smiled at him in a friendly way, and said, 'I was just wondering, Jack, whether you both think that it would be all right for Charles and me to go on the bus out to Sir Guy's studios. I don't want to be monopolizing Morgan when you and Elaine probably have a greater need of him,' she ended tactfully.

Jack's eyes met his wife's and Elaine said, with a degree of decisiveness that Daisy had not expected of her, 'I'm sure, Jack, that Daisy is very sensible. She's an adult now and she knows that she had to be responsible for herself. I think that we should trust her. In the end,' she added, in a thoughtful fashion, 'it's up to Daisy to look after herself and to think of the consequences of her actions.'

There was, thought Daisy, as she sedately thanked them both for the permission to travel unescorted on buses with Charles, a world of experience behind her mother's words. No doubt Elaine had been very closely chaperoned – her Aunt Lizzie would have made sure of that, but, nevertheless, she became pregnant and Daisy was the result. Now Elaine's eyes told Daisy that she was responsible for herself and that it was up to her to be worthy of their permission.

'I appreciate your confidence in me,' Daisy said, and she made sure that her voice was sedate and grown-up.

With that she rose from the breakfast table and went back upstairs to put on her most attractive frock with its matching coat and rather fetching cloche hat. Charles, she thought, should be wowed by the ensemble.

Rose's train from Dover had already arrived by the time that Daisy arrived at Victoria Station. She had been delayed by having to call for Poppy, who had been at Baz's mother's house, and then had to wait as Joan decided to come too. Daisy thought of saying that there would be no room in the Humber, but then remembered the packed taxis of the night before; in any case, Rose would love Joan.

'Have you heard?' were the first words that Joan spoke once they were in the cab. 'Mr Gossip from *The Daily Express* did us proud. Pity there wasn't a photographer. And there was I in all my finery. My dear, how too sick-making. Oh, I say, Daisy, did you take any still photographs? You might be able to sell them to the newspapers. Especially one of me, you know. I'm always popular in newspapers!'

'I'll wait till I'm married before I start selling pictures to newspapers,' said Daisy, thinking with horror of the damage it could do to her reputation and of Michael Derrington's reaction.

'Oh, I say,' said Joan. 'Do tell! Has Charles popped the question? That's even better than Caro – she got engaged two weeks after meeting her Rupert. I thought he was a bit tied up with Annette last night, but I suppose if you're sure of him, you can let him off the hook a bit, amuse himself until you tie the knot – is that the idea? It's very modern, you know. I know one couple who keep getting engaged and then breaking up and then getting engaged again. And what's so delicious about it all is that they do it by telephone. They ring each other up and say: "*Sorry, darling, the wedding is off.*" Too, too bang up-to-the-minute.'

'Don't be ridiculous, Joan,' said Daisy, glad that Maud was in the front seat beside Morgan and that the glass partition was shut. She wasn't too worried now about competition from Annette. She and Charles had had a wonderful morning and he seemed more in love with her than ever. They had gone out to the film studio and had a marvellous time selecting the best shots from yesterday's filming session and, coming home on the empty top deck of the bus, they had almost missed their stop because they were too busy kissing. She blushed slightly at the memory and turned to look out of the window at the red-brick facade of Victoria Station.

'Here we are,' said Morgan, opening the partition. 'I'll find a parking place and then come along for her luggage. Be with you in a minute.'

Rose was with a crowd of schoolgirls all dressed in dark brown gymslips and brown and gold blazers. A flustered-looking woman seemed to be signing over one of the girls to a middle-aged woman.

'Daisy!' screamed Rose. 'At last! You're hours late.'

'Now don't exaggerate, dear,' said the teacher reprovingly. She looked doubtfully at Daisy and then back at her list. 'Your mother . . . ?' she queried.

'Dead,' said Rose cheerfully. 'And long, long in her grave.'

'Oh, I see. Yes, of course.' The woman seemed embarrassed and Rose took immediate advantage of it.

'It's a matter of great sorrow for the family so we don't mention it,' Rose said solemnly, and Daisy was glad that Poppy was not beside her. Memories of their mother were still very raw in Poppy's mind and she winced away from any reference to her. Rose, however, was only four when Mary died so she barely remembered her.

'But Daisy, my sister, adopted me and I lived happily ever after,' continued Rose cheerfully.

'Oh, I see, you are Rose's sister.' The woman gave a harassed look at the crowd of girls, who were getting restless and making silly jokes among themselves, attracting a lot of attention. 'Our train was early,' she explained, desperately scanning the crowds for signs of parents eager to take her charges off her hands. 'Oh, and here is a letter about the return dates,' she said, producing an envelope. 'The headmistress has decided to give the girls an extra-long Easter holiday to make sure that they are all well when we resume. School will reopen on Monday the nineteenth of May and the escorted train from Victoria will leave at ten a.m. on Saturday the seventeenth. Now, could you please sign here that you have received Rose.'

'Like getting a parcel,' said Rose. 'Oh, I say, Maud, you do look smart. And you, Morgan. Oh, there's Poppy over there with Baz. *Quel beau garçon!* Forgive me if lapse into French from time to time,' she said, her clear voice carrying over the railway platform and causing several heads to turn. She beamed, and called over to them, addressing them in the fashion of minor royalty, 'How lovely to be in England again; I wept when I saw the white cliffs of Dover, you know.'

'Now run along, Rose dear, and enjoy your vacation.' The teacher handed a health certificate to Daisy with an air of relief and returned to the other girls. They would be easier to handle without her sister's presence, thought Daisy. Rose was already cheerfully telling Joan that the drains had gone wrong in the school and that was the real reason for the extended Easter holiday.

'We suspect that Francesca made away with the maths teacher and shoved his body down the sewer pipe,' she said gaily, to the startled amazement of a bowler-hatted gentleman waiting to board the boat train to Dover.

'I say,' said Joan admiringly. 'That was jolly enterprising of your friend.'

'Rose!' Daisy felt that she should exclaim as the teacher was looking helplessly at her, but she found it hard to suppress a giggle.

'Let's all go and have an ice cream,' suggested Morgan. 'My treat,' he added.

'What a lovely man you are, my darling St Clair,' said Joan when she heard of the offer. 'St Clair is this dear man's middle name, Rose. I bet you didn't know that. It's all too, too stuffy, this business of being formal and calling him by his last name, isn't it?'

'Too, too right it is,' chimed Rose quickly, and Daisy did her best not to smile.

'It's lovely having you back again, Rosie,' she said affectionately. 'I've missed you so much.'

'Not the same me though. All has been utterly changed. I am now a deeply serious and studious young lady – I speak French like a native – like a native of somewhere, anyway – oh, and Morgan, St Clair, I mean – I've learned to play the piano properly. Elaine paid for me to have lessons.'

'Just what we need; what a clever little thing you are, Rosie,' said Poppy.

'And what have you two girls been doing while my eye has not been on you?' enquired Rose in a schoolmistressy manner.

'Don't ask?' suggested Poppy, with a mischievous grin at Daisy.

'Making a film – a film about India,' said Daisy hastily. 'It's coming along really well. Violet is going to be the heroine.'

'Sounds good – by the way, where is Violet?' began Rose and then she gave a slight scream. 'I say, look at that headline on *The Daily Express* over there: "SECRET SOCIETY SCANDAL. POLICE PROBE PARTY-LOVING PEER'S POSITION." Oh, pray, pray someone buy that newspaper for this poverty-stricken child.'

'*The Daily Express* – oh, what a splendiferous idea!' said Joan with an elaborately casual air. 'Let's see if there is anything interesting in the gossip column.' She produced a coin from her slim purse-sized handbag and dashed across to the newspaper boy. When she came back she handed the whole newspaper, except for one piece torn from an inside page, to Rose.

'I say, that is jolly nice of you.' Rose opened her suitcase and put in the newspaper. There were several others already in there, Daisy noticed, and guessed that her sister had managed to find them in railway carriages, from benches on railway stations and lying round on the boat during her journey back from Switzerland.

Once they were seated in the ice-cream parlour Joan produced the article from her handbag.

'Now you might be a bit upset with this – being dear little country girls and all that, and not used to publicity, but . . .' She placed the article on the table between Poppy and Daisy.

'Pops knows what it says – she heard the newspaper Johnny telephoning it,' said Baz.

'You're from the country too, Joan; only a couple of miles away from us,' said Daisy coolly.

'But far, far more sophisticated than us three *dear* little girls,' said Rose demurely, looking up and down Joan's exquisite and most fashionable clothes. 'Let me read the article, since I seem to be the only one in the dark.'

'And me,' said Morgan. He had a slightly grim look about him. Daisy watched him anxiously as he read over Rose's shoulder, but in the end he shrugged. 'It could be worse,' he said. 'It's a good advertisement for the jazz club – just a pity there is that bit about Baz and Poppy.'

'Can't think where he got that!' Joan raised her elegantly plucked eyebrows.

'Oh, but it's wonderful,' cried Rose. 'At least, it gives me great hopes for my future. I know I can write better than that.'

'He was just making it up as he went along; I heard him when I was in the lav,' explained Poppy. She took the piece of newspaper from Rose and recited it with all the commas, full stops and spellings as she remembered them, and Daisy found it hard to stop laughing as she saw Rose's eyes grow enormous with envy. Her ambition to be a journalist was evidently still alive.

'So you've got on well with the piano, Rosie,' she said affectionately.

'I'm afraid,' said Rose, 'that I have to admit that I have got on brilliantly. Never was such a talented child known within the portals of that school, or so a little bird tells me,' she added with a glance down at the newspaper article. She looked across at Morgan. 'Do say that I can join the jazz band.'

'We'll start saving for a piano straight away,' he said gently.

'We need your advice, Rosie,' said Daisy hurriedly, guessing that Morgan wanted to divert Rose from the idea of playing in a nightclub. 'We're planning our coming-out ball and Joan says that we must make it different. She says that everyone is bored with ordinary balls.'

'Have jazz played at it,' said Baz.

'Poppy can't be playing in the band during her own coming-out dance!' Joan was so outraged that she almost shrieked the words.

'What date is it?' asked Morgan, and nodded slowly when he heard that it was on the eighth of May.

'Now don't get too excited, but around that time King Oliver and his jazz band, including Louis Armstrong, will be coming to London. I've got a few contacts and we might be able to get them to play.' He looked across at Daisy. 'You'd have to talk to your uncle about it – they wouldn't come too cheap. I heard the Savoy Hotel was negotiating with him, but it would make your party something special, wouldn't it?'

'Unique,' confirmed Joan. 'Oh, my dears, I'm getting all excited for you. Well, a famous jazz band for Poppy – what about you, Daisy? Would you like something different in the music line?'

'I'm not very musical,' said Daisy slowly. 'I'm happy with a jazz band, if that's what you want, Poppy. And it would be different.' What did she want from her coming-out dance? Charles, she thought. How can I put him at the centre of things?

'Didn't you say that you were making a film about India?' said Rose. 'Why don't you make it an Indian dance – saris and all that sort of thing?'

'That's it,' said Daisy enthusiastically. 'Rose – you are a genius.'

'A theme!' Joan's voice rose to an excited squeak.

'My dears, that is quite the latest fashion, dressing up as Indians – a friend of mine went to a party last week dressed as a rani – the trouble was that there was a real rajah there and he was not amused to see someone who looked like his wife come up and ask him to dance and then to find out that it was a man after all – too, too embarrassing. We all laughed ourselves silly!'

'Let's have the men in ordinary clothes,' said Baz, flushing slightly. 'I hate fancy dress. Feel such a fool.'

'Men look great in ordinary evening dress,' agreed Daisy, thinking of filming. The men in black and white looked so good in her films.

'Girls can dress up,' said Joan firmly. 'My dears, I'd so love a sari.'

'What about having a theme of the nine jewels of India: diamond, ruby, emerald, coral, pearl, sapphire, garnet, topaz and cat's eye – you know that greeny-goldy stuff . . . chrysoberyl,' said Daisy, remembering the glorious necklace Fred had made for her film from bits of coloured glass and wire painted gold. 'That would mean that people who liked veils and saris could wear those and others could just come in jewel colours. We could put that on the invitation cards.' Thinking of Fred and his clever fingers and inventiveness gave her another idea. 'What would you think of using the backdrop boards from my film – Fred has done some magnificent ones – the Taj Mahal and everything.'

'Potted palms,' said Joan, as one inspired.

'Spotted leopards,' said Rose, not to be outdone, and

then added dreamily, 'Could I be part of the background, heavily veiled, of course?' She gazed up at Daisy with pleading eyes.

'Why not?' said Daisy, making a note that she would be firm with Elaine and Jack about this. She wanted her little sister at this special ball. After all, the Duchess of Denton had a 'nursery party' at her eldest daughter's coming-out dance. Rose was tall for her age and no one would question her presence.

At that moment there was a flash of white light and a popping sound – a sound very familiar to Daisy. Someone had taken a photograph. She turned around quickly to see a man in a belted raincoat, with a trilby soft hat pulled down over his eyebrows, just escaping from the ice-cream parlour. He held a large camera. Poppy and Baz were blinking in from the explosion of light.

'The beast!' said Joan. 'He just took the back of my head. How too, too sick-making . . . But I am pleased for you two, my dears.'

Chapter Eighteen
Thursday 1 May 1924

'I do so love your study, Jack,' said Rose with a very serious face. 'It reminds me of that chapter in *Kim* when they are getting ready to put down the Indian rising. All those lists of tasks and telephone numbers and names of useful people. And the countdown calendar! A Military Manoeuvres Board, that's what it is. It's absolutely wonderful!'

'Now then, young lady,' said Jack. He said it with a grin though. Poppy annoyed him with her intensity and her stubbornness, thought Daisy, but Rose's quick wits brought a reluctant smile to his face. An intelligent man, he would have been bored by this holiday in London if he had not had The Ball to organize. He had got a carpenter to cover the whole of one wall of his study with a soft board and by now it was completely filled with sheets of paper, large and small, with tradesmen's cards, lists of names and hand-coloured postcards of India. He had been hugely enthusiastic about the Indian theme and had come up with lots of good ideas of his own. Clear and succinct instructions about dress and the significance of the 'Nine Jewels of India' had been sent out with every invitation. He had personally checked every one of Fred's backdrops and allocated each an appropriate place in the Ritz ballroom.

Now he looked appraisingly at the plan of the ballroom, added a series of small oblongs, marked them as 'Champagne Tables' and then stood back and gazed at his board, full of thought.

'You know, Rose,' he said, 'Napoleon had small models of all the notables at his court and he used to get the court dressmakers to make outfits for them; then when he saw how they looked in groups, he used to inform them what colours they were to wear to his next party. I'm beginning to feel a little like him.' He laughed, quick to see the ridiculous side of his obsession, but yet determined to make a huge success of this ball.

'Did he really, how wonderful! I must tell my history teacher about that. So much more fun than learning about the Battle of Salamanca. I shall have to get two little dolls and call them Poppy and Daisy. And there was I feeling sad that I had passed the age to play with dolls.'

'I like the countdown calendar,' said Daisy, looking up at the impressive sheet that took up a large portion of the board. The months of April and May had been ruled out into boxes – each day had its own box where tasks could be inserted and two dates had huge stars – one for their presentation on the twentieth of May and the other one, coming excitingly close, for their ball on the eighth. Jack was consulting his notebook and putting a neat tick before each task that had already been done.

'Why do you have those six capital *T*s in a row beside the plan of the ballroom, Jack?' Daisy didn't care much, but she knew that he was pleased at her interest and it was, she thought, kind of him to go to so much trouble.

'They're for the telephones in the press room.' His face lit up with pleasure at her question. 'You see, the one thing these reporter Johnnies hate is having to queue for a telephone box. Puts them right off what they want to say. I've made sure that there will be plenty of phones available – each with their own table – and they're all in the press room – a tray of drinks in there too. The manager of the Ritz,' he said with satisfaction, 'was very struck by the idea. I'd take a bet that he will do it in the future for all the top balls and events.'

'A press room!' Rose's voice was reverential. 'Oh, I say, how wonderful.'

'Yes, and the manager promised me that he would make sure that there will be plenty of jotters and sheets of paper, pencils, rubbers on each of the tables – all that sort of thing.'

'Dickens himself could not have asked for more,' Rose assured him. 'I remember reading about his desk – ah, me, if ever I could aspire to such a thing . . .'

'And the tray of drinks will put them all in a great mood,' said Daisy.

'I thought that was a good idea,' said Jack with a pleased smile. He seized a pair of library steps, clambered up them and added a label that said 'Press Room' beside the row of telephones. Then, looking from his pocketbook to the board, he began to tick off completed tasks.

'Rose, dear,' he said, without looking around, 'could

you pop into the morning room and remind your aunt that the girls have the final fitting of their ball gowns today?'

'*Salaam, sahib*,' said Rose, touching her folded hands to her brow and then dancing off. Elaine would have all the magazines in the morning room and that would give her more fun than trying to tease the imperturbable Sir John.

Jack waited until she had closed the door behind her and then, after putting a last tick opposite the words 'floral decorations', he came down from his steps and looked closely at Daisy.

'How are you and Charles getting on?' he asked with his usual directness.

Daisy smiled to herself at the question. She and Charles were almost like a modern married couple now, going off to work every day. And success was coming her way, with Sir Guy selling her film about the chickens almost as soon as she had completed it. She raised an eyebrow at Jack, trying to move just one of them in that way Joan did so expertly.

'Well. Very well.' She tried to convey that it was none of his business, but he ignored that.

'Not getting too serious, are you? You see . . .'

But then he was interrupted. Tellford was at the door with a list of champagne providers, and while they began an earnest conversation Daisy escaped, saying hastily that she had to remind Poppy about the appointment with the dressmaker. She didn't want to hear what Jack had to say. He wasn't too keen on Charles, she thought. Elaine had confided in her that Jack had given up the idea of getting him a job at the Foreign Office since Charles was not willing to work his way up but seemed to want to start at the top.

'If he has pots of money, why should he bother being a message boy for some big shot?' said Poppy when Daisy told her. She seemed to think that Charles was quite right not to do something that would bore him. Neither she nor Baz would ever dream of doing something that bored them.

Daisy tried to tell herself that this made sense, but she was worried that Charles might be depending on being a success in the film world.

Poppy and Baz both had great musical talent, but Charles . . .

'He'll never make a star,' Sir Guy had said to Daisy a few days earlier. 'He might get a few walk-on parts, or crowd scenes, but he's never going to make a living out of it. I'm afraid that he's like your sister – just can't act. Is he thinking of going back to India? He might be better off doing something back there. He must have picked up some skills over the last few years. Perhaps not the Indian Police, but something in the commercial line . . . Has he any thoughts about what he's going to do? '

'Not that I know of,' said Daisy. She pretended to sound indifferent, but she felt rather troubled. Charles had no interest in India, no interest in producing films either; he wanted to be in front of the camera, not behind it. Sir Guy was waiting for her to say something, to agree with him, to decide to drop this film about the rajah and the girl, but she bit her lip and said nothing. How could she drop it without talking to Charles first?

I must speak to him, she thought. It's not fair on Sir Guy to use any more of his resources on this film. He had faith in the other short film that she was gradually putting together, about the Bright Young People, but none in the Indian film. Something had to be said, and she was the one who had to say it.

And now, when she had a couple of hours before the dressmaker appointment, was the time to do it.

Quickly she grabbed her coat from the hallstand and slipped out of the front door, closing it very softly behind her and crossing the road.

'I'm not sure if he's up yet, my lady,' said the housemaid who opened the door. 'Lady Cynthia is out. Will you wait in the morning room?'

Daisy was pleased that Lady Cynthia was not there. She was a strange woman; had been effusively friendly for a while, but now seemed to be rather cold and distant. She sat down without taking off her coat. The room was cold, quite unlike the house across the road, where she continually felt too hot. Although it was almost eleven o'clock the fire had not been lit. She glanced at the invitations on the mantelpiece – Charles seemed very popular; there were lots of invitations for him – including one to a 'Bottle & Bath' party from Annette, which made Daisy open her eyes rather widely.

It was while she was gazing at the card that Charles opened the door and came in, looking very spruce and well groomed.

'I wondered if you would like a walk,' she said. She could hear the words coming out rather abruptly, but she didn't care. She needed to be alone with him. There always seemed to be people around them. 'Let's go down by the river,' she suggested.

'Yes, let's,' he said eagerly, and she was touched to see how much he wanted to please her.

On the way down they chatted about the ball and Daisy told him about Sir John's Military Manoeuvres Board. That did not make him laugh, as she had intended, and he looked at her rather uncomfortably.

'Did he tell you that I didn't want that job that he found me?' he said after a minute. 'You see—'

'You don't need to explain it to me,' she interrupted him quickly.

'I knew you'd understand.' He looked down at her with glowing eyes. 'You see, I want to put everything into supporting you, making films with you and helping you in every way that I can.'

He looked so wonderfully handsome as he said that. Daisy looked up at him, wondering what he meant. It sounded almost as though he was seeing a future for them as a couple – but perhaps he just meant a professional alliance. And then he gave a quick look around, bent over and kissed her. 'I can't resist you when you look like that,' he said softly. 'You know, you have the loveliest eyes. I used to dream of blue eyes like yours when I was out in India and homesick for England.' He looked around and steered her towards a bench sheltered behind a large bush of orange blossom. When they sat down, he put an arm around her and pulled her close to him and she put her head down on his shoulder.

She couldn't, she thought, talk now about abandoning the film. After all, she told herself, neither Charles nor Violet were being paid for their work – they had both been told that any payment would come as a percentage once the film was sold. Fred had already done all the work on the backdrops so now it was really only a matter of her own time and small amounts of processing materials. Sir Guy wouldn't press her.

While Charles was murmuring into her ear dreams about their own studio and about the films that they would make in the future, she could not possibly come back down to earth and be sensible. After all, she tried to tell herself, Elaine had said that he was rich, so he didn't need to make a living.

And the smell from the orange blossom was intoxicating.

Chapter Nineteen
Thursday 8 May 1924

Anything could happen to a person wearing a dress like this, thought Daisy as she gazed into the full-length mirror in her room. This electric light was wonderful, she thought. Its warm, even glow lit up the girl who faced her from the sparkling glass. A short girl, though looking divinely slim in the well-cut dress, a girl with large blue eyes, a smooth, shining cap of blonde hair that hung around a porcelain-pale face, lips delicately pink; a girl clothed in a gown made from silver lamé, spangled with tiny diamonds, fitted closely to her figure in the front, barely reaching to her knees and billowing out behind into ankle-length gleaming folds.

'What do you think?' Daisy met her mother's eyes in the mirror and was glad that Maud had gone to do Poppy's hair and that they were alone for the moment. Tears ran down Elaine's cheeks.

'My darling, you look wonderful. The most beautiful girl in the world.' She laughed shakily. 'I want to squeeze you in my arms, but I daren't touch such perfection. Now I must fly. Jack will wonder what's happening to me. He does so want everything to be perfect tonight.'

And then she was gone. Daisy took one last look at herself and then went into Poppy's bedroom. Poppy was still in a wrapper. Maud was just undoing an elaborate hairstyle where Poppy's long hair had been braided and tucked under to give it the appearance of a fashionable bob.

'I've decided to wear it loose – Baz likes it better down,' Poppy explained as Daisy came in. 'Is Jack jumping up and down waiting for me?' she went on. 'You look lovely, doesn't she, Maud?'

'Elaine has only just gone to get dressed,' said Daisy. She watched as Maud brushed out the long red hair and decided that Poppy was right. Short hair might be more fashionable, but Poppy's rippling dark red mane was so striking that it was a shame to hide it. Maud tied it loosely with a piece of silk while she slipped the dress over Poppy's head, freed the hair, adjusted the dress and then stood back to see the effect.

Poppy's gown was of gold lamé, embroidered all over with dozens of tiny green chrysoberyls, the cat's eye jewel – one of the nine jewels of India. It was short and made quite simply, figure-fitting and without frills. The sumptuous simplicity suited Poppy and highlighted the beauty of her hair. And the headband of gold lamé, embroidered with more chrysoberyls, made her amber eyes glow.

'You're beautiful!' They said it in unison and then both laughed. Maud slipped out of the room to fetch Rose and soon returned with her, looking exquisite in a coral-pink dress and with her long blonde hair floating out behind her.

'Girls! We're off. The taxi is here. It's waiting for you!' Jack had an unusually tense note in his voice.

'Wish Morgan was taking us,' grumbled Poppy. 'Why does Jack have to monopolize him?'

'He's only being kind,' said Daisy swiftly. 'He thinks we'll have more room for our frocks in a taxi. That's what he said.'

Jack, she thought, couldn't wait to get to the Ritz and make sure that every one of his meticulous arrangements was going with a swing.

'We'd better go,' she said. 'We need to be there first so that we can receive the guests. It's our party, after all.'

Sir John and Elaine were already in position by the time they arrived. Rose, who had been warned to stay in the background, went off to see the press room and they took their places beside the couple, he in his superb uniform and Elaine wearing a glorious gown of black velvet trimmed with gold embroidery. The cloak, which formed part of the gown, fell behind her, and at the back of her slender neck a large, stiffened collar of the dark velvet rose up to form a frame to her blonde hair, her pale skin and her blue eyes. She looked tiny but dignified beside her distinguished husband.

'Poppy next to me, I think; and Daisy next to Elaine.' He looked along the line and nodded with satisfaction. It was a good arrangement, thought Daisy. Ever since she had found out that she was not Poppy's twin, not her sister, she had been slightly self-conscious about the lack of resemblance between them. Standing side by side, they looked odd – one tall redhead; one small blonde.

Now with Poppy beside Sir John and she beside Elaine, they looked interesting.

'First taxis drawing up now, Your Excellency.' The manager approached Sir John, casting a last professional look around the ballroom.

Everything was splendid, thought Daisy. The Indian backdrops, painted by Fred, had been attached to the Ritz's own screens and the spaces between had potted palms placed at wide intervals, allowing those who sat on the gilt chairs to have a clear view of the ballroom. The ceiling was hung with chandeliers whose warm light enhanced the gold paint on the stately columns and the mouldings along the wall. The Ritz's own orchestra played gentle music – the jazz band would come at nine o'clock. She straightened up to greet the first guests: His Excellency, the High Commissioner, Sir Atul Chandra Chatterjee and his British-born wife, from the Indian Embassy in London.

Charles came late and Daisy was glad about that. It would have been agony to have to stand in line with Elaine and Jack greeting the guests while he, in his well-mannered way, danced with other girls. Poppy, of course, had no such worries. The jazz-band boys, Baz, Simon, Edwin and George, despised music that wasn't jazz, so they lurked among the potted palms just behind where Poppy stood on the end of the receiving row and made low-voiced jokes that only she could hear. Daisy envied her sister. She was so relaxed, so confident in Baz's affection. Would things ever be like that between her and Charles? The thought had just crossed her mind when suddenly she saw him. He was alone but he came forward with great confidence, bowed gracefully to Elaine, shook Sir John by the hand and then looked at Daisy.

'Dare I ask for a dance?' His dark eyes were so warm in the bright light from the chandeliers overhead and his well-shaped eyebrows formed two such perfect arcs that for a moment she wished that she had her camera in her hand.

'Yes, you girls run along; your aunt and I will receive the rest of the guests.' Elaine whispered something into her husband's ear and he gave Daisy and Poppy a paternal nod of approval while sending a keen-eyed look down the hallway that opened out of the ballroom. All the important guests – the people from the Indian Embassy and from the Foreign Office – had already arrived.

'I purposely came late; I couldn't bear to dance with anyone but you,' Charles murmured into Daisy's ear as he swung her on to the dance floor. The Ritz orchestra was playing a gloriously slow, languorous waltz and they moved to its rhythm, spinning down the length of the ballroom.

Daisy looked lovingly at him, though when he spoke it was only to say, 'I love your dress.'

'I love your costume too,' she said. Charles was one of the few men who had come dressed up, but the *churidar* and *dhoti* suited his dark good looks, and Daisy thought that he looked very dashing compared to the rest of the young men who were wearing the same evening clothes as their own fathers.

'Are you ever homesick for India?' she asked him.

'No,' he said with surprise. 'I love London – and,' he added, squeezing her hand gently, 'London has you and India does not.'

Daisy squeezed his hand back. She caught sight of Poppy and Baz exchanging kisses as they danced. Backwards and then forwards and then another kiss; it was a good job, she thought, that their father had refused all invitations to attend his daughters' coming-out ball. Violet was frowning at Poppy in an exaggerated way, but Poppy just laughed when she met her elder sister in the dance.

'Wonderful party!' called out Annette as they passed. 'I was just saying to Jeremy that I gave you the idea. Everything Indian is just too, too spiffing, my dear. I just adore everything about it.'

Daisy laughed and waved back. Perhaps, she thought charitably, the news that Annette was setting up a marriage-broker service as they have in India had planted the seed of an idea. In any case, she was kept too busy responding to all the compliments and the excited exclamations to worry about Annette. Charles had hardly looked at the girl; his gaze was fastened on Daisy's face and his gloved hand pressed her fingers in a close, intimate grasp. She half shut her eyes, seeing the scene as a swirl of lights and colours – ruby-red, emerald-green, sapphire-blue, set off by the glitter of diamonds and the glow of pearls. She wished that she could dance with Charles forever, wished that so many young men, introduced by Sir John, had not implored her to put their names into her dance card.

They had grown so close, she and Charles, during the past few weeks. The permission to travel to and from the studio had opened up the relationship, thought Daisy. The daily journeys had been extended by walks in Kensington Gardens to admire the blossom and the spring flowers, followed by kisses on benches under the pale green-gold branches of a weeping willow tree; by strolls along the riverside, hand in hand; the month that they had known each other seemed more like a year. Never, she thought happily, were two people more suited to each other. They thought the same on every subject; she had only to voice an opinion for Charles to agree, immediately and enthusiastically, with her.

'I'll remember this all my life,' she said to him as they came together again for the first dance played by the jazz band. No longer did she feel dreamy but full of energy, the beat stirring up feelings within her that she hardly knew she possessed. She looked across at Poppy, but her twin was gazing at Baz and oblivious to everything else so she looked back up into Charles's eyes and wondered whether the tumultuous beat of her heart could be felt by his gloved hand between her shoulder blades.

Chapter Twenty
Thursday 8 May 1924

Rose gave a quick glance around the deserted press room at the Ritz Hotel, so well equipped with tables and telephones, then took a fat notebook from her brand-new evening bag. She perched on one of the Ritz's gilt chairs and began to write:

Seldom have such spectacles been witnessed as tonight within the luxurious portals of the Ritz Hotel <full stop> *Frequent visitors stood aghast at the transformation from a staid and respectable establishment to a scene from the Far East* <ellipsis>
And what a scene <exclamation mark>
This magnificent ballroom <comma> *usually a setting for graceful waltzes* <comma> *was filled with people rocking and shaking* <comma> *twisting heads* <comma> *fluttering hands waving from every direction* <full stop> *Ladies and gentlemen of the older generation froze with horror at the wild scenes that occurred* <comma> *the contortions* <comma> *the gyrations* <semi-colon> *it seemed impossible that the human body could twist itself in so many hundreds of different fashions* <ellipsis>
<new paragraph>

Lord Toomanydrinks was witnessed swinging from the chandelier <comma> while Lady Bignose screamed with laughter <full stop> The young Baron of Beastlyden was overheard to ask for his fourteenth bottle of champers . . .

Rose sucked the end of her pencil and then started to write rapidly again.

. . . The Honourable Alice Hinwonderland waltzed pensively with her looking-glass while the jazz band played a tango <comma> but the most shocking figure of the evening was young Lady Rose Derrington <comma> clad in a striking thigh-length gown of coral pink <comma> fetched that very morning from the far Pacific Ocean <full stop> I observed the exquisite young lady dance <quote> The Cake Walk <unquote> while surrounded by a platoon of young men standing obediently on their heads in a circle around her <full stop>

The whole evening was a scene of unbridled debauchery . . .

Rose picked up one of the telephones, but the sharp 'Yes' from the girl in the exchange startled her. She pressed two fingers on to the bar to cut off the sound and continued. 'Social, please,' she said, and began to dictate fluently and clearly, condescendingly spelling out words for the stenographer who would be typing her piece in the press room of the gossip newspaper and dwelling with satisfaction on the 'quote, unquote'.

'That's it; nighty-night,' she said, remembering Poppy's story.

And then she tore out the page from her notebook, placed it carefully beside the telephone and went off to gather new material.

Chapter Twenty-One
Thursday 8 May 1924

'I say, Poppy, look what I got for you.' Baz fumbled in his pocket and took out a small box, which he handed to her.

Poppy opened it and stared. The jazz band of King Oliver had just replaced the sedate Ritz band, but for once she did not listen to the opening chords of 'Canal Street Blues'. King Oliver blew his cornet and Louis Armstrong his trumpet, Baby Dodds beat his drums, Johnny Dodds played heavenly notes on the clarinet, Lil Hardin ran her fingers over the piano keys, Will Johnson plucked the bass and Honoré Dutrey made the trombone sing, but Poppy just looked at what was in Baz's hand.

It was a ring. The diamond was tiny; nevertheless it glowed within the broad band of gold and the ring slid on to Poppy's third finger as though it had been made for her.

'It was part of my inheritance from my grandfather – it was a man's ring, but I got it cut down for you,' said Baz, flushing a deep red, but smiling down at her.

She flung her arms around his neck and kissed him in the middle of the dance floor.

'Oh, Baz,' she said, 'we're engaged.'

Never had music sounded so beautiful to her. 'It had to be you . . .' she crooned into his ear as, hand in hand, they spun across the well-polished floor of the Ritz ballroom.

'We'll have five children, won't we?' he said later, as they sat together and shared an ice from the same plate.

'Why five?' Poppy licked the last trace of ice cream from off the china dish and smiled blandly at the wife of the Indian Ambassador.

'Two girls to play the piano and the clarinet; and three boys to play the trumpet, the bass and the drums,' he said.

'Or the other way around.' Poppy spoke absent-mindedly. Suddenly she wished for a decision, for permanence. Resolutely she got to her feet and crossed over to the bandstand. Lil had just sat back down at the piano, Louis was joking with Baby Dodds, and King Oliver was polishing the bell of his cornet with a silk handkerchief when Poppy touched him on the arm. She spoke briefly in his ear and there was a flash of white teeth in his dark face as he nodded and spoke to the band. And then he stepped to the edge of the stage and addressed the audience.

'Ladies and gents,' he said in his strong New Orleans accent, 'the young lady whose coming-out dance this is tells me that she has just gotten engaged to the man of her dreams, and she wants us to play . . .' he paused dramatically and then said emphatically, ' "Sweet Lovin' Man".'

As the first notes were blown there was a buzz of conversation, but then the other instruments came in and all the young people at the dance swept on to the floor, twisting, swaying, jitterbugging and clicking to the rhythm of the beat. Cameras flashed into the faces of Poppy and Baz and she smiled her wide sweet smile, put her head closer to Baz's and turned him slightly towards the lenses that were aimed at them. Joan waved and beamed as she jigged her way past and then all the dancers were waving and smiling and laughing. Poppy was conscious of the appalled faces of Sir John and Elaine in the background and of how reporters were rushing to the door to get at the telephones, but she did not care. Baz gave a little wave to his mother and she waved back with a slightly amused smile. Baz, thought Poppy, was the youngest of eight eccentric children and his mother had had plenty of experiences to toughen her. She blew Lady Dorothy a kiss and then forgot about her. Daisy rushed up, flung her arms around Poppy and then went back to jitterbugging with Charles.

Suddenly Poppy was supremely happy. Everything was now out in the open. The words had been spoken in public and they could not be taken back. Her future was settled. She was going to marry Baz.

Chapter Twenty-Two
Thursday 8 May 1924

Once the jazz band had taken over, the whole atmosphere changed. Daisy held on to Charles's hand and swung to the beat. It was their first dance together for quite some time as several of Jack's friends had claimed her for themselves or for their sons.

And then came the drama! Daisy had seen her sister go up to the bandleader and whisper some words in his ear, but nothing prepared her for the shock announcement. Poppy engaged! Engaged to be married! As the catchy rhythm of 'Sweet Lovin' Man' mesmerized the dancers, she thought suddenly of Michael Derrington in his lonely home with the huge weight of his anxieties pressing down on him.

And yet, she thought – and it was a surprisingly new thought for her – perhaps . . . perhaps he would be relieved. He had been amazingly accepting of Violet's engagement to a penniless lawyer; Baz might be a youngest son, but his family were wealthy. The young couple would not be allowed to starve even if the jazz club was not a huge success.

And then she realized that Charles was steering her over towards the potted palms. One of his hands was in the small of her back and the other grasped hers firmly.

'It's stupid, I know,' he gasped when they were sheltered behind the greenery, 'and I've told myself again and again not to rush things, to wait until I had some sort of position, some sort of income to offer you, but I can't help asking you tonight . . . Daisy, would you, could you ever feel that you could marry me?'

The shock struck Daisy dumb for a moment, but she recovered quickly when she saw how sheepish and embarrassed he looked. It was a huge surprise, but yet, since their walks, their kisses under the trees in Kensington Gardens and their time next to the orange-blossom bush by the river, she had half expected this. After all, how else could his words about working together, about having their own studio, be explained?

She flung her arms around him. 'Oh, Charles,' she said, and that was all that was needed because he suddenly covered her hands and then her face with kisses.

'But no surprise announcements,' she said breathlessly when she finally extricated herself from his arms. 'Elaine and Jack will drop dead if that happens again. We'll keep it to ourselves until we can talk to our relations and make it clear that we are not rushing into anything.'

He laughed then. 'No,' he said. 'I think Poppy has been enough for one evening. In any case, we must talk to my mother before we tell anyone. I couldn't do anything without her blessing.'

Lady Cynthia, thought Daisy dreamily, had a very high opinion of Sir John and was always trying to flatter him. Surely she would agree. In any case, Charles was over twenty-one and his own master. She looked across at Poppy and saw her own happiness reflected in her sister's face.

This is the most wonderful evening of my life! The words were in her mind as she whirled around, exchanging smiles and jokes with the many friends that they had made since they came to London. She seemed to be floating in a kind of brightly lit, gaily coloured paradise, and looking across at Poppy she could see the same shining happiness in her face. Although it was three o'clock in the morning before the taxis arrived and they all left the Ritz, it seemed to her as though the evening passed in a flash.

Chapter Twenty-Three
Friday 9 May 1924

'And may I ask whether your father, or your uncle and *aunt*, know about this extraordinarily sudden engagement?' Lady Cynthia glared at Daisy, and Daisy glared back. The preliminaries had gone well, but now the gloves were off. Lady Cynthia had not wasted any time on Charles and his tentative explanations but had fixed her eyes on Daisy.

Daisy had been wondering whether she would need to be honest about her illegitimate birth and had steeled herself to talk to Elaine about it, but this antagonistic reception had stiffened her backbone and now she was determined not to yield an inch to this woman. What business was it of hers anyway? Presumably Charles had his own fortune.

It was Charles, however, who answered, and his voice, to Daisy's bewilderment, sounded conciliatory and a touch apologetic.

'No, not yet, no, we haven't told anyone yet. We wanted you to be the first to know, Mama, dear,' he said.

'And will your father make a substantial settlement on you, Daisy, may I ask?' Lady Cynthia ignored her son.

'No,' said Daisy, 'but—'

'And may I enquire whether Charles has told you that

he is utterly and completely dependent on me for every penny? Even his tailor's bill arrives addressed to me.' She waved a piece of paper under their noses and Daisy saw Charles flinch. She suppressed a gasp. This was a shock. She had thought that Charles had private means. Elaine had said – what was it exactly that Elaine had said? It was only, thought Daisy, that she had the impression that Charles was rich. And Charles himself had seemed to be a young man of fortune.

'We'll earn money,' said Daisy defiantly. 'In the last few weeks I've earned fifteen pounds. If I can keep that up it will amount to more than the average wage of an English worker.' Her godfather had told her that and she prayed that he was correct. The silly little film about the hens had sold to almost every cinema in England – had started off with children's matinee performances and then had moved on to evening showings. Sir Guy was keeping a nice little sum for her. At some stage, she thought, she would tell Charles about Elaine, but she refused to do it while everything was so uncertain. It's my business, she thought, tightening her lips resolutely.

'Ten pounds a week is what I should be able to reckon on if I go on having success,' she repeated firmly.

Lady Cynthia, however, did not query her figures.

'And Charles?' she asked with a sarcastic note in her voice. 'How much has he earned?'

Daisy was silent. As a matter of fact, the film *The Rajah and the Lady* seemed to be doomed to failure. She had hoped that Hollywood might buy it, might be seduced by some of the scenes showing the beauty of the two leads, but that had not happened. In fact, even the thousands of English cinemas, even the ones that had bought her short films, were busily rejecting this particular film. Charles's future as a star of the big screen was uncertain, to say the least.

'We'll have a breakthrough soon,' she said defensively.

Lady Cynthia looked at her closely. It was a long and a penetrating look and Daisy bore it as bravely as she could. After a few minutes the woman said abruptly, 'Charles, go and wait in the dining room. I need to talk to Daisy in private.'

He went without a backwards glance and Daisy felt sorry for him but at the same time ashamed of his lack of courage.

Once he had closed the door, Lady Cynthia sat down abruptly and signalled to Daisy to sit by her side on the sofa.

'I'll be very honest with you; I don't want this marriage to take place,' she said curtly. 'Charles must marry wealth and that is the end of it. I'm a widow and I need my money for myself. I spent enough on him with this India business and he hadn't the guts or the brains to make something of it. Marriage is the only answer – he has the looks – but not to you, my dear. Your father has nothing. His property is entailed. I hear that he has managed it badly and that his heir is after his blood. Not only will there be no money for your settlements or dowries but you will, all three of you, be left without a home or means to support yourselves.

But that is not all.' She drew in a deep breath and looked stonily down at Daisy.

'Even if you had means, you would be no suitable wife for my son. I have been making enquiries about you and I've found out *everything*. It's a small world, my dear, and there are enough people around that remember Elaine Carruthers and how she vanished from the London social scene in the middle of her season. My youngest sister was being presented that year and all the girls were talking about it. There were plenty of rumours around that she was pregnant and plenty of talk when her sister Mary came back from India the following spring with two babies looking quite unalike. There is nothing in this that is my business, you will say, but it becomes my business when you propose to marry my son and bring your disgrace into my family. I warn you that if you persist with this ridiculous engagement to Charles I will not hesitate to drag your name and the name of Elaine Carruthers through the mud. Don't think that you will be presented at court – an illegitimate girl like you! I have plenty of acquaintances who will drop a word into the Lord Chamberlain's ear. You will be rejected as unsuitable. London will seethe with gossip. And Elaine will be utterly disgraced. I don't think for a minute that my cousin Sir John will permit this, and if you do not agree to my terms, I shall see him instantly. He will want to protect his wife, such as she is, and he will not stand for any nonsense from a girl not yet eighteen years old.'

Daisy sat rigid. She forced herself to be cool, to speak in an indifferent tone.

'You must, indeed, be very against my marrying your son to have come up with that silly rumour,' she said, and watched carefully for a flutter of uncertainty in the woman's eyes.

But there was none. Lady Cynthia had the facts at her fingertips. She knew all about Clifford Pennington, Justin's unfortunate uncle; all about his sudden death on the hunting field; all about the relationship between Elaine and Clifford – she had the whole history, dates and all, off pat, and without pity she told it all to Daisy, who had to pretend to listen in indifferent disbelief.

For a long moment Daisy sat very still, wrestling with her feelings, with her conscience. '*It's not fair*' – everything within her screamed the words.

She steeled herself. 'I've nothing to say to you.' With more confidence she went on. 'You might as well call Charles back in and tell him that silly, spiteful story. And make all the threats that you want to. He won't take any notice of them. He's over twenty-one; he can do what he wants to do. We love each other. We don't plan to get married straight away, but after about a year I think that we can afford to rent a house and feed ourselves.'

That's if I can go on producing the sort of short films that the cinemas want to buy, she thought. And of course Charles will get a job, she tried to tell herself. He is well educated, handsome. Firms will queue up to employ him. But can I expose Elaine to all the old cats of London?

Elaine can go back to India, she told herself, but she was not comfortable. Elaine, she knew, would mind desperately about her reputation. After all, she gave up her own child to preserve her good name.

And what about Great-Aunt Lizzie? A scandal like that might kill the old lady – it was not impossible for gossip columnists to get hold of it; she could just imagine how they would do it with a sly innuendo, could just visualize the paragraphs where Elaine and her parentage would be pilloried and she, Daisy, ruined so far as polite society was concerned.

Still, it should be feasible to keep these sorts of newspapers out of Beech Grove.

But a strange question kept coming into her mind. Did they love each other enough to face all of these terrible problems?

'I must talk to Charles,' she said aloud, but she was conscious of a weakness in her voice.

'Very well.' Lady Cynthia had agreed almost before Daisy's thoughts had ceased to stream through her head. She went to the door and called, 'Come in, Charles.'

When he came in he looked very uncomfortable. It was obvious that he did not expect good news. Daisy's heart ached a little for him, but she wished that he were more of a fighter. He glanced uneasily at her, but then returned his eyes immediately to the stern face of his mother.

'Sit down,' she said coldly, pointing to a low chair beside the table. He sat instantly and obediently – just like a guilty small boy, and Daisy defiantly got up from the sofa and went and stood beside him. Lady Cynthia was standing in front of them; her back was to the window, her face shadowed, but the expression of unyielding severity was unmistakable.

'I've explained to this young lady that it is utterly impossible for any talk of marriage or even an engagement to take place between you both. Daisy understands me perfectly, don't you, dear? You know your position, Charles. You have nothing except what I bestow upon you, so I want your word that there will be no more talk of marriage and that you will cease to spend time in Daisy's company. Now give me your word, Charles, and no more will be said. You can enjoy the rest of the season and have fun going to parties and meeting other *suitable* young people.' And Lady Cynthia picked up the tailor's bill and fluttered it in her son's direction.

Charles did not look at Daisy. He almost, she thought, looking at him with dry eyes, shrugged his shoulders. 'As you wish, Mama,' he said, and left the room without a glance at Daisy.

A minute later she heard the front door open. The sound of the London traffic rushed in and then the door clicked closed. She sat for a moment. It was like the time she fell out of a tree when she was eleven years old, she thought. Wild panic, incredulity, and then nothing; just a feeling of confusion and a dull ache in her head.

He gave me up without a word of protest – asked for no reasons – just said, 'Yes, Mama,' like a small child.

She rose to her feet. 'I'd better be going,' she said. And

she went out into the hall with no more words spoken.

Did he ever even care about her at all? Or was he indifferent?

Had he only been interested in her because he thought she could offer him the chance to be a film star?

She didn't know the answer to these questions, but she had her suspicions.

Is that all I am worth? wondered Daisy, humiliation chilling her to the bone as she walked away from the house.

I've been such a terrible fool.

Chapter Twenty-Four
Friday 9 May 1924

There was no one in Daisy's room. Poppy yawned, stretched, tucked her pyjama jacket back inside the waistband of the trousers, stretched her arms again and opened her eyes as wide as she could to try to unglue them.

I'm engaged to be married!

That sentence had been running through her head since she had surfaced from a deep sleep. She said it aloud to hear what it sounded like and examined herself in the mirror.

And then she noticed a note on Daisy's pillow addressed to her. She opened the envelope and her eyes widened.

'*Gone to see Lady Cynthia with Charles – perhaps you won't be the only engaged twin when I come back, and what will Jack say to that!*'

Poppy grinned sleepily, and wondered. She had not realized Charles and Daisy were so in love. They had been keeping rather quiet about it, she thought, and then jumped as Maud's voice came from behind her.

'Sir John sends his compliments, my lady. He hopes that you have slept well and would like to see you as soon as possible in the breakfast room.'

'Oh, Maud!' Poppy threw her arms around the girl. 'Guess what! I'm engaged to be married. Look at my ring. I'll never take it off for the rest of my life!' She had been so tired the night before that she had just tumbled into bed while Maud had been attending to Daisy. Now she wanted to share her happiness with the world.

'Oh, my lady!' Maud's very green eyes shone with excitement. 'That's beautiful,' she said enviously. 'Oh, this is exciting! Did you have a wonderful time last night?'

'Wonderful!' Poppy hummed a bar from 'Sweet Lovin' Man' and danced around the room with the stool from Daisy's dressing table held stiffly in front of her. Maud grinned.

'I'll never forget it for the rest of my life,' said Poppy after a minute as she replaced the stool. 'I wish you could have come, Maud. You would have loved it.'

'You'd better have your bath, my lady,' said Maud, looking amused. 'Sir John was walking up and down and looking a bit impatient.'

'Oh, he can wait. Maud, will you do my hair for me? It's such a mess. I was thinking that I could have it like Lil Hardin's – she was the pianist last night; her hair was fantastic. I'll show you just how she did it.'

Sir John was, indeed, walking up and down the breakfast room when she arrived and he glared at her. Poppy smiled sweetly at him and twirled to show Elaine and Rose her new hairstyle.

'I'd like to have a word with you, Poppy, about that ridiculous business last night,' he said as she sipped some orange juice and refused, with a shudder, the butler's offer of scrambled eggs. 'Thank you, Tellford, that will do,' he said abruptly.

'About that friend of yours from the Foreign Office who got drunk and kept eyeing down the front of my dress?' asked Poppy, before the door had closed on the butler. She helped herself to another glass of juice.

'Don't be ridiculous!' snapped Sir John. 'What was the meaning of that announcement last night? How can you be engaged? You're not yet eighteen.'

'That doesn't stop people. Look at Violet's friend Marjorie. She was married before she was eighteen, and now she's expecting a baby,' Poppy pointed out.

'That was different, dear,' said Elaine nervously. 'Marjorie made a very good match.'

'What's that to do with it? And Baz and I must start a family soon as we plan to have at least five children and train them up to be a jazz band.'

'I say, do you mind if I have that?' said Rose, who was helping herself to a spoonful of the rejected scrambled eggs. She went back to the table and opened her notebook.

'*A little bird tells me*,' she murmured as she wrote, '*that the popular young couple the Honourable Basil Pattenden and Lady Poppy Derrington have ambitious plans for the future . . .*'

'I'll give you an exclusive news break about it,' said Poppy gaily.

'You are being absurd,' snapped Sir John angrily. 'If this is the way you choose to behave, then I must ring your father and tell him what happened. I can't take responsibility for you any longer. Rose, haven't you some study to do to make up for missing school? You remember that we promised you would do some of your school work every day.' He left the room, his lips tight with annoyance, and shouted to Tellford to get Morgan to take a parcel to the Foreign Office for him.

'Tell him to let Sir George know that I will be tied up with urgent family business this morning,' he called down the back stairway. 'Also that I won't need his services this morning, but I may need him to drive to the station this afternoon to meet the Kent train.'

'Oh dear,' said Elaine with a sigh.

'What are you doing, Rose?' asked Poppy cheerfully.

'Writing press releases,' said Rose.

'Oh dear,' repeated Elaine. 'I wonder what Michael is saying to Jack?'

'*Aggrieved Father Sends Out Challenge to Careless Chaperone: I'll Have You Horsewhipped for This, Sir.*' Rose had turned over a new page of her notebook and was printing her headline in large block letters.

'Let's change the subject; you're upsetting Elaine.' Poppy examined her ring lovingly.

'Yes, let's,' agreed Rose obediently. 'I'll probably work better later on in the solemn silence of my cloistered bedroom. In the meantime, Elaine, let me distract you by telling you that I know all about a terrible secret from your dim and distant past. I heard about it from a girl in my dormitory in Switzerland.'

Poppy looked up in time to see Elaine's face turn completely white. Her aunt's hand was stretched out appealingly towards Rose, who was finishing off her headline in her notebook by drawing an ornamental border around it.

'Why don't you read us something from your own writings instead, Rose?' Poppy suggested quickly. It was all that she could think of to say in this emergency. Rose normally could never resist reading out her latest story whenever she could persuade her sisters to listen.

'I think you should hear this story first,' said Rose reprovingly. 'Nell's mother told it to her. It's like something from one of the Brontë novels. It's the tale of a poor young governess who lost her heart to the son of the house and was expelled into the snow by her angry employer.'

'Oh, poor Miss St Clair,' said Elaine. To Poppy's ear the relief in the woman's voice was unmistakable, but Rose didn't seem to notice anything.

'Nell's mother was in school with you and she said that was why you were sent there – to get away from the scandal.'

'It was hardly a scandal for me,' pointed out Elaine. 'I was only eleven years old at the time. Robert, your father's younger brother – he was only about twenty years old – he fell in love with my governess. They used to write to each other and my governess used to hide the letters under a loose board in the schoolroom. Little wretch that I was, I used to take them out on her afternoon off and read them to myself. They were very romantic. One afternoon – it wasn't snowing, Rose, but it was very cold so I was sitting by the fire with the floorboard prised up, indulging myself with reading the letters from the first to the last, when Aunt Lizzie suddenly popped in.'

'Like the witch in Hansel and Gretel,' put in Rose with a bland face. 'What was your governess's first name, Elaine?'

'I think it was Lucinda,' said Elaine after a moment's thought.

'Lucinda,' said Rose rapturously. She wrote it carefully into her notebook. 'How wonderful! Just like the doll in the Beatrice Potter book *Two Bad Mice*. A much better name for a romantic heroine than Jane Eyre or Agnes Grey or something like that. Go on, Elaine, I am riveted by your tale.'

'Well, I can't remember too much about it,' said Elaine apologetically. 'I must have been a very heartless child because I recollect feeling pleased that I had no lessons to do – and then it was Christmas. And after Christmas I was sent to boarding school in Switzerland. Aunt Lizzie knew the owner of the school. She took me herself, by boat and by train, and it was exciting because suddenly I had so many girls to make friends with – I had been quite lonely at Beech Grove Manor after Mary went out to India with your father, you know. I'm afraid that I don't remember worrying about poor Lucinda, though I was sorry that Robert did not come for Christmas. He was always fun and very nice to me. The next I heard of him, he had been killed in the Boer War.'

'And you buried your doll in the same place as the letters were hidden,' said Rose suddenly. 'We found her in the schoolroom.'

'That's right.' Elaine smiled and then her face changed as her husband came back into the room. 'What did Michael say, Jack?' she asked anxiously.

Poppy didn't think that she wanted to hear her father's opinion on her announcement the previous night. He was bound to make a fuss in the beginning, but he would come around eventually. Anyway, Daisy said that he was spending hours every day preparing for the court case that was coming up later in the month. Let him concentrate on that and allow his daughters to get on with their lives.

'I think I'll just walk across to Lady Dorothy's place and see what she's thinking about the engagement,' she interrupted. She got up quickly and raced out of the door before Jack could say a word.

'Coming, Rose?' she called over her shoulder, then grabbed her coat and hat from the hallstand and had the front door open in a second.

Chapter Twenty-Five
Friday 9 May 1924

'Is anything the matter?'

Daisy blinked away the hot tears that had begun to well up in her eyes as the big Humber car slid to a halt beside her. Morgan had stuck his head out of the window.

Daisy blinked rapidly. 'No, nothing, Morgan, just tired after last night.'

'Fancy a spin?' he suggested. 'Your uncle says that he doesn't need me this morning. What's going on? I've been hearing rumours about a surprise announcement last night. Get in and tell me.'

Daisy got into the front seat beside him. Great-Aunt Lizzie would have a fit, but she didn't care. There was something very comforting about Morgan's steady gaze and his quiet, reassuring voice. He looked at her searchingly a couple of times after he had pulled out into the traffic, but it was only when they reached the comparative quietness of the Embankment and were driving beside the Thames that he spoke again.

'What's the matter?' he asked again.

Daisy opened her mouth to tell him all about Baz and Poppy, but then shut it again. A sob was rising into her throat and she thought that she would not manage to keep a quiver out of her voice. She dug her nails into her hands and fought to recover herself.

'Something to do with Mr Charles de Montfort? Or his mother?' Morgan's voice was harsh and Daisy realized that he did not like either Lady Cynthia or her son. He was always very wooden when Charles was in the car, although he treated their other friends with the casual friendliness that he showed to the jazz band and was, she thought, amused by Joan and, in fact, rather fond of her too.

The slight contempt in his voice steadied her. She wound down the window, thrust her face out into the cold, damp air, breathing it in deeply until the sobs subsided and her hot eyes had cooled.

Then she pulled her head back in and as steadily as she could manage gave him an account of the sensational announcement of the engagement between Baz and Poppy. He did not scrutinize her again – for which she was grateful – and he laughed when he heard of Poppy's choice of music to celebrate her engagement. Daisy laughed too and was relieved to find that she felt a bit better.

'I like Baz,' she said. 'He looked so thrilled with himself.'

'He's a nice young fellow,' Morgan said judiciously, 'but your father will have a fit. Now, stop worrying about them and tell me what the matter is. You looked as white as a sheet when I saw you standing there outside the de Montforts' house. What happened? Remember, a trouble shared is a trouble halved.'

'It was nothing,' said Daisy, trying to make her voice sound indifferent. 'I made a mistake, that's all.'

'Let's go for a walk,' he said, pulling the car into the side of the road by the river, parking it efficiently and winding up the window. The sun had come out.

Daisy sat rather still for a moment, and then turned her head to look at him when he came around to the passenger door. It was a face that she had known for a long time. As she took the gloved hand held out to her her mind went back to the picture of herself and Poppy as pigtailed twelve-year-olds, when Bob Morgan had first come to Beech Grove Manor. They were a wild pair, everyone used to say, but looking back she thought that they had been rather neglected. Violet always got on much better with Great-Aunt Lizzie than they did, and Michael Derrington, shell-shocked and still in deep mourning for his wife, had come back just a few weeks earlier and caused a deep tremor of unease to run through the household, who could not get used to the violent fits of temper and the consequent moods of black despair.

Morgan had been a calm, humorous refuge for the girls; he had joked with them, teased them, played music to them, taught them both all the new dances that were coming out after the war, picked them up when they fell off their ponies, suggested things to do, built tree houses and always made them welcome in his little cottage, where he played the drums and all four of them danced. Soon Baz, Edwin, Simon and George had taken to visiting there and had persuaded their parents to buy them jazz instruments.

Morgan had even got permission from the Earl to take them to the cinema in Maidstone, and once the first visit had been negotiated had followed up with a series of Charlie Chaplin comic films, romantic films, films with jazz accompaniments, films from Hollywood, films from Germany, from France, from the new London film studios. He bought them ices out of his small salary and never seemed to mind that his cottage was overrun with kids.

And yet, thought Daisy, I've never really looked properly at his face before. She stayed in her seat for a moment longer, her hand still in his, and studied him.

A dark man – dark-haired and dark-eyed; a man with a square chin and broad shoulders – no Greek god, but with a kind face, a strong jaw, tanned skin and – Joan was right – beautiful dark eyes.

Daisy swung her legs out of the car, still holding the hand that he held out to her, and then straightened up, but she did not let go. It seemed to her almost like a lifeline, something to hold on to – something that might pull her free from . . . *from the sea of despair*, she thought and then smiled slightly at herself. Perhaps she was overdramatizing. It sounded like something that Rose would say.

'Morgan,' she said, 'do you remember this time last year when you parked in about the same place and Poppy and I went up here? We climbed up this bank and we went into Somerset House . . .' She hesitated for a moment, but somehow she wanted to unburden herself. She knew that she could trust him. 'Poppy and I went into Somerset House and we asked for our birth certificates. I had begun to suspect from lots of things that I was not actually her twin, and when I found that only one child was born to Michael and Mary Derrington on the eleventh of October 1906, well, I knew the truth.'

He nodded. 'You're Lady Elaine's daughter,' he said.

Daisy looked up at him quickly. 'How did you know?'

'I knew that you had had a shock that day. And I saw the way that she looked at you. And Maud had some story about an old nanny at the Duchess's house who said that you were very backward for a three-month-old baby – more like a six-week-old one. I put two and two together. And no one thought to tell you; you were left to find it out for yourself, you poor thing.' He stopped for a minute and then said shrewdly, 'And I suppose Lady Cynthia got hold of the story and now young Charles has cried off.' There was a note of savage anger in his voice but his eyes were gentle.

Daisy was conscious of an enormous feeling of warmth. It was both confusing and lovely to have someone care so much for her. She felt as if she were suddenly seeing him with new eyes. Perhaps it's Joan's influence, she thought, with an inner laugh, but in a way he is more attractive than all of those elegant young men that attended our coming-out ball. There's something quite magnetic about his decisiveness, his broad shoulders and his direct gaze . . .

'Let's sit on the bench there in the sunshine,' she said.

'I love looking at the river. And I have nothing to do this morning. I told Sir Guy that I would not come into the studio today. Poppy and I thought that we would sleep in this morning.'

And then she thought of Poppy and her surprise announcement and she knew that she should get back, should be on hand to soothe matters, to speak to her father if necessary.

But the sun was warm and the river enchanting with the reflections from the boats showing dark navy blue on its surface and suddenly she felt happier than she had for a long time – a strange feeling, rather as though someone had taken a heavy weight off her shoulders.

'Well, never mind,' she said lightly. 'Perhaps some day my prince will come – and if he doesn't, well . . .'

'He'll come,' said Morgan. 'Whether you'll want him or not – well, of course that is a different matter.'

'You think that I should forget all this romance and go back to my notion of earning my living by being a film director.' Daisy turned her eyes towards him and was surprised to see an odd expression in those dark eyes so admired by Joan.

'You could do,' he said, and his voice was a little unsteady. 'Don't push love out of your life though, will you, because you are a very lovable person.'

Daisy sat very still. There was a note in his voice that made her hesitate. She looked at him, but he looked away from her and kept his gaze fixed on the river and its boats. An impulse made her put her hand out and grasp his. He had taken off his chauffeur's gloves. His hand was hard and callused in places from the work that he did on the estate, but its grip was firm.

'Who would marry me – a girl with no father and whose mother abandoned her when she was a baby?' she said. She was pleased to hear that there was no note of self-pity in her voice.

'You'll find someone – everyone is in love with you,' he said lightly.

'Do you mean that?' asked Daisy unsteadily. A strange idea had come into her head and she looked at him.

'That's right,' he said, his eyes still fixed upon the river. 'You'll be able to choose the pick of them all, Lady Daisy.'

'Don't call me that,' she said, and she heard the hurt in her voice.

He heard it too and he looked at her penetratingly. 'Hush now,' he said gently. 'You're upset and you don't know what you are saying.'

She laughed unsteadily. 'Did you know, I was in love with you when I was twelve years old?' He gave a grunt and his eyebrows moved down to form two bars over his dark eyes.

'That's just it,' he said cryptically and got to his feet. 'Twelve-year-old girls get crushes on everyone and anyone. But you're not twelve any more. Don't rush into things next time.' He gave her hand one slight squeeze and then dropped it.

'Feeling any better?' he asked as if he had picked her

up from a fall from her pony, and she could only nod and follow him back towards the car.

'Would you like me to drive you to the film studios?' he said when she had got in. At least he made no fuss about her sitting in the front seat, thought Daisy. She felt slightly dazed. Was I really in love with Charles? she wondered. Or was I just in love with the idea of being in love, and a good-looking, supposedly rich young man came along? When she thought of how easily he had thrown her over at a word from his mother, at a threat that his tailor's bills would no longer be paid . . .

'I should go home,' she said reluctantly. 'I suppose there is a huge fuss going on about Poppy and Baz. I should be there to help smooth things over.'

Unexpectedly he laughed. 'I'd stay out of it, if I were you,' he said. 'Poppy is a determined young lady. If you go back home now, well, you'll probably find that she's gone out and left them all to fuss without her.'

'I'll tell you what we'll do,' said Daisy. 'Let's go to Bethnal Green and find that orphanage of yours. It's nice to have someone with you when you find out about your past. I'd have died if I hadn't had Poppy with me, that time.'

'I don't think that I will be finding out anything too dramatic,' he said with a grin, but then he shrugged. 'Why not?' he said, and Daisy echoed his words.

'It will be about four miles – out the East End way,' he warned. Daisy guessed that he had looked on a map to find where his orphanage had been and was glad that she had suggested going there.

'Doesn't matter,' she said, snuggling into the cushioned seat. 'You're right; I'm just as well out of the house this morning. Jack will be organizing everything like a military campaign. I suppose at least it will take Father's mind off the court case.'

'That may not go too well,' said Morgan with a sidelong glance at her. 'Bateman was talking about it to me – shouldn't have, really, I suppose, but the old fellow worries about your father. He wishes that the Earl would come to some agreement with Sir Denis. Apparently the last time that he visited – about sixteen years ago or even longer – they had such a row that Sir Denis went off and stayed in the village inn, so it's never been an easy relationship. The housekeeper hinted about something scandalous, but Bateman stopped her. He got all haughty and said that as butler he couldn't allow gossip about any member of the family.'

'Sixteen years ago my mother, I mean Poppy's mother, was still alive,' said Daisy. She felt puzzled. 'Rose wasn't even born then, so why did Denis think that he might be the heir?'

'Strictly speaking, he was the heir then, since your father had no son, but it probably wasn't too tactful to turn up and start causing trouble, whatever he did,' explained Morgan. 'Don't think of it any more. Look, there's the Tower of London – we'll bring Rose there one morning; she'll have some great tales to tell, I'm sure.'

He went on pointing out various landmarks and sights

to her until they came into an area of small crowded streets and then his voice changed. 'Here we are; this is the orphanage. I remember it well.'

'Were they kind to you?' asked Daisy. She heard the tentative note in her voice and knew that she had little idea of what Morgan and Maud had endured, being brought up in a place like this, with no parents, no brothers or sisters for support or company.

'They were all right,' he said, but there was a dead, toneless note in his voice.

How would I have fared in an orphanage? she wondered, and knew that the honest answer was – not nearly as well as at Beech Grove Manor. She looked at the man beside her, a man who had grown up without any family at all, and a warm feeling swept over her. She reached out and touched his arm and saw him smile. What a nice smile he has, she thought. There was something very attractive and boyish about his expression.

But what had he meant when he said that *everyone* was in love her?

The woman at the reception desk of the orphanage was welcoming and helpful. She took them both into a private parlour while she went to look up the records. When she came back she was brisk and addressed the issue instantly and in plain language.

'You were brought here when you were three years old,' she informed Morgan. 'There had been a terrible accident. The gasworks on Albert Row had blown up and three streets of houses had been demolished. Almost everyone in the neighbourhood was killed, but you were found wandering. Look at the map here.' She crossed the room, encircled an area on a map and then came back to them again. 'You were identified by the fireman who brought you in – I've got his testimony here . . .' She peered at the pages. 'He felt sure that you were the son of Annie Morgan – a love child, it says here.' The woman cast a quick glance at Morgan and then averted her gaze. 'The fireman said that she had a job scrubbing out a public house called "The Welcome Stranger". He thought that your name was Edward, but you . . .' she peered at the handwritten entry and read out: "'*the child persisted that his name was Bob so it was thought that perhaps Edward might have been his first name, and he was called by his middle name* . . ." That's signed by the superintendent of the orphanage at that time, and so,' she concluded, 'you were known as Bob Morgan all the time that you were here.' She turned over some more pages while Morgan stared straight ahead and Daisy's heart ached for him.

'Ah, yes, found it,' said the woman. 'You did well,' she concluded. 'You passed your labour certificate at the age of eleven, rather than at the usual age of fourteen, so this meant that you were allowed to leave school early. You got a job at a local foundry and of course you left the care of the orphanage at that time, so the record ends there.'

The woman shut the book and beamed at Morgan, and then, somewhat uncertainly, at Daisy.

'Would someone have looked after him?' asked Daisy

tentatively. *Eleven*, she thought. *Imagine being thrown out into the world at the age of eleven!*

'Oh, he would have been getting a small wage,' said the woman quickly. 'And, suitable lodgings would have been found.'

'I remember dividing up my money after I paid my rent,' said Morgan with a grin. 'I had a box with seven compartments in it and labelled them with the days of the week; I didn't allow myself to spend any more than the day's allowance.'

'You should have been a banker,' laughed the orphanage woman, but she put away the book with an air of finality and Daisy knew that the interview was over. Morgan had found out the little that was known about him and that was it.

But did it matter? she asked herself. Wasn't it what you made of yourself that mattered in the end? He was hard-working, honest, kind and talented. Although she didn't want him ever to leave Beech Grove Manor, she had to admit that if Baz and Poppy's scheme came to fruition, then Morgan might have a great future in front of him. King Oliver, now the most famous musician on the jazz scene, had been a poor man once, and as for Baby Dodds, now renowned all over the world as a drummer, he had started off playing on some empty tin cans.

And as Daisy thought about this, suddenly she made a decision about herself.

Morgan, she noticed, with warmth in her heart, passed some money over to the woman, stipulating that it was to be used for a treat – perhaps some ice cream – for the orphans at present under the roof of that ancient building.

'Your name might not really be Bob Morgan,' she said once they had gone outside. 'It was just that meddlesome fireman who thought you were Morgan. You could be anything.'

'Bob Nothing,' he said with a wry grin, but he was frowning now, his heavy eyebrows overshadowing dark eyes.

'It would be interesting to find out about your actual past,' admitted Daisy. She hesitated for a moment. Perhaps he should not be the first person to know about her decision, but somehow in the last hour they had grown very close and she wanted to say something that would perhaps turn his thoughts from the gloom of feeling unknown and without family. She took a deep breath.

'I've been thinking,' she said, 'that when Elaine, my mother, goes back to India – when all this fuss about the presentation at court and the season – when all of this is over and done with, I'm going to call myself by my real name. I will be Daisy Carruthers – Miss Daisy Carruthers. I'll have to talk to Elaine about it, I suppose, but I'm sick of lies and sick of wondering whether people might guess the truth. I could perhaps let Elaine think that the title is a nuisance to me in the world of business . . .' She hesitated for a moment and then rushed on, looking up at him anxiously for his approval, but he said nothing, just looked at her searchingly as though he were seeing her in a new light.

'When that ghastly Lady Cynthia brought out the story about Elaine,' she continued, 'about her being pregnant, I mean, and me being her illegitimate daughter, she thought that was enough to blackmail me into silence, that the threat of disgrace would make me give up the idea of marrying her son.' She gave a little laugh – to her own ears it sounded unforced and not bitter, and she was pleased about that. 'But of course she need not have bothered. The mere threat that she wouldn't pay his tailor's bills was enough for Charles – he backed off instantly. But, you see, Morgan, I don't ever want to be in that position again. I want to be open and honest. I want to say to the world, "I'm not an earl's daughter; I'm a talented film director." And if someone asks me to marry him, then I'll tell him the truth immediately, if he doesn't know it already of course . . .'

'Good for you!' Now the smile was back on Morgan's face – for a moment she thought that he might be going to hug her, but he just put his left arm around her shoulders in a brotherly fashion and squeezed them in the way that he used to do when she was twelve years old. Does he still think of me as just a child? she wondered.

'Did you feel very bad when he rejected you?' The words were blunt, but the expression on his face was tender. His right hand touched her cheek gently but he withdrew it immediately.

'I thought I did,' she said, 'but I've realized that he

wasn't in love with me, not really. And what's good is that now I realize that I wasn't in love with him either. I was in love with the idea of *being in love*, if that makes sense. My pride has been crushed and I feel very foolish, but now, a few hours later, I find that I don't really mind as much as I thought I would.' She laughed suddenly. 'Perhaps now I'm ready to *really* fall in love,' she said, and raised her eyes, watching his face. There was a sudden flush on his cheekbones that enhanced the tanned skin that stayed with him through winter and summer alike. His dark eyes glowed and then he looked away.

'As long as you remember that you're too old for fairy tales,' he said abruptly, and then turned away and started to look around the narrow streets.

'Do you know,' he said suddenly, 'I remember that gasworks the woman mentioned. It was enormous – like a giant drum, a tall and enormous drum; I can remember looking up at it.'

'Let's go and see the place where you were living when you were little – I know that it will be different, but you never know – some other memories might come back to you,' said Daisy. Somehow she wanted to prolong the morning. Perhaps it was the interest of finding out about Morgan's past, or whether it was his undemanding company, but the bitter humiliation of the interview with Lady Cynthia had been soothed and she was conscious of feeling genuinely happy.

'Come on,' she said turning back towards the car. 'Let's go to Albert Row.'

Albert Row had never really recovered from the explosion. There were still rows of ruined tiny terraced houses, back to back with each other, with only narrow, weed-filled yards separating them from each other. Here and there a couple of houses had been rebuilt, but the place was filthy and derelict. They both got out of the car and walked around.

'Mustn't have been much fun living here,' commented Morgan.

'Do you remember anything?' asked Daisy. 'See that place up there . . .' She went a bit nearer to a big building and made out the words 'LABOUR EXCHANGE' beneath the burned-out roof.

'Nothing; it doesn't seem a bit familiar.' Morgan looked around him. 'It's funny, but I thought we had a garden. I seem to remember a garden. Yes, I do!' He stopped suddenly and thumped a fist against a letter box. 'We did have a garden. I remember having my birthday in the garden. And the sun was out. I was born in June, like she used to sing to me, not in December! They've got the wrong boy! I'm sure of it now. This wasn't the place where I lived.'

Daisy looked at him with excitement. 'Let's have a look around – just walk around and see if anything comes back to you. This is like a detective story – like one of those books by Agatha Christie where Tommy and Tuppence were going around London picking up clues.' To while away the time as they walked, she chatted about the film that she was editing with the Bright Young

Things pouring out of the taxi and dancing in the jazz club. 'I need a good name,' she finished. 'Can you think of anything?'

'Perhaps just call it *Jazz* or *Jazzy* – it's the most fashionable music at the moment,' he suggested, but he wasn't giving her his full attention. 'There!' he exclaimed. 'That's where the gasworks used to be – see, it's a coal yard now, but you can still see the remains of it.'

'How near were you to it?' Daisy found herself getting excited.

'Not very, I don't think. I remember going for a walk and smelling it before I got close. I don't think that we could see it from our garden. But of course I was only three.'

'Look over there – something that wasn't burned down.' Daisy pointed to a church. 'I'd say that's a few hundred years old. Great-Aunt Lizzie used to teach us about different styles of church building.' Suddenly an idea came to her and she said quickly, 'You can't find your birth certificate if you don't know your real name or your real date of birth, but we could look at the records of children baptized in the parish in June ... what year was it?'

'1900,' he said, and then grinned. 'I lied about my age to get into the army and then had to lie to your father when I went for this job. I'm twenty-three, nearly twenty-four now though – a nice respectable age if they want to start another war.'

'Let's go to the vicarage,' said Daisy.

The vicarage was a newly built house surrounded by a moss-infested lawn with the stump of some ancient tree in the middle of it. They rang the bell twice before it was answered by a maidservant in a dirty apron.

'Yes,' she said snappily.

'We'd like to see the vicar.' Daisy took charge. She sensed that Morgan was almost reluctant to uncover the past any further. Perhaps, she thought, he feared the destruction of his memories of a happy and pretty young mother singing songs to him and holding a party tea for him in a garden full of June flowers.

'What about?' The maid sounded most unfriendly and Daisy saw Morgan take a backwards step.

'We'd like to look at the baptismal entries for June 1900,' she said, trying to sound a little like Great-Aunt Lizzie. The girl's eyebrows shot up and she gave Daisy a wondering look. Daisy stared back haughtily. *None of your business*, she said to herself.

'Well, you can't. Vicar's away on his holidays – won't be back until the second of June. Mr Hardiman from the next parish comes to take the Sunday service, but he won't have no time for looking at registers.'

'Well, we'll make an appointment for the first week in June, perhaps the fourth?' said Daisy firmly. 'Three o'clock. Perhaps you would be good enough to write it down.'

'What name?' asked the maid reluctantly, taking a large, leather-bound diary from the hall table.

'Carruthers,' said Daisy. 'Miss Carruthers.'

Chapter Twenty-Six
Friday 9 May 1924

'Oh, my dear children,' said Lady Dorothy. 'Oh, Basil, how could you? Poppy, you naughty, naughty girl. People keep phoning me! Now what are we going to do? Your brother is going to be so, so furious with you, Baz.'

'Sorry,' said Poppy demurely.

'Oh, Mama,' said Baz, 'you don't mind really. You're just worrying about what Ambrose will say.'

'Oh, goody,' said Rose. 'You've got the papers.'

'Yes, indeed. Joan was up early and she bought them.'

'Dearest Mama, I cannot tell a lie,' said Joan, yawning. 'In truth I was out so late that the morning papers were already on the streets when we were coming home. Some of my crowd went on to Mary's party after yours finished,' she explained to Poppy. 'It's just too sick-making to go home early.'

'Oh, pray, look at this!' said Rose, enraptured. '*Earl's Daughter Drops Bombshell* – and a great picture of Elaine and Jack with their jaws dropping – pity you're not a duke's daughter, Poppy. It would have sounded so much better – *Duke's Daughter Drops* . . . now what can I use instead of "bombshell"? I know – this is better. *Shock Disclosure from Duke's Daughter – Dashing Debutante*

Dares All in Her Desperation. This Is the Man I Love, Says *Lady Poppy Derrington.*'

Poppy smothered a giggle and turned a bland face to Lady Dorothy, who was shaking her head and repeating the words 'my dear children' over and over again.

'Don't fuss, Mama,' said Baz, dropping a kiss on top of his mother's fashionably cropped hair. 'We'll be all right.'

'It's what your brother will say,' mourned Lady Dorothy. It was amazing, thought Poppy, how elderly relations continually repeated themselves.

'Well, Ambrose wanted me to go to Oxford, the silly chump, and that would have cost him a packet – all those Oxford fellows get into debt all the time. Let him give me what he would have spent on my getting a BA from Oxford, and that will keep us going until the Jazz Club makes a fortune.'

'Failing a BA, probably, dearest,' said Poppy gently.

'Oh, don't do that, you beast. Lady Dorothy, rescue me!'

'You are a silly pair.' Lady Dorothy shook her head sadly and Poppy pulled herself away from Baz, threw a velvet cushion at him and began to think hard.

'How much?' she demanded. 'How much was your brother going to give you?'

Baz shrugged his shoulders. 'Dunno,' he said. 'I didn't want to go.'

'*Honourable Basil Pattenden Disdains Oxford Honours.*' Rose had her notebook open and was busy scribbling, murmuring to herself as her pencil moved along the lines. '*Lady Poppy Is More Precious Than Academia, Says Son of Earl.*'

Poppy thought hard for a moment and then went across and sat on the sofa beside Lady Dorothy. It was important, she felt, that her future mother-in-law be swiftly reconciled to their engagement.

'Dear Lady Dorothy,' she said, stroking the woman's hand, 'you are so understanding. I do love you so much.'

'It will have to be a very long engagement,' said Lady Dorothy. Her tone was intended to be severe, but Poppy could hear that she was weakening.

'We'll do whatever you say,' she murmured submissively. Baz, she thought, looking across at him lovingly, was adopting the pose of a man of the world, with his thumbs stuck into his waistcoat pockets, but his eyes had the faraway look which showed that he was thinking of a jazz tune.

'Baz and I,' she said appealingly to Lady Dorothy, 'we love each other very much; we will just be so happy together.'

Lady Dorothy kissed her affectionately. 'My dear, you two are like the little babes in the woods,' she said, but there was a soft look in her eye and she looked helplessly across the room at her daughter.

'We need Chomondley,' said Joan firmly. She crossed the room, picked up the telephone and asked for Mayfair 3493. She waited.

'I don't care if you were asleep,' she said when the speaker at the other end of the line had spluttered into action. She listened for a moment and then said firmly, 'Dearest man, if you are going to take that line with me, then I shall just put this telephone down and you'll have to do your own job, instead of me giving you the most wonderful piece of copy for the evening newspapers. Now stop talking nonsense about the pain in your head and complaining about the racket the birds are making. Just take your pencil and write this down and then you can phone it through and go back to sleep for the rest of the day. Ready?'

'A little bird tells me . . .' prompted Rose, and Joan nodded and repeated the words: '*A little bird tells that the owner of the latest and most fashionable jazz club* . . . its name? – I don't know . . . wait a minute.' Joan covered the mouthpiece of the telephone with one hand. 'What's the name of the club, Baz?'

'Dunno,' said Baz after a few seconds' thought.

'Very Heaven.' Poppy had suddenly remembered the line of poetry: 'To be young was very heaven'. It had come true, after all. She hugged herself, kicked off her shoes and began to shimmy across the floor, rotating her hands vigorously backwards and forwards, keeping her fingers spread open with the palms facing out and facing first to one side and then to the other while maintaining the rhythm with her pointed feet.

'*To be young is very heaven!*' she sang, fitting the words to a jazz rhythm and noting with pleasure that Lady Dorothy was now smiling.

'*The owner of the latest and most fashionable jazz*

club, VERY HEAVEN, SUTCHELEY STREET, BELGRAVIA – put all of that in capital letters, Chomondley, won't you? Yes, yes, put the address. I don't care if the Social Editor doesn't like addresses; do as I tell you – we want people to come . . . Where was I?'

'*Has presented his new fiancée to his mother,*' whispered Rose.

'Yes,' continued Joan. '*The honourable Basil Pattenden has presented his new fiancée, Lady Poppy Derrington, to his mother. I have been reliably informed that Lady Dorothy is enchanted by the romantic match.*'

'"*My dearest wish has been fulfilled,*" said Lady Dorothy,' prompted Rose.

'"*My dearest wish has been fulfilled,*" Lady Dorothy told a close friend,' Joan amended and then waited, impatiently tapping her foot, while Chomondley took the words down.

'Joan!' exclaimed Lady Dorothy helplessly, but Joan, prompted from time to time by Rose, was on a roll, and was not going to be easily stopped. Baz had by now pulled off his shoes also, and together with Poppy danced noiselessly around the morning room while phrases such as *lifelong romance, stunning sensation, jazz geniuses, rumours are rife* drifted to their ears.

It's true; it's true, thought Poppy. Baz and I are going to get married. We are going to have the best jazz club in London and we will make a fortune and live happily ever after and have a large family of musical children who will be playing tin whistles and drums in their cradles.

Chapter Twenty-Seven
Friday 9 May 1924

'Ah, there you are, Morgan. I was just coming down to see whether the car was back. Could you fetch Lord Derrington from Victoria Station at three o'clock?'

Daisy's heart stood still for a moment. So her father had been told about Poppy's shock announcement last night. She felt very guilty. If she hadn't rushed out to meet Charles, if she hadn't gone to his mother's house with him, perhaps she could have talked Jack out of informing her father so soon. Perhaps things could have been smoothed over.

'I wish you had waited,' she said to him in a low voice as he helped her out of the car. Who did he think he was? she thought resentfully. He had no authority over Poppy or herself. He wasn't even a real uncle.

'My dear girl,' he said in those smooth tones that he used when he was really annoyed, 'don't you realize? It's in every paper this morning – there are even boards up on Westminster Bridge – saw them when I went out for my early-morning walk. Your father had to be told. I had to explain that your sister consulted no one and took it into her head to do such a silly thing. The manager of the Ritz is most upset. "If it had only been our own band, Sir John," he kept saying to me, "our bandmaster would have known better. Those Americans don't understand. The young people there are all wild and out of control" – that's what he said to me,' said Jack running out of steam as Daisy glared at him angrily.

'Well, I'm going to meet him at Victoria, not you,' she said firmly, and was emboldened as Morgan gave her a grin from behind Sir John's stately back. She stopped herself from saying that it was none of his business. After all, her mother's husband did feel responsible for the girls – they were guests in his house, and Poppy should not really have made that impulsive announcement. 'I think it will be best if I talk to him alone,' she said quietly, trying to give the impression of being adult and in charge. 'I'm sorry that you have been so troubled in this matter,' she ended on a stately note and went into the house to speak to Elaine.

'Why don't you and Jack go out for the afternoon?' she said when she had listened to all of Elaine's self-justifications, which she was obviously practising on Daisy ahead of the arrival of her brother-in-law. 'Go out straight after lunch, and by the time that you are back at dinnertime I may have calmed him down.'

'But Jack—' began Elaine.

Daisy quickly interrupted her. 'Don't let Jack talk to him before I have a chance to,' she begged. 'Please, Elaine. Tell him not to. Father will feel obliged to be even angrier if he sees that Jack is angry. It's important to calm everything down now.' She glanced out of the window and saw a quick flash of red hair as its owner bounced up the steps and put her finger on the bell.

'Well, young lady?' Jack was in the hall before Daisy had opened the door of the morning room.

'It's all fixed up,' said Poppy, flashing a smile at him. 'Lady Dorothy is delighted. Baz's brother, Ambrose, is going to give him an allowance. And he's got a house already so that's all settled. And of course, once I am a married woman it will be quite respectable for me to play in jazz clubs, side by side with my dear old husband. I'd better go and get ready for lunch. Coming, Daisy?' Rapidly she ran up the stairs before Sir John could say a word, and Rose followed, her cheeks pink with excitement.

'In a moment,' called Daisy after her. She could hardly prevent herself laughing. How like Poppy all of this was. She always managed to get her own way.

'It will work out all right,' she said reassuringly to Jack. It was, after all, good of him to concern himself so much about a pack of girls to whom he was not related. She was glad now that Lady Cynthia wasn't going to make trouble for him.

'The Pattendens are rich and very respectable,' she added, and saw with satisfaction that he shrugged his shoulders with the air of a man who has done all that could be reasonably expected of him.

'I'm afraid that Father is on his way up here,' she said when she reached Poppy's bedroom. 'Jack phoned him.'

'I'm glad,' said Poppy carelessly. 'I wouldn't want to tell him myself as he would make such a fuss, but

I don't want it kept a secret.'

'Secrets,' said Rose wisely. '*Beech Grove Manor: A House Full of Secrets* – that may be the title of a book that I shall write this summer. Doubtless it will sell a million copies and then I shall be fabulously rich . . . Oh, Daisy, you don't know one of the secrets, do you? Elaine had a governess called Lucinda . . . think of it, *Lucinda*!' she said rapturously. 'Anyway this poor girl, just like Jane Eyre and Agnes Grey and all those other governesses, fell madly in love with the son of the house, Robert, and was turned out into the snow by Great-Aunt Lizzie—'

'Beg your pardon, your ladyships,' said Maud, tapping on the door and putting her head around it, 'lunch is ready.'

'It'll work out all right,' said Morgan on their way to the station. 'To be honest, I was a bit afraid of . . .' He gave her a sidelong glance and then said, 'Well, you can probably guess. Now that it is all out in the open, and as long as the wedding isn't delayed too long, then it should all work out. He's a nice little chap and they're like a pair of bluebirds together – very much in love. How's the money situation with the Pattendens?'

'Not at all like us,' said Daisy promptly. 'They'd be quite rich, really.'

'They'll probably be all right then,' he said. 'He's a bit young for marriage but he's a gentle fellow. Will make her a good husband. She'll be the boss of course. She has a lot of determination for one her age. But I still think that eighteen is too young for a wedding – for a man anyway. Women grow up more quickly. Still, it can't be helped.'

'So how old do you think that a man should be for marriage?' asked Daisy, watching his face.

'Twenty-three, twenty-four,' he said promptly, and she chuckled.

'So you're just the right age,' she observed.

He made no comment, just steered the car carefully into the station car park, keeping his eyes fixed firmly on the road ahead. When he had parked, she got out without waiting for him to come around to the passenger door. She had an odd feeling of being rebuffed, almost as though the happy, confident feeling that she had always had in his presence was now a thing of the past and that he was putting up a barrier between them.

In silence they walked towards the platform for the Kent trains. They were in good time and it was five minutes before the train pulled in, snorting and puffing, the steam billowing from the funnel. It seemed a long five minutes, thought Daisy, looking up at the station clock and then down the platform at the people pouring out from the train.

'He'll probably wait until everyone else gets out of the carriage,' said Daisy eventually, as there was no sign of the Earl. It was odd, she thought, and she began to worry a little. Only a few stray figures were still on the platform, and one by one the carriage doors were being slammed closed by the railway staff.

They waited another five minutes, but by then no one

was emerging and the train was beginning to fill up with passengers for the return journey back down to Kent.

'We'd better go home,' said Daisy eventually. 'Perhaps he missed his train.' She didn't believe it though. Michael Derrington was meticulous about matters like this. Morgan was worried also, she thought, as she took her place beside him. His eyebrows were knitted in a frown and his lips compressed. Neither spoke during the journey back, and it was a relief when he drew up in front of number twelve.

'Come up with me,' she said. 'Something is wrong; I'm sure of it.'

And so he was beside her when she went into the hall and when Jack came out from the small sitting room that he and Elaine liked to use after lunch.

'I'm afraid we've had bad news; your great-aunt rang just after you left.' His voice was formal and businesslike and Daisy was grateful for that. She could not have stood it if he had fussed or prevaricated.

'Tell me,' she said.

He hesitated for a moment, glancing at the chauffeur, but then faced her honestly. 'It sounds to me as though he has had some sort of breakdown,' he said. 'According to Aunt Lizzie, he was all ready to come to London when a letter arrived in the post.'

'The lawsuit,' said Daisy instantly and he nodded.

'Yes, nothing to do with young Poppy and her antics. Apparently the heir, Sir Denis, has heard of the sale of one of the woods and has brought an action against your father – what they call a stay of execution. It will be heard in London on Monday the twenty-sixth.'

'What's wrong with him?' she asked, and then when he didn't reply immediately, she said impatiently, 'Tell me the truth, Jack.' She was conscious of Elaine coming forward and placing her hand on her daughter's arm, but Daisy kept her eyes fixed on Jack. 'Aunt Lizzie used the word "catatonic",' he said reluctantly. 'Do you know what that means?' Without waiting for an answer he rushed into an explanation. 'It means that he is sort of frozen – not able to talk; apparently he is just sitting there, gazing straight in front of him, and blind and deaf to all around him.'

Daisy turned to the chauffeur. 'How long will it take us to get to Beech Grove at this time of day?'

'An hour and a half – two at the most,' said Morgan. 'You should pack an overnight bag. Do you want to go now? There's plenty of petrol in the car.'

'Yes, please,' said Daisy. She thought of going upstairs to pack and realized that it might involve her in explanations and queries. She didn't want to talk to Elaine, nor to Poppy and Rose. 'Let's just go now,' she said, and looked an appeal at him.

'Fair enough,' he said readily and held the hall door open for her without a single glance in the direction of Sir John.

As they went out, Daisy heard his voice calling her back, but she took no notice. Sir John Nelborough might be a big chief in the Indian Police, but he had no control, no authority over her. She knew the right thing to do and she was going to do it. She thought briefly about Violet – perhaps she should collect her on the way, but then she rejected the idea.

I'll see for myself first, she thought desperately. Perhaps he will be fine by the time I arrive.

Chapter Twenty-Eight
Friday 9 May 1924

'Darling boy, you and dearest Poppy can't possibly live in this tiny little house – in a mews!' Lady Dorothy's plucked eyebrows rose to their utmost height as she kissed Baz. She shuddered artistically as she looked around, and Poppy bit back a smile wondering what her future mother-in-law would have said if she had seen the house before Maud and the boys had scrubbed it and before the recent painting and decorating.

'Come and see the cellar, Lady Dorothy,' she coaxed.

'Dear child, don't call me Lady Dorothy – I'm determined that you shall be my little daughter. Call me . . .'

Poppy stiffened. She didn't often allow herself to think of her dead mother, but an image of herself sobbing the word 'Mama' had just shot into her mind. She clenched her hands, digging the fingernails into the palms.

'You could call her Bazmama,' put in Rose. 'You know; *Baz's mama.*'

'Bazmama!' Poppy relaxed, and when she spoke she could hear her voice sounding light-hearted and careless. 'I like it. I'll call you Bazmama. It's really hip and cool.'

'Too, too modern, and bang up to date,' said Joan enthusiastically.

'*The fashionable world has been taken by storm at the appearance of a new face and a new name: Bazmama. Her origins are suspected to be from an exotic island in the Far East, but she is chic, stylish, and has a true understanding of the needs of the Bright Young People on the London scene.*' Rose's voice was dreamy, but then she added, 'Turn on the gas lamp, Poppy. I want to write that into my notebook before I forget it.'

'Oh, I say,' said Lady Dorothy with a girlish giggle. 'You're making me feel young again.'

'You look about twenty, Mama,' said Baz affectionately.

'I love your dress,' said Poppy, lighting the gas lamp above the steep stairs going down to the cellar. 'I've decided that I am going to wear a really short dress like that for my wedding. What do you think, Bazmama?'

'I don't see why not, darling Poppy. Make it properly short though. The dress worn by the Duchess of York for her wedding was the wrong length – neither one thing nor the other. Short and sewn with crystals – what do you think, Joan dearest?'

'Light all the candles in the cellar,' whispered Poppy to Baz as Joan and her mother went into an earnest discussion about dresses and dressmakers and where to get the best choice of materials.

'Darling pet, you and my sweetest Basil cannot possibly live in this terrible little house, but I've had such a brilliant idea.' Lady Dorothy broke off her discussion with Joan and put her arm around Poppy's waist. 'You know how Ambrose is planning to get married and he wants to live in Kent and that I was thinking of building an extension for myself?' Lady Dorothy didn't wait for an answer but rushed on. 'But I've changed my mind. I really do not think that I could bear it. A Berkeley, my dear! Can you imagine? So I've decided that I'm going to move to London and live permanently in my own house in Belgravia Square. Now why don't I get a couple of builders in and turn the top floor into an apartment for you and my little boy? You can live up there, just like two little birds. Do say yes. It will be just so, so lonely for one when Joan goes off and gets married.'

'Yes,' said Poppy promptly and immediately. She was never one to hesitate when a good offer came her way. Baz, she knew, was fond of his mother, and this was an ideal situation for them both and solved all problems instantly – such as how they were going to eat and what they were going to live on. 'But don't bother about a kitchen,' she said helpfully. 'We'll eat with you. I'll be too busy with my music for all that housekeeping. Your maids will keep the place tidy – pick up things and that sort of thing, won't they? And your food is always glorious; we'd love to have all of our meals with you – stop you getting lonely if Joan gets married, won't it? You won't want to come down to an empty table at breakfast-time, will you?'

'How sweet of you to think of that!' Lady Dorothy sounded genuinely enthusiastic, and Poppy beamed at her. She liked people who fell in with her plans without fuss or alterations.

'*Lady Poppy Derrington, well known to all of her admirers as the philanthropist of the year,*' murmured Rose, but Poppy ignored her. Baz had come to the stairs and was signalling to them to come down.

And the cellar really did look marvellous, thought Poppy. The little house faced north and the black panels of artificial silk completely blocked what little light came in through the small, below-ground-level windows, but the candles lit it all up beautifully and the red material shimmered. The floor had had a second coat of paint and now shone so that pools of light were reflected in it.

'Oh, I say, what fun!' Lady Dorothy clasped her hands together girlishly.

'We're going to save up for a piano,' explained Baz.

'But, darling boy, why don't you take the one from the schoolroom in Belgravia Square? No one ever plays it these days – with all you great creatures so grown-up, and...'

'And turning into Bright Young People,' put in Rose quietly, while Poppy and Baz stared at each other with widening eyes.

'I know what we'll do.' Lady Dorothy turned to Joan. 'Joan, dearest, on our way back let's call in on those charming people in Curzon Street – the furniture removers. They'll have it over here in two shakes of a lamb's tail. Oh, dear, I wish I wasn't so old! What fun you young people have these days. When I think of my young days and all those boring dances, all that stuffy etiquette...'

'Well, now you're Bazmama; and Bazmama can do what she likes,' said Poppy firmly. 'You're a new person now. You must come here tonight with us. Let's go and get the piano first, and then we'll teach you all of the latest dances. And you can come, too, Rose; Morgan can't fuss if my mother-in-law is here to look after us.'

'But you mustn't drink anything except orange juice,' warned Baz. 'If you do, Morgan will be furious. He might ban you forever.'

'Who is this Morgan?' asked Lady Dorothy curiously.

'Morgan? Oh, he's an impresario from New Orleans,' said Joan carelessly. 'My dear, he's quite a person. The whole of London is talking about him. Got gorgeous eyes!'

'Oh, how too, too exciting it all sounds,' said Lady Dorothy with a giggle.

'I've just thought of something,' said Joan. 'Dearest Mama can be the club sponsor, can't you, Mama?' Without waiting she ran upstairs to the telephone. A minute later they heard her fluently dictating:

'I have been reliably informed that the newest fashionable figure on the London scene,' she began to dictate, *'has invested a substantial sum in the latest stylish jazz club* <full stop> *I am speaking, of course, of Very Heaven* <comma> *that charmingly individual place in Sutcheley Street in Belgravia* <full stop> *Ever one to take up the latest craze* <comma> *Bazmama* – I'll spell that, Chomondley:

B-A-Z-M-A – no, no – no title – no Mrs or Miss –
just Bazmama – where was I? *Ever one to take up
the latest craze* <comma> *Bazmama has thrown her
reputation and her fortune into the enterprise and I
venture to predict that all London will be queuing to
gain admittance* <full stop> <new paragraph >'

Joan changed tone and squinted down at Rose's
notebook.

'*I need not tell my knowledgeable readers that
Bazmama is the chic and stylish lady that all of
London is talking about* <full stop> *Her origins are
hinted to be from an exotic island in the Far East
and her lineage is only whispered about by those in
the know* . . .'

'Quote, unquote,' suggested Rose.

Chapter Twenty-Nine
Friday 9 May 1924

It was raining heavily when Morgan turned into the gates of Beech Grove. As the big car drove up the winding avenue Daisy craned her neck to catch the first glimpse of the house. She had been so totally immersed in London, in the film studio, in the coming-out ball, that it seemed almost years since she had last seen it.

And there it stood, graceful and beautiful, its cream-coloured stone framed by the golden brown of the beech leaves and with the lake shimmering in the background.

'You know, Morgan,' she said quietly when he came back from closing the gates, 'there was a time when I would do anything to get out of here, and yet, when I look at it now I think it is the most beautiful place in the world.'

But what problems were hidden behind that magnificent facade, she thought as she listened to the purr of the idling engine.

He glanced down at her. 'I feel the same,' he said. 'When I came here first – just after the war – it seemed the most marvellous place. You can imagine – coming out of the trenches, of the stink and the mud and the bleeding bodies, and then to come to such a peaceful place. Well, you saw where I grew up, and then working in the foundry was no picnic, and then the war – though I have to say that I got good training there; they were desperate for men by the time that I joined up, and because I had been working metals they put me into the Royal Engineers. I was good with engines – that sort of thing.'

'And now you are a chauffeur,' said Daisy.

'And lucky to get a job straight after I was demobbed. A job with a cottage – I didn't know my own luck. Your father was very good to me. I remember what he said: *"All you young fellows want to get married at some stage. Wait till you're in your twenties and then, if you find a nice girl, you needn't worry. The two of you will be very snug in that little cottage in the woods."'*

'And now you are in your twenties,' observed Daisy, looking sideways at him. 'Have you found a nice girl yet?' She gave a little laugh and was glad to hear that it did not sound forced.

He laughed, too, but she thought she detected a slight strained note in his voice. 'The trouble with me,' he said, 'is that I am too presumptuous. I'm looking at somebody outside my range.'

'Not a . . .' Daisy hesitated, but then made herself go on. 'Not a girl with no father and no proper birth certificate?' she forced herself to say.

He waited for a moment before replying. 'I know when someone is way above my reach,' he said quietly.

He pressed his foot on the accelerator and moved slowly forward down the avenue. 'No smoke from the chimneys. Why is that?'

Daisy sucked in a breath. No, there was no smoke from

the front chimneys. That meant that the dining room, the hall, the library, the drawing room were all without fires. And what about the bedrooms? Great-Aunt Lizzie was a very elderly lady and she had not been in good health since that winter.

With a feeling of dread in her heart Daisy got out of the car as soon as the handbrake had been pulled up. She ran up the steps and pulled the doorbell. It took two pulls before Bateman answered it. His old face was white and his eyes dark shadows under them.

'Oh, Lady Daisy, I'm glad to see you,' he said. 'And Morgan too.' He looked past her and then turned and waved a helpless hand around. 'I don't know what to do,' he said in a broken voice, ignoring the fact that Morgan was, sin of sins, coming in through the front door rather than going round to the back like a well-trained servant should do.

Daisy looked around her. In six weeks the place had become very shabby. She felt a moment's shame. If she and Poppy had not insisted on going to London, on having their season, on experiencing the fun that the big city could offer, then things might not have got into such a state. They had removed Bob Morgan and Maud – the two youngest and most able members of the staff. Maud had tirelessly scrubbed and polished, lit fires, carried buckets of coal and cans of hot water and Morgan had chopped wood at every available second and had kept everything running as efficiently as possible.

'Where is my father?' she asked in a low voice.

'In the library, my lady.' Bateman took a step to block her path. 'Don't go in there, my lady. Not immediately. I'll try to get him to take a sip of brandy. That sometimes helps.' He hesitated for a moment and then, as though the words were being dragged out from him, he said with a sob in his throat, 'He won't know you, my lady. He doesn't know anyone. He looks at me like he's never seen me in his life.'

'And Great-Aunt Lizzie?'

'Her ladyship has gone to bed, my lady. She had a heavy cold that has turned into a cough. She's eating nothing. After she had telephoned Sir John, she just went up the stairs to bed. Nora has just brought her up a couple of hot water bottles. They ease the pain in her side, she says.'

'Pain in her side?' repeated Morgan. 'You don't get a pain in your side with a cough and a cold. Sounds like pneumonia to me. Have you had a doctor?'

'Lady Elizabeth did not wish the doctor to be called,' said Bateman with dignity. 'And his lordship was most upset when he heard Mrs Pearson even mention the word "doctor".' He shut his lips firmly, but Daisy could guess. She had seen and heard her father in these fits of rage and she had no desire to provoke him with talk of doctors. On the other hand, Great-Aunt Lizzie sounded really ill.

'I'll go up and speak to her and then you can fetch the doctor if necessary. Wait for a minute, would you?' she said in a low voice to Morgan. The telephone was in the library and there would be no way of phoning without upsetting her father, but the doctor lived just outside the

240

village and could be fetched easily. Her heart felt like lead within her.

There was a smell of damp, perhaps even of mould, in the air when Daisy climbed the stairs up towards her aunt's bedroom. It seemed impossible that in a few short weeks things had deteriorated so dramatically. Her father must have put an embargo on unnecessary fires as soon as his daughters left – probably the coal had run out, and wood burned very rapidly in those huge fireplaces.

As soon as Daisy opened the door of Great-Aunt Lizzie's room she could hear the old lady's laboured breathing. She tiptoed across the room. Great-Aunt Lizzie was awake and staring at the ceiling. She expressed no surprise at seeing Daisy – there was, perhaps, even a small flicker of relief in her old eyes.

'I fear that I am quite unwell,' she gasped and then her face contorted with pain. By the bulge in the bedclothes she had one of the big stone hot-water bottles by her side, but that would not be enough to account for the crimson flush on her cheeks. Daisy touched her forehead gently. It was burning hot. Some aspirin lay beside her and a mug of Mrs Pearson's special cough-and-cold remedy made from turnips, brown sugar and lemon juice, but Great-Aunt Lizzie was beyond such simple treatments. Daisy took her hand and held it for a moment. The pulse was tumultuous.

'We'll get the doctor to you very soon,' she promised, replacing the hand under the blankets.

'Your father,' gasped the old woman, and Daisy

nodded understandingly. 'Don't trouble yourself, Great-Aunt Lizzie. I'll look after everything.' She felt tears come to her eyes as she ran down the stairs to where Morgan stood waiting for her in the hall.

'You go for the doctor, instantly, Morgan. Tell him that she needs to be in hospital. She's burning with fever and she has a terrible pain. Tell him . . .' She lowered her voice. 'Tell him that my father . . .' she hesitated, glancing at Bateman's impassive face. 'Tell him everything,' she ended. She had complete trust in Morgan and she saw his face warm with understanding as he looked down at her. He nodded – a world of sympathy in his eyes – and then was gone.

'I'll go down to the kitchen, Bateman, and have a cup of tea there before I see my father,' she said when the door had shut behind Morgan. She didn't wait for a protest, but went straight down, leaving him hovering in the hall. Mrs Beaton, the cook, would be easier to talk to about what was really going on. Bateman had such huge loyalty that he would not even appear to question any decision the Earl might make.

Even the kitchen was not as warm as usual. Probably because the vast old oven was being fuelled with wet wood rather than coal. Mrs Beaton was whisking up some eggs and gave a little scream at the sight of her.

'What happened to my father, Beaty?' asked Daisy bluntly as she pulled out a stool and sat herself as near to the stove as possible.

'Just opened the letter from Sir Denis's lawyer – that's

what Mr Bateman says – and once he had read it he just sat there and didn't move.' The cook looked around furtively and then whispered, 'Don't tell anyone. I saw the letter when Nora brought down the waste-paper basket. They want to take Beech Grove Manor away from him and use the rents to repair the house and put the estate in order. It gave him a terrible shock. That's the way he's been ever since – just sits there staring into the empty fireplace. When Nora tried to make up the fire he sent her out. We've been so worried about it all; not for ourselves – us old folk want to retire and Nora will easily get another job – no, it's for his lordship.' It seemed to be a relief to Mrs Beaton to talk, and everything poured out – all about the stubbornness of Great-Aunt Lizzie and then orders about unnecessary fires, about how the coalman was turned away when he came with his usual delivery.

Things can't be that bad, thought Daisy. Her father should not condemn the mainly elderly servants, as well of course as Great-Aunt Lizzie, to lead that sort of existence in his house. After all, he had been ridiculously insistent on paying for their presentation dresses. He need not have done that. Elaine would have preferred to do it herself and certainly she had plenty of money. In fact, Daisy knew that she planned to give the money back to him by some means or other.

She looked around the huge kitchen. There just were not enough servants to run the place. Would it perhaps be best, after all, if her father were forced to leave it – perhaps came to some agreement with Sir Denis and

243

retired to a small house in the village, or even to a flat in London? These things happened to other landowners. It was a bad time for farming.

And yet, she knew his stubborn nature and she knew how much Beech Grove Manor meant to him.

To please Mrs Beaton she had some scrambled eggs piled on top of home-made wholemeal bread with her cup of tea. 'Good old hens, still laying those nice brown eggs,' she said lightly. And then, anxiously, 'Does my father eat anything?'

Mrs Beaton shook her head with a heavy sigh. 'I send some up,' she said, 'I'll set a tray for him, but it'll come back untouched. Same with Lady Elizabeth. If it weren't for the servants, there would be no need for me to be here.'

'You'll always be here,' said Daisy, trying to smile. 'It's this wretched court case that is upsetting my father. They are having a hearing in just over a fortnight, and perhaps when that is over and done with he will feel better.' I'll get Justin to go with him, she thought, and wished that she had telephoned Violet before she left London. Still, she would see her father first – perhaps Morgan might be able to persuade him on some pretext to leave the library and give her time for a few phone calls. Elaine should know how ill her aunt was, she thought, and then remembered that Elaine hated her. And Violet would not want to leave London; and Poppy was just engaged . . . and Rose – well, Rose was a darling, but only a little girl despite her long words.

Me and Morgan, we'll just have to cope on our own,

she thought, and turned her attention back to Mrs Beaton, who was explaining how the previous earl had kept everything to himself. 'The trouble was that the present earl, your father, always had his mind on the soldiering and he had no interest in the estate,' said Mrs Beaton confidentially. 'Now his brother, Mr Robert – the Honourable Robert Derrington, I should say; how he used to laugh about that title, poor fellow, saying that it sounded so stuffy – well now, Mr Robert, he had a great interest in the estate and he knew everyone and was full of ideas for farming for profit – that's what he used to say. He'd come in and sit there, just where you're sitting, and he'd say, "If only Michael would come home and take an interest in things. My father is still stuck in the eighteenth century" – that's what he used to say. He managed everything for the old earl, but he had no liberty to carry out his own ideas. That's what he used to say anyway, but he was only nineteen or twenty years old. As time went on he would have been trusted more and more, I dare say. It was a terrible shame that they quarrelled – father and son falling out over that silly business.'

'The governess, wasn't it?' asked Daisy idly. She forced herself to swallow some more scrambled eggs. She didn't feel hungry, but she did not know what the coming hours would bring.

'That's right – that Miss St Clair. Pity she ever came to the house, though she was nice with the child, with Lady Elaine – I'll give her that. But she should have discouraged Mr Robert from hanging around the nursery so much. Any pretext would do him. Making the child, Lady Elaine, I should say, laugh with his old one-eared rabbit or telling her jokes. But of course it was the governess that he had his eye on. And she had a couple of afternoons off as Lady Elizabeth liked to do educational things with the little girl – and I suppose that was when the trouble started. He taught the governess to ride, and goodness knows what happened out there in the woods.'

Daisy smiled. She could just imagine. How many love affairs had those ancient woods seen? she wondered.

'But then things came to a head,' continued Mrs Beaton. 'There was the big row with the old earl. Mr Robert took himself off to London – and I did hear that his father stopped Mr Robert's allowance – trying to bring him to heel, I suppose – but it didn't work. Mr Robert just went off and joined the army – the second battalion of the Buffs here in Kent, and the next thing we heard was that he was killed in that nasty Boer War. Don't know why they have to have all these wars, and that's a fact. People getting killed before their time and leaving the old people behind to mourn them.' Mrs Beaton sighed heavily and put some goose fat into a large pan. A pot of potatoes simmered on another part of the stove and Daisy guessed that dinner this evening was going to consist of scrambled eggs and potatoes. What would Sir John and Lady Elaine make of that? She got up from her stool and went towards the door.

'I think I'll go up and see Great-Aunt Lizzie again,' she said. 'Morgan has gone for the doctor. I'm sure that they'll want to send her to hospital. She's very ill. I'll pack a few things for her, just in case. Thanks for the lovely scrambled eggs, Beaty.'

Mrs Beaton made some enquiry about London as she went out, but Daisy pretended not to hear. She did not feel like any gossipy conversation about balls. All of that seemed to be light years away. She would not endeavour to see her father just now, she decided. She would wait for the doctor's arrival and then just usher him into the Earl's presence.

Had Michael Derrington slipped over the edge into madness? she wondered as she climbed up the back stairs. Stories she had heard of his father had often suggested to her mind that he had been slightly insane. How absurd to make such a fuss because a young man flirted with a pretty governess.

Robert, of course, was probably destined to marry Elaine and to keep the other half of the Carruthers' fortune in the Derrington family. It would have all been very neat. Two brothers marrying two sisters – and both of them heiresses. That was why there had been such fury when he had fallen in love with . . .

Suddenly Daisy stopped on the stairway. With a governess called Miss St Clair. Rose had told the story, but she had called the governess Lucinda.

Lucinda meant nothing, but St Clair . . .

Great-Aunt Lizzie was fast asleep, moaning slightly, but her eyes were closed and her breathing heavy. Daisy moved around the room quietly packing a couple of night-dresses and a toilet bag and some other necessities into small suitcase which she found on top of the wardrobe.

And then, as the old lady still slept, she went quietly out of the room and up the stairs to the gallery where hundreds of framed family photographs decorated the walls.

'There were none of the governess – but then Great-Aunt Lizzie had removed all pictures of Elaine when the scandal of the seventeen-year-old girl's pregnancy had become known to her relations. No doubt, somewhere in the old lady's secret desk drawer there would be a photo of the blonde little girl with her governess.

But there were plenty of Robert Derrington – from a child of about three, clutching a soft toy, a one-eared rabbit; to a school boy with a cheeky grin; right up to a dark-eyed, dark haired young man with a nice smile, though none of him in the uniform of the famous Kent regiment, the Buffs. By that stage the break with his father must have stopped the exchange of photographs. And Great-Aunt Lizzie, of course, would have been furious at the young man's refusal to fall in with her plans.

He would have been my uncle if he had lived, thought Daisy and then, suddenly, another thought came to her.

No, she was the child of Elaine Carruthers and Clifford Pennington, who was killed in a hunting accident aged only seventeen. Robert Derrington had, of course, no blood relationship to the illegitimate daughter of his brother's sister-in-law.

Chapter Thirty
Friday 9 May 1924

'Daisy, your father . . . he's not well . . . shell-shock . . .'
Between bursts of painful coughing Great-Aunt Lizzie
clutched at Daisy's sleeve and fixed her fever-bright eyes
on the face of her great-niece. Daisy had managed to
make her swallow a draught of Mrs Beaton's home-made
cough syrup and her breathing was a little easier.

'Don't worry about anything, Great-Aunt Lizzie. I'm
home now and I'll look after Father.' Daisy endeavoured
to make her voice calm and reassuring. She dabbed a
cloth soaked in lavender water on the woman's burning
forehead and wished that the doctor would hurry. At his
own request Dr Taylor had gone alone into the library
and he had been a long time shut up with the Earl. One
part of Daisy wished that she could hover in the hallway
and try to find out what was happening, but the other half
wanted to call him out and get him to attend the more
urgent case of the elderly woman who was in immense
pain.

'Don't worry, Great-Aunt Lizzie,' she repeated. 'Don't
try to talk. Talking makes you cough and coughing hurts,
doesn't it?'

The only answer was a moan. The incoming breath
seemed to squeak in the woman's lungs. Daisy got to her

feet resolutely and went out of the bedroom, closing the door quietly behind her and running lightly down the stairs. Morgan was kneeling on the floor in front of the huge fireplace in the hallway. He had carried in a large dusty log and was lighting some newly split pieces of kindling under it. Despite her feelings of anguish and terror, Daisy almost smiled at the sight. Morgan was never one to sit still for a moment. He had only been back in the house for about fifteen minutes and already he had managed to organize some heat.

'I've lit a fire in the dining room also,' he said looking up at her, 'and I have some wood in the basket for one in the library.'

'Oh, Morgan, we'll have to get the doctor to Great-Aunt Lizzie; she's very ill.' Daisy held herself very straight, trying to stiffen her spine and resisting a surprising impulse to throw herself into his arms. She thought for a moment. Dr Taylor's soothing tones, talking about a horse that he had bought, came from the library, but her father did not seem to be responding. There is no time for this, she thought impatiently. She felt a little ashamed at her lack of sympathy, but Great-Aunt Lizzie's need was greater. Unfortunately her father's troubles could not be cured by a bottle of medicine. It might be half an hour before the doctor could coax him to say a word, and then what?

'Morgan,' she whispered, 'would you go in and get the doctor out? If . . .' She hesitated, but then went on, 'If my father sees me, it will alarm and worry him and he'll think

250

of Poppy and then he'll feel guilty about us.'

'Write the doctor a note and I'll just walk in and deliver it,' said Morgan. Daisy gave a nod of understanding. That was the best way to do it. She went into the drawing room, took a sheet of paper and an envelope from Great-Aunt Lizzie's desk and penned the note quickly, sealing the envelope and writing the doctor's name in block capital letters in case her father was alert enough to recognize her handwriting. She waited in the shadows in the hallway and listened. Morgan did it well, she thought. There was no outburst from her father at the sudden appearance of his chauffeur whom he had supposed to be in London. She heard Morgan say, 'For you, sir,' and then as the doctor came out of the library, she heard the rattle of the logs in the fireplace and smelt the sharp smell of sulphur from the match. A fire had finally been lit in the library.

'Where is she?' Dr Taylor was by her side and he patted her hand reassuringly. 'Don't worry, my lady,' he said. 'She's a tough old lady. I'm more concerned about your father, to be honest.'

'In her bedroom.' One thing at a time – Daisy sent a fleeting thought in the direction of all those girls whose parties she had attended during the past few weeks. They would be shrieking over the latest gossip column or the photographs in *Tatler* magazine and trying to decide which one of their dresses would be the most suitable for tonight's dance; chatting about the young men at the dance before, secretly speculating on offers that might be made by eldest sons – second sons and below that would not be considered at this stage of the season.

Reality, for her now, on the other hand, was a desperately sick old lady and a middle-aged man who had been getting steadily more deranged over the years and who now seemed to have been driven into a catatonic state by the threats from his heir.

'In here,' she said, opening the door to the bedroom. And then, in a lower tone, 'I've packed some things in case you think that she needs to go to hospital.' She left him to go in on her own. Great-Aunt Lizzie was a very private person and would not want her niece around while the doctor examined her. Daisy, thinking back, could not recollect ever seeing her in bed before. She had suffered from colds and coughs throughout the years in the damp, draughty house, but she had battled through them.

And yet, thought Daisy, going across to look out of the tall window, this is such a beautiful place. If only money on essential repairs could be spent, if only there was enough to finance the proper running of the house, modernize it, heat it properly. She smiled to herself as she remembered all of their dreams last year. Violet was going to marry a prince – but had settled for an impecunious young lawyer. She and Poppy were going to make a fortune – Poppy in the jazz world and she in Hollywood . . . well, she had earned a few pounds and Poppy was having fun in the jazz world, but she hadn't yet made any money from it. That was about as far as things had gone in a whole year.

And how much would it cost to put Beech Grove

Manor on its feet again? she wondered, and then turned to face the doctor who had come down more quickly than she had expected.

'I'm going to phone for an ambulance from my house so as not to disturb your father,' he said, and then paused. 'There's not much that I can do for him now,' he went on. 'But now that one of his daughters is back home, that might be the very thing that he needs. Tender, loving care; that's what daughters are for, God bless them,' he said, and went towards the front door, leaving Daisy feeling uncomfortable and guilty.

'Hope your lordship will soon be feeling better,' he called into the library, and then in a peremptory tone to Morgan, 'I'm ready to go now, my man.'

When Morgan had left to take the doctor back home, Daisy went back upstairs and into the sick woman's bedroom. Her great-aunt was moaning, but she seemed to be asleep. Daisy went across and sat beside the bed and felt very helpless. There were some paper packets on the bedside table and she could see traces of powder clung to them. The doctor had given some sort of draught to her aunt and she hoped that it had eased the pain a little. The hot-water bottle was still warm, so there was nothing that she could do for her until the ambulance came.

Nor for Michael Derrington, who sat downstairs in his library with his mind seething with agonies of guilty and anxiety.

A resolution came to her. She could not go away and leave him there, and it would do little good for her to see him and try to talk to him. When Morgan returned, and the ambulance had taken her great-aunt off to hospital, they would take the Earl, with his permission or not, and they would drive him up to London. He could not be left here with just a few elderly and nervous servants to deal with him. His family needed to care for him now.

Chapter Thirty-One
Friday 16 May 1924

Poppy stared at her father with apprehension. She couldn't get used to his appearance. When he had arrived at the house in Grosvenor Square last week she had been frightened by the sight of him. He seemed to have aged by years during the six weeks that they had been away. Jack's valet had shaven him neatly and trimmed his hair, but there were heavy, dark pouches under his eyes and his thin hands shook continuously. What was she going to do with him until the others came back?

'Talk to him,' Daisy had urged. 'You're his favourite. You look like mother and you both share a love of music. Try to get him to open up and speak about his worries. I have to go out. We must see the lawyer and find out if there is any chance of postponing this court case on the twenty-sixth.'

Then Daisy was gone, flying down the steps to where Morgan was already cranking up the engine of the old Humber with its angular starting handle. And then Jack, looking efficient and businesslike, came bustling down the steps and Elaine, looking hesitant and unsure, trailed down after them, and she and Rose were left in charge of their father.

Poppy almost felt panicky. There is something almost

terrifying about a person who doesn't speak, she thought. Especially someone who looks as though frightening thoughts are simmering behind their eyes. She looked across at Rose sitting pensively at the piano, touching the odd note here and there and shooting anxious glances at the Earl. He had said very little since he had arrived, almost nothing to his daughters, though he had made an effort with Jack. Daisy, however, said that he was better than he had been at Beech Grove and that he wasn't to be left alone.

'Doorbell,' said Rose, and then, with a note of relief, 'Oh, it's Joan. She's come to say goodbye. She knows that I am to be incarcerated from tomorrow onwards.' She rushed out into the hall and Poppy heard her exclaiming over a present – a make-up bag with rouge, mascara and eyeshadow, apparently. Joan and Rose were great friends, which was funny because Rose, it was generally considered, was the cleverest of the Derrington sisters, and Joan, thought Poppy, was pretty empty-headed and very silly.

Still, Poppy was delighted to see her. It was impossible to be quiet or anxious when Joan was in the room. She came in now – danced in, as a matter of fact, her feet beating out a rhythm. She twirled around, shrieked greetings and waved her hands in the air, then tossed her close-fitting cloche hat into a corner and unwound her feather boa from about her neck.

'Poppy, dear old girl – guess what? Got the music for "I Wish I Could Shimmy Like My Sister Kate" – pity we don't have the drums, but Rose can have a go at marking the beat on the . . . Oh!'

Poppy almost giggled at the expression on Joan's face when she realized that the Earl was present. He said nothing but had risen to his feet politely, giving a half-smile and a nod in the direction of his neighbour's youngest daughter.

Joan called across one of her speciality greetings – '*Hillo*' – twinkled her fingers in his direction and then promptly forgot about him.

'See, here it is,' she said. 'Look at it, Poppy. Baz got hold of it yesterday – he'll be coming over himself, but he had to see Ambrose – they're talking about allowances – something like that – discussing how much you two will need to live on, I suppose – anyway this is a great dance and a great tune. I'll be the dancer – where's Daisy? – she could be Kate, or could she? Perhaps I'd better be Kate – I'm a better dancer – oh well, we'll manage without her. Rose, you do the beat on the piano.'

'Try playing all four beats on two notes with your left hand,' said Poppy authoritatively. She had almost forgotten about the silent presence of her father in the excitement of this new piece of music. She rang the bell imperiously.

'I say, Tellford, could you ask Maud to come up?' she said once the butler appeared, and then went back to instructing Rose not to lift her fingers too much.

When Maud came in she gave a sidelong, slightly scared glance at the Earl out of the corner of her large green eyes, but Joan hummed the tune to her and sang:

'*Oh, I wish I could I shimmy like my sister Kate;*

She shimmies like a jelly on a plate . . .'

– all in a slightly breathless voice as she shimmied across the floor and swung her feather boa around her hips.

'You've a terrible voice, Joan,' said Poppy impatiently. 'Maud, you do it. Rose, you just mark the beat, don't get too fancy.'

That was almost perfect, thought Poppy, listening to Maud's husky voice critically as the notes slid from her clarinet. But then she stopped. Something was wrong.

'You're not doing it right, Rose,' she said in annoyance. 'You're doing all those cascading things with your right hand and you're getting in the way of the clarinet. Keep those notes quieter or else play the left hand louder.'

'My left hand is not strong enough,' complained Rose.

'Wish we had Morgan on the drums – why did Daisy have to take him off like that?' wailed Poppy. 'Or Baz. We need the drum or the bass.'

Her father's presence had set her on edge and suddenly it seemed essential to her that this playing of 'I Wish I Could Shimmy Like My Sister Kate' would be a success. In her mind she heard exactly how it should sound.

'I'll do the left hand.' Suddenly the Earl rose to his feet and went over to the piano. Rose, with a slightly nervous look, slid along the piano stool to make room for him beside her, but Poppy just gave a satisfied nod and put her clarinet back into her mouth. Her father was quite a musician and he had often accompanied her in the past.

And they were all still playing it and Joan was still dancing when the party came back from the visit to the lawyer. Maud sidled out the instant they came into the hall, but the others continued. Poppy looked at her father strumming the piano and then across at Daisy and took her clarinet from her mouth in order to laugh at Jack's astonished expression. But then she put it back again straight away. Her father needed to lose himself in the music; he needed to play that incessant beat until his mind, his heart, his blood was saturated by it and nothing else in the world mattered. The music had to be kept going. In the beat lay salvation. Poppy knew that from her own experience.

Chapter Thirty-Two
Saturday 17 May 1924

'*Then England's ground, farewell; sweet soil, adieu;*
My mother and my nurse that bears me yet!
Where'er I wander, boast of this I can:
Though banish'd, yet a true-born Englishman . . .'
declaimed Rose to the astonished crowd queuing to
present their tickets at the gate to platform ten at Victoria
Station.

'Shakespeare,' she added, and then she spotted
another girl in the brown and gold uniform and waved
vigorously.

'I say, Sheila,' she yelled, 'did you have a good time? I
had an absolutely splendiferous holiday – balls, parties,
cocktails, orgies . . .'

'Rose!' remonstrated Daisy, but despite the raised
eyebrows of the respectable-looking mothers and
fathers handing over their daughters to the harassed
teacher inside the barrier, she was glad to hear her
little sister back on form again. The silent, brooding
presence of the Earl had had a bad effect on Rose.
She had been white and worried-looking and had even
given up inventing dramatic newspaper headlines.
Despite her protests about being sent into exile, it
would do her good to be back to normality with other

girls for company and teachers to tease.

Rose, was, of course, too young for all the invitations that poured into the house at Grosvenor Square so she was alone with her father for a lot of the time while Daisy and Poppy, happily chaperoned by Elaine, were enjoying themselves at balls in the evenings, as well as luncheon parties and afternoon tea at the Ritz during the day.

'I'll put the luggage in the guard's van,' said Morgan in her ear as Daisy dug out Rose's health certificate from her handbag and presented it to the teacher. In a minute he was off, efficiently organizing a harassed-looking porter and making sure that all Rose's cases and her tuck box were piled neatly on top of her trunk.

'Bags I the window seat,' shouted Rose, swinging her overnight bag dangerously near the bowler hat of a gentleman who was bending down to give his daughter a farewell kiss.

'C'mon, Charlotte, Ellen, Wilhelmina, Ann! C'mon, everybody! Bye, Daisy, Bye Morgan. Do make sure when I die of sorrow that my bones are carried home and buried in English soil, won't you?'

And then she was gone, filling the carriage that she had chosen with a group of her best friends. Daisy could see how the girls were all laughing and leaning forward and could imagine the tale of some invented wild orgy with which Rose was entertaining them.

'She'll be better off back in school,' said Morgan as the guard blew his whistle and the train snorted and then slowly puffed out of the station.

'I know,' said Daisy. She realized that he had seen the tears gathering in her eyes and she wiped them with a laugh. 'I'll miss her though. It's funny how she was talking about English soil,' she continued. 'I was just thinking last night about Beech Manor Grove. I miss it, you know. I know it's damp and cold, but I miss the woods around the house, I miss my pony and the dogs.' She gave a little laugh. 'I even miss collecting the eggs from the hens.' And of course the breathtaking beauty of the house set among the woods and the lake, she thought.

'How did the visit to the lawyer go?' asked Morgan as together they strolled back through the barrier.

'Not good.' Daisy shook her head. She said no more until they reached the Humber. She felt that she could not trust her voice.

'I suppose I've been thinking of Beech Grove Manor since the visit to the lawyer,' she said once he got in beside her. She looked across at him. He had cranked up the car, but he left the engine running and made no move to set off. His eyes were on her and he had an understanding expression on his face.

'Bad as that, is it?' he asked.

'The lawyer says that he has breached a court order and laid himself liable to a prison sentence for contempt of court. The best that can happen to him will be that he will get a heavy fine, and of course, according to the lawyer, he has to pay Denis Derrington back the money that he got from the sale of Binton Wood.'

Morgan gave a long, low whistle. 'Has he still got the money?' he enquired.

Daisy shook her head. She felt tears well up in her eyes.

'He gave it to Elaine to pay for our coming-out dresses and party,' she said. 'He won't consider taking it back. He yelled when she tried to offer it. He told her that she was trying to rob him of a last remaining shred of pride, so Jack . . .' Jack, she thought as she choked back her sobs, had not really understood, but he was sensitive enough to comprehend that Michael Derrington was a man balanced on the edge of sanity. He had made a decisive signal to Elaine and she had immediately changed the subject.

'You see, he was told quite clearly by the judge that he could sell nothing without the consent of his heir, but he went ahead and did it – all for the sake of this season.' Her voice was now choked and tears poured down her cheeks, but she had ceased to care. It was comforting to be able to let go, to be able to stop pretending that everything was well.

Morgan touched her hand with his and then withdrew it. She wound down the window and put her head out, gulping in some fumes as she did so. For a moment she remembered with a feeling of nostalgia the fresh smell of the beech woods of her home, and then she closed the window again and said as steadily as she could, 'There really is only one option, and that is to accept the offer that Denis Derrington has made that Beech Grove Manor

House is handed over to him. He will repair the damage and renovate the house while my father continues to receive the rents from the farms. And of course, when he dies, Denis will inherit all so it makes good sense for him to prevent any further damage to the house – the roof is in a very bad state,' she added, though she knew that Morgan knew all about that. He had often climbed up on the roof to replace lost slates, but he had once told her that the whole thing needed to be stripped and the timbers renewed.

'Of course, he will make things even worse if he doesn't turn up at the hearing on the twenty-sixth,' she added.

'Well, that's still a while away,' said Morgan encouragingly. 'A lot can change in a week. I'll tell you what I'll do; I'll try to get him to come out for a spin in the car – down to Greenwich or something like that. Take his mind off things. I'll just turn up and pretend that I thought he ordered the car. A bit of air will do him good.'

'Perhaps,' said Daisy, trying to sound cheerful. 'We'd better go now, Morgan. I want to spend this afternoon with him as we are going to Joan's coming-out dance tonight. You know, Morgan, I feel very guilty that we have pushed him into this,' she added impulsively as the car slid out into the traffic of Victoria Street. 'Every time I look at my presentation dress, hanging up there in my dressing room, I just wonder whether this dress has cost him his reason.'

'Don't think like that.' Morgan's voice was almost

rough. 'You had a right to have what others of your kind have. You had a right to look for your own happiness. If you want to blame anything, blame the war. That's what wrecked the Earl – not the cost of a dress and a few parties. Now stop thinking like that and concentrate on the party tonight. Going to be very splendid, I hear.'

'Yes, it's all top-secret, but Joan assures me that it is going to be the most stunning event of the season.' Daisy tried to smile, but she couldn't help thinking that she might not enjoy the evening. Of course, when the invitations went out she and Charles had been a couple, but now . . . She just hoped that, given the circumstances, he would send an excuse.

'I should get plenty of material for my new film, *Bright Young People*, at least; it's coming on really well. Joan suggested that I bring my camera tonight – and made me promise faithfully that I would never, ever film her right profile or her left knee.' She laughed at the memory of Joan's detailed instructions.

'And of course you will be there, won't you?' She turned to Morgan with a sudden feeling of pleasure.

Chapter Thirty-Three
Saturday 17 May 1924

Joan's coming-out party had been more than a year in the planning. Everything, she had told her mother firmly, had to be different. It would be the sort of party that people were going to go on talking about for years. Dowagers shrieked in horror, fathers threatened, mothers agonized, but the Bright Young People screamed with laughter when the gold-edged cards arrived, inviting everyone to an underwater party by Westminster Bridge.

Elaine had been very enthusiastic and excited about this party and had insisted on buying the girls new outfits for it. Daisy had a dress in deep, rich ocean blue, adorned with a matching fluffy boa, fringed like exotic artificial seaweed. Poppy chose a very short scarlet dress sewn all over with tiny, cup-like coral shapes. They dressed and admired each other and showed off their outfits to Maud while Elaine got ready, but they both felt heavy-hearted that their father had once more sunk back into a dark depression of despair.

Only Morgan was in the hall when they came down the stairs. He looked up, startled, and lifted a hand to shield his eyes from the impact of Poppy's explosion of colour. She made a face at him before going into the library, where Jack and Elaine were having a conversation with some friend.

'You look gorgeous,' whispered Morgan to Daisy, his eyes on the still-open door. 'Looking forward to it, are you?'

'Not really,' said Daisy. 'They're more Poppy's friends than mine.'

'Well, I'll be there, and I'm more *your* friend than anyone else's.' His voice was still a hushed whisper and he looked around hurriedly as the sound of voices saying goodbyes showed that the others would be coming out at any moment.

'I'll come and sit by the drums,' she promised, and felt cheered by the light of pleasure in his eyes and the warmth in his voice. Joan was going to have jazz played right through her party, but she had engaged another jazz band as well, so that Poppy and Baz could have their fair share of the dancing. Would Morgan dance too? Daisy wondered.

A long line of taxis was dropping off young people at the quayside when they arrived at Westminster Bridge. Daisy leaned out of the window of the car, pointing her camera at them and wishing suddenly that someone would invent colour photography so that she could do justice to the bright dresses as the girls teetered across the gangplank to the boat in their impossibly high heels.

When they got inside the riverboat she wished it even more. Lady Dorothy had engaged the services of the stage designer from Drury Lane Theatre and the effect was magical. The ceiling of the large saloon downstairs was hung with bunches of coral in blue, red, pink, green and gold. Trails of exotic seaweed draped the windows and light glowed through shades of green and blue glass. The floor itself had been painted dark blue and sprinkled with glitter, and Daisy saw with amusement how Poppy, unselfconscious as always, bent down and rubbed her finger on the sparkling surface to see whether any would come off. But then she forgot the floor, forgot to film, as she gasped in amazement at the sight at the far end of the room. A floor-to-ceiling pale blue translucent voile curtain hung a few feet away from the end wall. Behind it, but clearly to be seen, were dozens of tiny blue balloons flecked with silver. They rose continuously, looking like bubbles beneath the sea.

'Jolly clever, isn't it? Filled with hydrogen gas, of course.' The voice from behind her was wonderful. Quite deep and very musical. Automatically Daisy swung around and found herself staring into the very beautiful eyes of Charles de Montfort.

'Oh! Charles!' she gasped, and was instantly mortified at her reaction. She had planned to greet him in a polite but distant manner, and now she was standing gaping into his face. He was with a girl that she did not know and his arm was around her waist. He glanced at Daisy and instantly turned away.

'Come and see the lobsters, dearest,' he said to his companion. 'They are just too, too killing.'

Daisy did not move. She felt a sudden stab of

humiliation. Why had she not cut him, rather than allowing him to cut her? She felt her cheeks colour and was glad that the light was so dim. She gazed after Charles pushing his way through a crowd, who were, she supposed, looking at the lobsters. The music was starting – not Baz's band, she thought, hearing a piano instead of a drum.

And then there was a sudden exclamation of pain and a well-known voice – a voice that she had known since she was twelve years old – saying indifferently, 'Sorry, old chap, did I tread on your foot?'

Charles's voice, sounding uncertain, replied, 'Don't worry, old chap. No harm done.'

And then Morgan was beside her, looking very smart in his evening dress.

'Are you all right?' he asked.

Daisy nodded. 'Only my pride was hurt,' she said. She looked around. Everyone was pairing up and beginning to move to the music. 'Dance with me, Morgan,' she said pleadingly. 'I don't know anyone here, and I don't want to just stand there filming. It's too early in the evening anyway. They'll all be looking at me.'

For a moment she thought he was going to refuse, but then he nodded. Without a word, he took the camera from her hands, went across to the bandstand and placed it on his drummer's stool and then came back holding out his hand. 'Let's do some jitterbugging then,' he said.

He danced well, marking the beat firmly, thought Daisy, and then smiled to herself as she overheard one of their neighbours from Kent say in penetratingly loud tones to Lady Dorothy, 'Who's that fine-looking young fella dancing with little Daisy?'

'I say, St Clair, save the next dance for me?' called out Joan, twirling around in the arms of languid young man. 'I'm the hostess, you know. If anyone displeases me, I have some stalwart sailors here who will immediately throw them into the river.'

Morgan smiled but made no reply. There was a glint in his eye and Daisy laughed. It would be a brave man who would try to throw him into the river. Even under the smooth cloth of his well-cut jacket it was easy to see the impressive swell of his strong arms.

'Our band is going to be playing the next few tunes,' he said to her, 'but after that . . .' He broke off and twirled her around but did not finish the sentence. She wondered whether he had been going to ask her to dance again, but he said no more and the pace was fast and furious and they were breathless and laughing by the time that dance finished. He spoke then, but it was only to remark in an amused fashion, 'I notice that Mr Charles de Montfort did not dance this last number. I wonder, could he have a problem with his foot?'

And then he gave a formal end-of-dance bow, quickly returning her camera to her before taking his place on the bandstand behind his drums.

It was, thought Daisy, filming happily, an extremely beautiful evening. The misty blues and greens set off the nets of bright orange and deep pink starfish and the tiny scarlet fish that seemed to swim through the waving strands of emerald and purple seaweed – everything made a fantastic background to the girls in their exotic colours and the men in their black and white. She danced a couple of dances with some of Joan's friends – even the eldest brother, Ambrose, the young earl, danced a tango with her, and all of the jazz-band boys in turn led her on to the floor in the intervals between filming, but Morgan did not ask her again and she wondered why. Had Joan embarrassed him? When it came to supper time she filled two plates and took them over to where he sat, softly tapping out a muted rhythm on the drums.

'All right now?' he asked, accepting the plate with thanks.

'All right?' She looked at him genuinely puzzled, and then understood. 'Oh, him,' she said, looking across at Charles with his arm around the expensively dressed female. 'It makes me seem very silly,' she confessed, 'but I look at him now and wonder what I saw in him. Do you know what Sir Guy said one day a couple of weeks ago when I was picking out shots?' Without waiting for his reply she went on. 'He said, "Don't use that shot, Daisy, he's a bit of a chinless wonder – and when you shoot from that angle you make things worse." I was furious with him at the time, but now I see what he meant.'

'I'm pleased.' Morgan laughed. 'Don't think of him any more; just enjoy the evening. You dance very well, you know.'

'So do you,' said Daisy. And then she plucked up her

courage. After all if Joan could ask him to dance, then she could do the same thing.

'Will you be dancing again, for the last three songs of the night, when the other band take over?' She tried to make the words sound casual, but couldn't help a slight blush.

'Only if a girl in blue with blue eyes asks me.' His tone was easy, affectionate and teasing and it relieved her of her embarrassment.

'Will I do?' she asked. 'Or. . .' She stopped as Joan came tripping across.

'Oh, lord,' groaned Morgan. 'Save me! I don't mind, but her grandmother and all the other titled ladies sitting over there will have a fit if she dances with me.'

But Joan had a tall, broad man in tow. She waggled a finger at 'St Clair', threatened to sue him for breach of promise and said breathlessly: 'Daisy, this is Sam. He's American and his father is a film producer. He thinks it's fantastic that you make films. Sam, darling, here is the girl of your dreams.'

'Excuse me,' said Morgan. He got to his feet, plate in hand. 'Are there any lobsters to eat, or are they all just for display?'

'Darling St Clair, come with me,' said Joan, tucking her arm into his. 'Just say the word and every one of those lobsters will be cast into a vat of boiling oil.'

She turned back to Daisy and whispered in her ear, 'His father is very, very rich, darling. Oh, and that girl that Charles is dancing with is another American, called

Millicent, an extremely rich heiress. So forget him, darling. Sam is a sweetie, a much better choice!' And with that Joan beamed at the tall American and dragged Morgan away.

'Will you take a glass of champagne with me, Lady Daisy?' Sam's accent was rather attractive, and there was no doubt, thought Daisy, after she had gulped down a few mouthfuls of fizz, that champagne did give you a wonderful feeling.

'Are you a film producer too, Sam?' she asked as he examined her camera with a professional air.

'No, not me, that's my father; I'm not that keen on film-making. That's just Joan shooting her head off as usual. As a matter of fact, I'm still at college – what you folks over here call university. I'm good with a camera though. It comes in useful in my work.'

'Your work?' queried Daisy. She was conscious of feeling a little disappointed. He was probably studying photography and intended to be one of those press photographers. And yet he had an intelligent-looking face with sharp grey eyes.

'Yes, I'm studying to be a doctor,' he said. 'This year is mainly about dissection, so it's quite handy to be able take some good photographs of corpses before and after I take the scalpel to them. I'm fiercely ambitious, you know.' His voice warmed and his eyes glowed as they beamed down on her. 'I want to be the best doctor in the whole of the United States,' he said. 'Skeletons are fascinating, you know,' he declared so loudly that a few people turned around to look at him. 'The individual variation in human bones is amazing. You'd never guess. But we all have the same bones and the same number of them. I'll bet you don't know how many bones there are in the human body – two hundred and six, and every single one of them is essential. I bet you didn't know that, did you?'

'No, I didn't,' said Daisy, and began to laugh. 'I must say that I never really thought about bones. What made you want to be a doctor, rather than a film producer like your father?' Especially if he is so very rich, she added silently to herself. Joan was usually very accurate about matters of rank and fortune. She had all the gossip in London at her fingertips. She looked at Sam and found his grey eyes fixed on her.

'Do you know, Lady Daisy, your face has a very perfect bone structure?' he said, gazing down admiringly and ignoring her question. 'Your nose is just perfectly shaped. And your cheekbones, and those frontal bones.' Gently he touched her eyebrow. 'That would be a beautiful face even without the skin and flesh. And of course with them, w-e-e-l-l-l –' he dragged out the word 'well' in an exaggeratedly American fashion and ended up by saying in quite a simple manner – 'it's the most beautiful face in London. Will you dance?' he went on before she could gasp or even blush. 'The band is coming back. Your camera will be quite safe here. I won't guarantee to keep an eye on it because I'll be staring at you, but . . . I say, Mr Bandleader,' he addressed Morgan, 'would you be a good guy and keep an eye on the lady's camera for me?'

'So what did make you become a doctor?' asked Daisy again as they stood on the dance floor and waited for the music to begin. What a difference from Charles, she thought. Charles had no money and his only ambition seemed to be to live off some woman, first his mother, then Daisy, when he thought that she was wealthy, and now this Millicent, the American heiress.

And yet Sam, with all the money in the world, went off and studied those two hundred and six bones – not to mention flesh and skin, she thought mischievously, and then the smile died from her face when he said quite simply, 'My mother. It was because of her. She died of tuberculosis when I was twelve years old. I thought that the doctors should have been able to cure her if they had only known enough. I swore I'd be better than them and now, here I am.'

At this moment the music started, very loud and very energetic. There was no opportunity to talk, but in between dances they drank more champagne and chatted like old friends. From the chaperone chairs Daisy could see a fond smile on Elaine's face and she and Lady Dorothy had their heads together.

'Let's go and have a breath of fresh air; there'll be an interval before they swap over bands again,' said Sam when the third dance finished. He took her by the arm, saying gaily as they went out on to the lower deck, 'What a pretty little radius you have, straight as a die.' And then, before she could make a joking reply, he bent and put his lips to hers.

She kissed him back for a moment, overwhelmed by his sudden closeness, but a thought of Morgan's dark eyes filled her mind and gently she disentangled herself.

'I'm sorry, Sam, I must go in now,' she said quietly. 'I've promised the last three dances to someone else.'

'I see.' He stood back, looking very tall in the overhead light from the spar on the deck. 'So there *is* someone else, is there?' he asked. 'I suppose I should have guessed it.'

'I'm afraid there is,' said Daisy. He was too nice for her to flirt with, she thought. She liked him immensely, but, just in case he became serious about her, she would not raise false hopes. 'I hope you have a wonderful holiday in London,' she said softly, and went back inside. He held the door open until she went through, but did not follow her and she was pleased about that.

The music had just begun when she came in. Morgan had his back turned to her and was chatting to one of the jazz-band boys when she approached. She went up and touched him on the arm.

'Excuse me, Simon,' she said. 'Sorry to keep you waiting, Morgan. Let's dance, shall we?'

As they danced together, Daisy felt a sudden certainty about the feelings growing in her heart. There were no worries in her mind – just the music, the beat, and the feeling of Morgan's strong arms holding her.

Chapter Thirty-Four
Tuesday 20 May 1924

This could be my wedding dress!

That was the thought that was in Poppy's mind as she endured her sister Violet's fiddling with the folds of her train and pulling up the white kid gloves as tightly as she could so that they almost reached Poppy's shoulders. Elaine was doing the same thing to Daisy, but Daisy was enduring it with more patience.

They had eventually gone for identical gowns.

It was Violet who, with the impeccable taste that made her younger sisters forgive much of her imperious manner, had decided on the pattern and selected the material for this gorgeous creation in pale cream and magnolia silk. It had a demure upper bodice and short sleeves of lace. The body ended at one side of the thigh and dramatically angled upward to the hipbone, the sharp geometric line accentuated by a border of embroidered swirls and circles in the art deco style. The daring design was made acceptable by an underskirt of thick, richly coloured magnolia silk which fell to the knees in graceful folds, and a three-yard train of the same heavy silk swept behind the dress.

Yes, thought Poppy, I'll be able to wear this dress for my wedding in the summer. She looked intently at herself in the mirror and her eyes widened with excitement. It was a perfect dress for a wedding – creamy-white, with a dropped waist, very, very short, but disguised with that dramatic underskirt of pure silk and the stately train. With a pair of sleeves added it would be perfect in church. Nothing had been said yet about a date, but Poppy's mind was firmly fixed on a summer wedding. July, she thought. That would give everyone time to get used to the idea. She stood patiently while Violet, standing on a chair, fixed the three ostrich feathers to the headband around her forehead. She could just about wait until July, she thought. And July in Kent was usually a warm, sunny time. All the old-fashioned rambler roses that her mother had planted would be in flower. One of them, an enormous giant rose called Wedding Day, which had turned into a twenty-foot high and eight-foot wide bush smothered with tiny white roses, had been planted when Poppy was seven years old and had rambled further and further and higher and higher ever since. The garden would be spectacular then; she and Baz would have such a pretty wedding.

'You go first; you're older,' Daisy said, and so Poppy walked out of the room. She heard Violet say something about gathering up her train, but she didn't care about what happened to the underside of the long sweep of silk that trailed behind her. She wanted to look beautiful for Baz. Slowly and carefully she trod the steps, her head held high, her ostrich fan in her hand and the three feathers on her head moving slightly in the breeze from an open window. Now she was pleased that she had not cut her hair, as Baz found it so beautiful. She could feel the heavy weight of it as it fell down her back and imagined his hands running through the ripples of dark red waves.

As soon as she reached the top of the stairs she saw only him. She was dimly conscious that others were there – her father and Jack. Morgan and most of the servants were gathered in the back hallway and peering up through the banisters, but her eyes were on Baz, and his, those beautiful golden-brown eyes, blazing with excitement, were on hers. If only this was their wedding day, she thought, and wished passionately for a magic wand to wipe the intervening months away.

When she reached the bottom of the stairs she held out her hands and Baz took them, drawing her slightly towards him, but then nervously releasing them as Violet squealed 'don't touch' from the landing above and Jack came forward, picked up her train, efficiently folded it and draped it over her arm.

Jack seemed to want to bustle her out to the car straight away, but Poppy drew Baz back to one side and waited. She had had her moment and now it was Daisy's turn to come down the stairs. She looked up and saw how Daisy's mouth trembled and how pretty she looked in the white satin sheath, with her blond hair curving like a gleaming cap of gold.

'Ready to go now, Morgan.' Jack's voice was clipped and authoritative, but he received no answer. With amusement Poppy realized that Morgan was going to wait until Daisy stepped on to the hallway. He wasn't going to be taking orders from Jack. She and Daisy had stayed up talking half the night after Joan's party, both curled up in Poppy's bed. Poppy knew that Daisy would want Morgan's eyes to be on her as she came slowly down the stairs.

And then her father's arm went around her, and his voice, husky and broken: 'You look lovely, Poppy, my darling.' He moved across to Daisy once she was safely on the hall floor and said the very same words to her. Poppy hugged Baz's arm for a moment and then released him and said, 'Let's go, Morgan. Let's get this stuffy affair over and done with.' She was glad to see her father so much more cheerful. They had spent hours practising jazz tunes today, her father thumping out the beat on the piano and she playing the clarinet. It seemed that he would never tire of playing and his fingers had regained all of their old agility. Perhaps, after all, he would agree to go to court next Monday and all their problems could be sorted out.

Poppy was the only one in the house who was not astonished at the change music could make in him. She knew how jazz played as loudly as possible drowned out all thought, all anxieties and all fears. When she reached the door she turned and looked back at him and smiled. He returned the smile and she was reassured. Baz, she saw, had moved over next to him. He had promised that when they were gone he would try to persuade the Earl to go to Belgravia to try out the schoolroom piano, now safely installed in the jazz club.

'We must wait for Joan when we get there,' said Daisy when she slid into the back seat beside Elaine and Poppy. 'She says that we must be either the first or last, and that it's better to be last as they will speed things up after the first dozen or so.'

'I'll have to drop you off at the Buckingham Palace railing; I can't wait, my lady,' said Morgan over his shoulder to Elaine. 'I walked around last night and had a word with one of the taxi drivers nearby; they said the Mall is murder, so I am taking a short cut, but once we're there I'll have to drop you off.'

They had to wait for some time before Joan arrived. She looked unexpectedly demure in a long full skirt that swept the ground, but her face was full of mischief.

'Wait till we get rid of the chaperones,' she whispered to Poppy. 'Then we'll have some fun.'

'Dearest child, how lovely you look.' Lady Dorothy kissed Poppy, admired their dresses and then started to call greetings to her numerous friends. Poppy giggled at the helpless expression on Elaine's face as Baz's mother introduced her to everyone as 'my new little daughter'. Jack had decreed that there was to be no talk of an engagement in the household at Grosvenor Square until the Earl returned to full health and could deal with his daughter's absurd notions. But it was beyond Jack's well-known diplomatic gifts to rein in Lady Dorothy.

'Oh, so you are the Derrington girls,' said a jolly-looking woman, mother of one of Joan's friends. 'I remember your Uncle Robert, my dears. When I was about eighteen I was madly in love with him – I cried my eyes out when I heard of how he died in the Boer War.'

'Tell us about him.' Poppy was surprised to find Daisy so eager for details about Robert, Michael Derrington's younger brother and uncle to Violet, Poppy and Rose – though not to Daisy, she thought suddenly. Why was she so interested? Still, they had to occupy themselves in some way, standing in a queue under the scrutiny of the palace officials.

'He was such a charming boy,' said the woman fondly. 'I remember one party at Beech Grove Manor where he set up this toy rabbit with one ear on the top chair of the table and we all had to come and bow to him and shake his little paw.'

Funny the things that amuse older people, thought Poppy, and stopped listening, though Daisy went on talking to the woman and asking questions about Robert.

Joan, in the meantime, amused herself by spreading salacious rumours about a liaison between the prime minister and Princess Mary, warning her unlucky victims that she would be consigned to the deepest dungeon in the Tower of London if the story got out.

'But I know I can trust you as we have been friends for the last twenty years or so,' Poppy overheard her say to one prim-looking girl.

'You're only just nineteen,' pointed out Poppy in a whisper. 'Who is she anyway?'

'Never saw her before in my life,' said Joan non-chalantly, and moved on to tease one of the bodyguards, asking him if he had to keep his chin pointing to the ceiling in order stop his helmet sliding off.

'Joan, leave the poor man alone,' said Lady Dorothy, breaking off the animated conversation about Robert Derrington. Her tone was resigned rather than angry, but Joan got bored easily and soon moved on to other debutantes, picking out, with an unerring eye, those who were newly up from the country, or those who looked shy and anxious, and proceeding to drop bits of scurrilous gossip in their ears and laugh loudly at the shy gasps of horror.

'How do you like my gown?' she asked Poppy, and she twirled around in a small space, causing everyone around them to take one step backwards.

'Very nice,' said Poppy. It was, she thought, rather old-fashioned for Joan's taste. Still, perhaps it belonged to her sister or something.

'I got it made to my own design,' said Joan demurely. 'Oh good, we're separating from the oldies. Come on; I know what happens now – all us little girls are put into one room on our own and the chaperones get to eat cake in the white drawing room and exchange scandalous hearsay without little ears overhearing the stories of their mothers' and fathers' affairs of the past.'

Joan was up to something, thought Poppy as she followed her future sister-in-law into the antechamber, the supper room for the ball. While the other girls *ooh*ed and *aah*ed over the magnificent ceiling or rushed to secure one of the small, spindly-legged gilt chairs, Joan went straight to the middle of the room and twirled so that the wide loose skirt of her dress flew out around her, displaying her white stockings and prominent knees.

Then, to Poppy's amusement, she unfastened a string on the waist of her skirt and showed that she was really wearing a white silk shift-like dress with a dropped waist and a skirt so short it barely touched her knees. It didn't, like Daisy and Poppy's dresses, have an underskirt to hide its deficiency in length; it was almost indecently short.

And then, ignoring the gasps of horror, she took her place on one of the gilt chairs and arranged the detached long skirt across her knees, just like a rug.

At that moment the major-domo came into the room and looked frowningly around at the helplessly giggling girls. However, by the time that he had finished making a pompous speech about what a great honour it was to be presented to their majesties and that he understood how nervous they all were, everyone had managed to control themselves – although all eyes were pointed towards Joan.

Joan herself was now deep in conversation with a friend of hers called Eve, a very beautiful girl with high cheekbones and enormous blue eyes, who was wearing a gorgeous silk dress with a dropped waist – very short, but disguised with a long lace fringe that fell below the knees. She, the Derrington girls and Joan were the only four in the room with short dresses – all the others had stuck nervously to pre-war fashion, which was daring if it showed a glimpse of an ankle, or, at most, the very bottom of someone's calf.

Every time the major-domo went out of the room, Eve and Joan did a little shimmy together, humming in low voices, '*I wish I could shimmy like my sister Kate . . .*' and every time that the door opened again they were back on their chairs with their legs tucked out of the way.

What a farce, thought Poppy, and then she shook herself. There were a hundred girls around her and at least half of them could be potential customers for the latest and most up-to-date club in London.

'Have you been to the Very Heaven jazz club yet?' she enquired of a chatty girl who seemed to be the centre of attention.

'My dear, of course . . . my favourite place in town . . .' drawled the debutante, and Poppy smiled her wide, charming smile and remarked mysteriously, 'I thought you would have; you look the type that knows all the latest places!'

And then she moved on to another group.

By the time that they were called into the Throne Room, the words 'Very Heaven' were buzzing through the debutantes like the murmur of bees on a summer eve.

Chapter Thirty-Five
Monday 26 May 1924

'I'm not going; I'm not well.' The Earl stared angrily at Jack and then pushed his chair back, leaving his breakfast untouched. In the silence that followed his exit from the room, they heard his heavy footsteps stomping up the stairs and then the slam of a door overhead.

'It might be just as well to go without him,' said Daisy quietly. Everyone in turn had tried to explain to him the importance of going to court today, but it had not worked. Daisy tried to console herself with the thought that the Earl was not very good at dealing with people like judges, and that his presence would probably only serve to make things worse rather than better. He might have been successful at the court in Maidstone if he had been able to be a bit conciliatory instead of treating the judge as though he were a servant on the estate.

'You don't know what you are talking about, Daisy,' snapped Jack. 'A man can't just not turn up for no reason. It's very likely that he will be jailed for contempt of court if he just doesn't show up there.'

'What if he had pneumonia?' asked Daisy. The news about Great-Aunt Lizzie was not good. Daisy would have to go down to Beech Grove again – it was terrible that no relation of the poor old woman seemed to be showing concern; the housekeeper, Mrs Pearson, was her only visitor in the hospital. Still, thought Daisy, if only Michael Derrington had pneumonia, everyone would be full of sympathy for him.

'But he doesn't have pneumonia,' pointed out Jack. 'If he did, all would be simple. We would get a doctor to certify that he was too ill to attend and then the hearing would be postponed.'

'We must get a doctor,' said Daisy decisively. 'Even if Father won't see him,' she went on, 'he may be willing to give a certificate to say that he is suffering from shell-shock.'

Was shell-shock still considered to be a valid excuse? she wondered. She had read in one of Jack's newspapers that there was no such thing – just nervous depression, the paper had said – and she had a suspicion that people like Jack – people like judges, perhaps – thought that men should be able to control their feelings and their emotions.

'Very well then!' Jack slapped down his knife and fork in the centre of his half-eaten fried egg. He glared across at Daisy. 'I'll go and see about it,' he said irritably.

'Oh, dear,' said Elaine as the door clicked firmly closed after him, but she patted her daughter's hand consolingly. 'Jack will do his best,' she said.

'When we are in court, you must play jazz as loudly as you can. Don't try to get him out of bed – that doesn't work; if wants to get out, he'll do it of his own accord, but don't put any pressure on him,' said Daisy, and

Poppy nodded. She was being very understanding about her father's plight – not at all like the usual Poppy, who seemed to be a bit closed off in her own world.

Armed with a few reluctant lines from the doctor, Jack and Daisy set off for the court, picking up Justin on the way. Jack had sent Morgan in to collect him from the little house and the chauffeur had obviously told him about the Earl's refusal to come, because Justin said nothing, just patted Daisy's hand when he got into the car.

'Violet wanted to come but I thought it might be best not. It's bound to be upsetting and . . .' He hesitated for a moment and then said, 'She's not very well at the moment. She'll tell you all about it herself when she sees you, I'm sure.'

'What's the best thing to do, Justin?' Daisy wondered whether Violet might be pregnant, but at the moment her father's problem was paramount in her mind.

'It's not really my business,' he said after a minute. 'You have your own lawyer, but –' here he looked across at Jack – 'I would feel that it would be best to put a member of the family in the witness box – someone who will make a good impression on the judge – and who will be able to explain about the Earl's . . .' he hesitated a little at that, and then finished bravely, 'would be able to explain his mental problems.'

Jack slightly preened himself. 'Well, of course I would be happy to do anything to help.'

'No, no, no, we couldn't ask that from a man of your position.' Justin's voice was soothing and held a note of deference to an older man, and one in a higher position. 'I was thinking of young Daisy here. She looks younger than she is and she will appeal to the judge's paternal instincts. It won't be difficult, Daisy, you just—'

'Don't tell me what to say,' interrupted Daisy. 'If you do, it might sound like I have learned it off by heart. I'll just get up and I'll do my best.'

There was something far more intimidating about this London court than the one at Maidstone, thought Daisy when they went in. The lawyer's face grew even longer when he heard that the Earl wasn't coming. He looked at the doctor's certificate dubiously and sighed heavily.

'He should have come,' he muttered. 'Does he realize that he can lose everything?' He stopped and his eyes went to Daisy.

'He doesn't realize anything,' said Daisy boldly. 'He's just not capable of coming here and . . .'

'We thought that if his daughter Daisy here went into the witness box and gave the explanation to the judge – if you could call her – we thought that might influence him. What do you think, sir?' Justin waited deferentially for his senior's opinion.

'Might work,' said the lawyer after a moment's thought. 'How old are you, my lady, if I may ask?'

'Eighteen,' lied Daisy decisively, and saw that he looked relieved. It had occurred to her that there might be something against putting someone under eighteen in the witness box.

He nodded with a sudden air of cheerfulness. 'We'll

do that,' he said. He studied her again and asked her to take off her hat.

'Yes, better without – a golden-haired innocent,' said Justin with a grin, but Daisy did not smile back. This was no game. It would kill Michael Derrington if he was put in prison. Whatever happened, she must try to avoid that plight for him. There was one more card left in her hand.

When they left the lawyer's office and went into the corridor, where barristers in wigs joked with each other, lawyers with worried expressions scurried around and frightened-looking members of the public paced up and down, she looked all around until she spotted Denis Derrington at the end of the long passageway. He had been talking to his lawyer, but now both sides' lawyers had gone to talk in the privacy of a window alcove and he was alone.

'Excuse me,' said Daisy to Jack. Justin had been taken under the wing of their lawyer and was being treated by him as a junior colleague. She walked steadily in the direction of a notice marked LADIES, then glanced over her shoulder. Jack had taken a small pocketbook out and was making a note in it, so Daisy rapidly changed direction and walked purposely towards Denis Derrington.

He pretended not to know her, though she guessed that he had been aware of her presence at the court in Maidstone, and also seen her beside the lawyer this morning. However, she introduced herself briskly and went straight to the point.

'My father is extremely unwell and cannot attend this

morning.' The words were crisp and to the point and she cut through his muttered expressions of regret with a decisiveness that pleased her.

She got straight to the point. 'I want you to agree to a postponement of this hearing,' she announced.

'My dear cousin Daisy, we cannot waste the time of the court like this. Your father chooses not to attend; that's for him to decide, but I don't see why I have to go to all the trouble and expense of another hearing.'

'There would be no trouble or expense if you withdrew,' she pointed out.

His face darkened. 'I'm not going to do that. Goodness knows what the man will do next – sell Beech Grove Manor House to an American.'

Clearly this man cannot be reasoned with, thought Daisy. She would have to go out on a limb and hope that she was right.

'I would insist that you agree to a postponement or else . . .' She purposely allowed the end of her sentence to dangle unfinished.

'Or else what?' Obligingly he rose to her bait.

'Or else I will tell the court that you are a man of bad character and that the last time you were at Beech Grove Manor House you seduced a servant girl, and that the present scullery maid, Maud, is your daughter – the living image of you, I may add.' She listened patiently to his splutterings, but knew, as she gazed up into the unusual green eyes and the winged eyebrows above them, that her guess had hit the mark. The housekeeper's gossip about Denis Derrington's visit sixteen years ago, which Morgan had told her about, had lodged at the back of her mind. Then inspiration had dawned yesterday when she was watching Maud sing. When she had seen Denis Derrington in Maidstone he had reminded her of someone, but she had supposed it must be some relative. Yesterday, in a blinding flash of certainty, she had realized that person was Maud.

'I will also inform the court that, despite your wealth, you do not pay one penny towards her maintenance and that she was brought up in an orphanage and sent out to work at the age of twelve. Of course,' she conceded, 'I suppose all this will be ruled out of order, but I can assure you that I will get as much of the story out as possible before I am silenced. Are you willing to take the risk?'

And then she left him and rejoined Jack, who was still making notes.

'Not nervous about speaking in front of the judge, are you, Daisy?' he asked in a kindly way.

'A bit,' she said just to please him, 'but I'll be all right.' She was feeling rather pleased with herself and added, 'You're very good to us all, Jack. I'm sorry that you've had so much bother.'

She registered that he looked touched, but most of her attention was on Denis Derrington. His lawyer had been talking with Denis and had now approached their lawyer.

A few minutes later Denis and his lawyer departed and their own lawyer, accompanied by the barrister, was back, with Justin beaming happily behind them.

'Good news,' said the solicitor rapidly as soon as he was beside them. 'The other side have agreed to postpone the hearing for a month in order to give the Earl a chance to recover.'

'They must have heard a rumour that we were going to put you in the box, Daisy, and they ran scared,' said Justin with a grin.

'It solves nothing though, just postpones the inevitable,' warned the lawyer. 'Unless the Earl can find some way to repay the money he obtained by the sale of timber and of a very valuable piece of woodland, then any judge in the country will bring in a verdict in favour of Sir Denis.' He stopped for a moment and then said significantly, 'There is, of course, another way, if you, Sir John, as the representative of the family, feel that, given the Earl's state of mind, this should be pursued.'

Jack looked at him through narrowed eyes. 'I think I understand what you are driving at,' he said slowly. And then with a sudden change of tone he said, 'Daisy dear, would you go back to the car and wait for us there. Here, take this,' he produced a pound note. 'Buy yourself a magazine and a newspaper for Morgan. 'He took another look at the lawyer and then said to her, 'We may be some time, but you will be quite comfortable in the car and Morgan will look after you.'

For a moment Daisy thought of refusing, but then decided against it. She made as if to walk briskly away, but stopped as soon as she had reached the corner and stole back to stand behind one of the marble pillars.

'Get him certified?! A lunatic asylum!' Justin's voice rose up high and astonished. The lawyer said something inaudible in reply. Daisy moved closer to the shelter of another pillar.

'Of course, a man who is out of his wits cannot be deemed responsible for his actions,' came Jack's voice, measured and considering, with none of the horror that had sounded from Justin. 'It is a point.'

'The Earl could always recover,' said the lawyer, 'and then of course there would be no problem with reversing his certification. At least the house and such income as there is would be retained for his dependent daughters, for the moment.'

'Worth trying,' said Jack.

'Let's just step into this room – we'll be undisturbed here. We need to make a few notes of occurrences and things said by the Earl – anything to back our case.' The lawyer sounded his usual self, urbane, sensible, businesslike . . .

Daisy could not bear to listen to any more. She wanted to confront them, to shout at them, but she was shaken by sobs and knew that she would just be put aside as a hysterical child. She had to think what was best to do. Far, far better to give up Beech Grove than to have her father imprisoned in a lunatic asylum. That would kill him. He was not insane, just depressed and shaken by fits of nerves. She would look after him, she decided – just as he and his wife had looked after her when her own mother did not want her. Stifling her sobs, Daisy ran down the steps and flew towards the narrow side street where the Humber had been parked. Morgan saw her coming and got out of the car instantly.

'What is it?' His hands were on her shoulders and as she threw herself against his chest she felt his arms tighten around her.

'Oh, Morgan.' She could say nothing more. Sobs were choking her.

'Try to tell me.' His voice in her ear sounded hoarse.

'They're plotting to have my father declared a lunatic, to have him put in an asylum.' She choked over the words. 'The only thing that will save him from that will be for him to give up Beech Grove Manor.'

There was a silence for a moment. She stood there with his arms around her, her cheek resting against his broad chest. She could hear his heart hammering against her ear and somehow the sound soothed her. After a minute she raised her head. He dug a large clean white handkerchief from his pocket and offered it to her, but still kept his other arm around her. She dried her eyes and nestled into his warmth while her thoughts moved, sifted themselves and clarified inside her head.

'Once Elaine and Jack go back to India,' she said after a minute, 'I'm going to get myself a couple of rooms in London – they're not expensive out near where the film studios are. I'll keep Father with me, and Violet can look after Great-Aunt Lizzie – though she'd probably prefer to go to her cousin. Rose can spend her holidays with Poppy, Lady Dorothy and Joan.' She was pleased to hear how firm her voice sounded, but when Morgan said nothing she looked up at him a little defensively.

He was not looking at her, just gazing ahead with a strange frown on his face.

'Father will be just as well off without the responsibilities of Beech Grove Manor,' she assured him, 'and you know that Baz and Poppy will want to employ the band in the club. Lady Dorothy is very rich, you know. There'll be money for everything to do with the jazz club now.'

'I'm not worried about that; I've had an offer from the Savoy Hotel for the post of drummer for three nights a week. That will be enough for me to live on – enough to get married on too,' he added softly.

'Married?' Daisy let the word fall.

He said nothing and she forced herself to go on. 'Have you found someone that you would like to marry?' she asked.

He hesitated for a moment, looking around the deserted street. She moved back into the shadow of an archway and he followed her. In a second his arms were around her again, holding her very tightly and his burning lips were on hers, not a tentative kiss, but passionate and demanding, sending excited ripples running through her. They stood there for a long moment, locked in each other's arms, until the sound of newspaper boy crying the evening papers made them break apart.

'I may be a nameless nobody,' he smiled, 'but if you marry me I'll love and cherish you for all of your life. You will never want for anything while I have a breath in my body.'

Daisy lifted her lips to his and, oblivious to the grinning newspaper boy, they kissed again.

'I, Daisy Carruthers, do take thee, Morgan the Impresario, as my lawful wedded husband,' she said softly.

Chapter Thirty-Six
Wednesday 4 June 1924

It's been nine days, thought Daisy as she and Morgan walked silently towards the vicarage, nine days of contrasts. Bliss and deep contentment whenever she thought of Morgan, whenever they stole a moment together and discussed their future home and their plans. And frantic worry when she thought of Michael Derrington. They had decided to tell no one of their engagement. It was essential that no word of it should come to the Earl's ears while his mental state was so precarious. Now he was lying in his bed and obstinately refusing to eat. The doctor had talked of removing him to a mental hospital where he would be force-fed, but Daisy had argued strongly against it. His momentary flicker of interest in jazz had given her hope, but that had fizzled out, and when Poppy had bravely taken her clarinet into his bedroom he had shouted at her to go away and to stop tormenting him, before drawing the bedclothes over his head.

It was lucky that Rose had gone back to school. The sight of her father in this very much worse state would have deeply upset the child. Now she was happily back with her friends and writing outrageous letters about *'The Case of the Mysterious Disappearance of the Mad*

Maths Teacher', which amused everyone at breakfast table, making Jack laugh so much that he choked over his coffee.

But Michael Derrington only turned his face to the wall when Daisy offered to read Rose's latest epistle to him.

She sighed, averted her mind from the unsolvable and went back to Morgan. She tucked her arm into his and steered his reluctant feet towards the vicarage.

'I wonder what we will find out,' she said. 'Perhaps you might be the son of someone married to a rich American. Who knows? Perhaps you might be Morgan from New Orleans after all.'

The vicar was surprisingly young – and harassed. There was the noise of a baby crying loudly upstairs and of a toddler scampering around overhead. He gave one glance upward but then ushered them into his study.

'I've prepared for your visit,' he said. 'I've got out the church baptismal records.' He pulled out a heavy, thick, leather-bound book and placed it on the table. 'Now let me see . . .' he said and looked expectantly at them.

Morgan pulled from his pocket the birth certificate he had received from Somerset House and silently held it out to him.

'It was filled out by the people at the orphanage when he was three years old,' said Daisy, when the silence had lengthened without a word from Morgan.

'Yes, orphanages will do that if there seem to be no records for the child,' the vicar explained. For such a young man he had a kindly manner, thought Daisy, but she braced herself against a disappointment. 'I fear that the chances of your having been baptized if there was no birth certificate registered are fairly low. Nevertheless . . .' He checked the date of Morgan's birth and turned the pages.

'No,' he said, 'I'm sorry. There is no record of a child of that name being baptized here in this parish. With that address you would have definitely been christened in this church.'

'The only thing is,' said Daisy urgently, 'that he thinks that his first name was Bob, not Edward as it says here on the birth certificate – on the evidence of a fire officer – that's what the orphanage said – and he was the one who thought the child was born in December. But Morgan thinks . . .'

'So you think this might not be you?' The vicar turned to Morgan.

'I thought . . . I think that I was born in June,' said Morgan huskily.

'And that his middle name, or more likely, his *surname* is St Clair,' said Daisy, taking her courage in her hands.

Lucinda St Clair, she thought, picturing the pretty young governess turned away from Beech Grove Manor by the virtuous and horrified Great-Aunt Lizzie. She might well have been already pregnant.

The vicar turned the pages back to June. It seemed to

have been a good month for baptisms; there were two pages of them.

'No, I'm sorry,' he said looking up from the book. 'There is no child of the surname St Clair here.'

'Wait a minute,' said Daisy. Her eye had caught something. A familiar name had jumped out at her. 'Turn back the page,' she said urgently.

She could sense that he didn't like her looking over his shoulder, but she persisted until her eye found what she was looking for. And she read aloud the familiar name: 'Derrington, Robert St Clair.'

Morgan said nothing, just stared at her with white lips, so Daisy read on, her mind whirring with the thoughts that dashed into it.

'Mother: Lucinda Derrington, née St Clair.

Father: the Honourable Robert Derrington.'

Still Morgan said nothing. His face was pale under his tan, giving him a sallow look. The young vicar looked from one to the other. He picked up the baptismal records saying, 'I'll leave you to yourselves for a moment. This seems to have come as a bit of a shock.'

And then he was gone, and Daisy took Morgan's hand.

'It did cross my mind that you might be the illegitimate son of Lucinda – because of your connection with the name St Clair – Rose had a story – Elaine confirmed it – that Lucinda St Clair, the governess, was having some sort of love affair with Robert – the younger brother of . . . my . . . of Michael Derrington. Great-Aunt Lizzie found Elaine reading her love letters – Elaine was only a child at the time – and . . .' Daisy stumbled over the story, still holding his hand and telling how Robert had left Beech Grove Manor and had joined the Buffs and gone to fight against the Boers – and how he was killed in that war. 'And of course your mother talked to her baby son, about Kent and about the woods and the bluebells, which are so wonderful in beech woods and so, when you saw Beech Grove Manor, Kent, you applied for a job there as a chauffeur,' she finished up.

'You're saying that I am the illegitimate son of Robert Derrington . . .' Morgan was so dazed that he hardly noticed the vicar coming back into the room, the leather-bound book still tucked under his arm and followed by the maid, carrying a tray with some teacups and a teapot with a chipped spout.

'You must have a cup of tea,' said the vicar hospitably, pouring some into the cups and adding apologetically, as he looked dubiously at the watery mixture that came through the strainer, 'It's not very good, I'm afraid.' He waited until the maid had closed the door behind her, before saying, 'Let's have another look at that entry. You said something about "illegitimate" – you were mentioning that as I came in – but this document states that your father was the Honourable Robert Derrington and your mother was Lucinda Derrington,' he said, his voice firm and decisive. But he cast a dubious glance at Morgan's chauffeur uniform.

'Perhaps . . . Perhaps she said that because he was the father . . . Perhaps she hoped that they'd get married?'

Morgan's voice broke, and Daisy went across and sat on the arm of his chair and stayed there with her hand on his shoulder.

'Not possible.' The vicar was brisk and decisive now. 'She would have had to produce the marriage certificate in order for the baptism, for the child to be registered in the name of Derrington rather than St Clair. I wonder whether they were married at this church. It's worth a try. I'll go and fetch the volumes for 1899 and perhaps for 1900 as well. Not earlier, you think?'

'No earlier,' said Daisy. Her mind went back to the photographs in the gallery. Robert's eighteenth birthday had been marked as 23 February 1897. To get married without his father's knowledge or permission he would have had to be twenty-one. February 1900 would have been the month of Robert's twenty-first birthday.

'Try February or March of 1900,' she said when the vicar came trotting back, a little out of breath but looking quite excited.

'There! I've got it. Twenty-third of February,' he said after a minute. And then continued, 'Yes, they were married in this church: "Marriage between the Honourable Robert Derrington of Beech Grove Manor House, Kent, aged twenty-one, and Lucinda St Clair, spinster, aged twenty-three, of 27, Waterside Gardens, of this parish." I'm not sure where that is – may not exist now – but it definitely says "of this parish" – witnesses are the caretaker of the church and the wife of the caretaker – they didn't have any friends or family around them, poor young things.'

'Is it legal?' asked Daisy. Morgan seemed too dazed to say anything. So Robert came back from the Boer War on his twenty-first birthday, came back to marry the woman that he loved, the woman who was bearing his child – due to be born that coming June, by which time his father would already be lying dead on the battlefield out in Africa. In fact, thought Daisy, I think that he was killed in March of that year.

'So far as it goes.' The vicar was cautious. 'The marriage was certainly legal. They were both of age. The banns had been called three weeks previously. They both must have shown their birth certificates. However, I'm not a lawyer, but if it were a matter of any property, I can see two problems. One would be the short length of the marriage – only three months – before the birth of a son, Robert St Clair, and the second, of course, would be the proof that you –' he addressed himself to Morgan – 'are indeed that same Robert St Clair Derrington, son of the Honourable Robert Derrington of Beech Grove Manor in Kent and not Edward Robert Morgan of the birth certificate that the orphanage furnished you with.'

'There's no way of proving that, is there?' Daisy asked the question, as Morgan still said nothing.

'Might be – mothers who abandon their children often leave something with them to identify the relationship if they can ever come back to reclaim them.' The vicar's face had a sad look and Daisy felt a slight lump in her throat as she thought of all the unfortunate girls who were forced to abandon their babies. 'Of course, in this case the mother was lost in that terrible accident, that dreadful explosion, but the orphanage will have kept . . . do, by law, keep the clothes and anything else that was with you when you were found. I should go back there, if I were you.'

'We'll do that,' said Daisy decisively. She rose to her feet and they thanked the vicar and made their farewells. If only there were some proof, she thought. Her mind went back to Lucinda St Clair, who had told her son that he was born in June, with a silver spoon, and that Kent was a lovely place with beautiful bluebell woods. And the son, as an adult, saw an advertisement for a position as chauffeur at Beech Grove Manor in Kent and had applied for it because of the never-forgotten words of his mother.

The lady at the orphanage was not best pleased to see them again. 'If there had been anything significant like a name on the clothes, that would have been recorded and I would have told you about it the first time that you came,' she grumbled. 'Still, I'll get them and you can take them away with you; one less dusty box for us to keep.' She took from Morgan the birth certificate made out in the name of three-year-old Edward Robert Morgan, thought to be born in December of 1900, and then disappeared, coming back with a box from which only the top layer of dust was blown off which she thrust into his hands.

Morgan made no attempt to open it and Daisy understood why. This would be something almost sacred to him. On the morning of the gasworks explosion his mother would have dressed him in those clothes – would perhaps have sent him out to play in the garden that he remembered, in Waterside Gardens – the fact that he was not in the house would account for the mother being killed but the child surviving.

She held his hand tightly, but waited until they reached the car before saying, 'Open it, Morgan.'

Slowly and reluctantly he opened the boot of the car and laid the box into the empty space. For a moment he hesitated, but then he took the lid off. It held a small boy's romper suit, a pair of shoes, two white socks, a blue jersey and . . .

On top of everything was a threadbare toy – a pocket-sized rabbit with one ear missing.

It was the exact match of the toy rabbit held by the Honourable Robert Derrington in the photograph taken in 1882, when Michael Derrington's brother was about three years old.

Robert had carefully preserved his rabbit – and his widow had handed it on to his baby son.

Epilogue
Sunday 27 July 1924

'*The wedding of the twin daughters of the Earl of Derrington, so lately and so romantically restored to the fortune of his forebears, has proved to be the event of the year. Even the royal wedding of the year before could not have outshone the occasion.*

'*And yet there was no red carpet, no marble columns, no princes and princesses attending the event, no archbishop blessed the pair of happy couples; only a humble rector performed the ceremony, in a simple country church strewn in tasteful profusion with almond-scented blossoms of creamy meadowsweet wild flowers by the youngest sister of the brides.*

'*The two brides were attended by the Lady Rose Derrington, who was dressed in an exquisite frock of priceless Parisian lace with a string of oriental pearls slung around her slender neck. Her naturally blonde hair was enclosed with a simple coronet, and a pair of sheer white stockings veiled her slim legs and complemented her silver shoes.*

'*The wedding feast, presided over by the venerable great-aunt of the two brides, took place in the newly decorated drawing room of Beech Grove Manor House (flower arrangements by the same tasteful hand as that* which had adorned the church) – and the guests were too numerous to be mentioned without tedium. Sufficient to say that they included Mrs Justin Pennington, the brides' eldest sister (a little bird has told me that she is happily expecting an interesting event – that is a baby) and her husband Justin, who was so useful in sorting out recent legal formalities for the Earl, as well, of course, as the very many relations and friends of the Derrington and the Pattenden families, from the Indian subcontinent as well as the old country.

'Conspicuous by his absence was Mr Denis Derrington, who had formerly been heir to the earldom. He was not missed and Sir Guy Beresford, godfather to Lady Daisy, whose film company was kept busy recording the happy event, took his place in the line-up for the family photograph. The cinema impresario proved to be expert at calming the fears of those Bright Young People from London who were afraid that their correct profile might not be recorded.

'With glasses of champagne in hand the guests strolled around the newly mown lawns that fringed the lake – a few, who had imbibed deeply, even took to the boats and rowed across its "shining levels" (Tennyson). It is rumoured that the Honourable Joan Pattenden and her friend the Honourable Evelyn Dickinson were seen to strip off their party dresses and to dive down into its depths "where the ripple washed among the reeds" (Tennyson), but rumour often lies and your correspondent's lips are sealed.

'When eventually all were sated (although enough

food was left over to feed the army of servants who had been engaged for the happy event) the four young people changed into their honeymoon attire. The brides kissed their father. The Honourable Robert Derrington (known as Morgan) shook the hand of his new father-in-law – his uncle, the Earl – left a few instructions about the selling of Binton Farm to a grateful tenant and then stepped into the ancient Humber at whose wheel he seemed singularly at home. The Honourable Basil Pattenden kissed his mother, Lady Dorothy, who, a little bird tells me, is looking forward to the young couple making a very protracted stay in her London house when they come back from their honeymoon. He then shook hands with the Earl, his new father-in-law, leaned in the window of the Humber and said something about drums to his brother-in-law, then jumped into his brother Ambrose's car, reversed it rapidly into a piece of marble statuary – of no particular value, according to the Earl – and then set off, speeding down the avenue in hot pursuit of the Humber.'

Rose put down her pencil, read through what she had written, then picked it up again and added the words:

'And that's all.'

Acknowledgements

I am deeply grateful for all the help that I have received in the writing of this book, from my two editors the two Rachels: Rachel Petty and Rachel Kellehar, whose joint infinite capacity for taking pains must approach genius level; from my agent Peter Buckman of Ampersand Agency Ltd, whose prompt, astringent and witty emails always make my day, and also from all those authors, such as P. G. Wodehouse, the Mitford sisters and Evelyn Waugh, who lived through the 1920s and wrote about those years with a verve and wit that keeps their books on the bestseller lists.

DEBUTANTES

CORA HARRISON

IT'S 1923 AND LONDON IS A WHIRL OF JAZZ, DANCING AND PARTIES.

Violet, Daisy, Poppy and Rose Derrington are desperate to be part of it, but stuck in an enormous crumbling house in the country, with no money and no fashionable dresses, the excitement seems a lifetime away.

Luckily the girls each have a plan for escaping their humdrum country life: Rose wants to be a novelist, Poppy a jazz musician and Daisy a famous film director. Violet, however, has only one ambition: to become the perfect Debutante, so that she can go to London and catch the eye of Prince George, the most eligible bachelor in the country.

But a house as big and old as Beech Grove Manor hides many secrets, and Daisy is about to uncover one so huge it could ruin all their plans – ruin everything – forever.